SHADOWS

ACROSS

CAPE YORK

Genre: Historical Fiction /Adventure

Cover design created by Cat Petersen

Cover picture design by Nick Green at PC Place.

Shadows Across Cape York

Published at Ingram Spark
by Elizabeth Rimmington. 2022.
Queensland
Australia

 A catalogue record for this
book is available from the
National Library of Australia

ISBN

978-0-6485257-9-0 (Print)
978-0-6454944-0-2 (Epub)

Disclaimer
This novel is a work of fiction. While some of the names, characters and business places mentioned may have existed, their interaction with the story characters is pure fiction. All incidents are either the products of the author's imagination or have been used in a fictitious manner. The opinions expressed or beliefs held are those of the characters and should not be assumed to be the opinions or beliefs of the author.

SHADOWS

ACROSS

CAPE YORK

Written by

Elizabeth Rimmington.

About ***Shadows Across Cape York***:

Drifting on a timber yardarm following the shipwreck of the *Pink Pearl* in the Arafura Sea in 1892 had not featured in the plans of the doctors for their triumphant return to their Australian homeland.

Cooktown, the ultimate destination for Doctor Henry George Carson Baldwin and Doctor Edward Benton, floated as an unattainable goalpost on the periphery of their minds.

Even if they survived the dangerous waters of the Gulf of Carpentaria, landing on the western shores of Cape York Peninsula, with the monsoon season only weeks away, did not offer substantial hope for a safe return to civilization.

APPRECIATION

To Caroline and Margaret for your invaluable input.
To Staff and patrons of the Cooktown Library.
To Alberta at Waalmbal Birri (The Boat House) Cooktown.
To Vicki and the staff at Cooktown Nature's Powerhouse.
To the fellowship of good friends within the local writing groups.
To the staff at the Gympie Library.

PROLOGUE

Cooktown

1882

The grassy hill on which he stood guarded the mouth of the Endeavour River. Not a breath of air stirred the early morning with its dawn yet to rise above the horizon. The cloak of eucalypt fragrance swathed his body. From the decks of *The Northern Orchid* in the wispy mist below, the captain's voice drifted up to where the native watched. Emerging from beneath rolled-up trousers, thick scars ran down the legs of the dark-skinned youth who remained as still as the trees around him.

On the water, smoke from the ship's auxiliary engine hung about like a child reluctant to leave for school. The noise of the motor sounded loud on the quiet morning. Sails, released by the human figures racing across the yardarms, hung limp waiting for the wind to stir.

On the hill, the youth's head lifted. He sniffed the air. The breeze and the sun burst over the sea in unison. The sails billowed with the sound of stockwhips bringing a herd of recalcitrant cattle into line. Smoke from the auxiliary engine lifted and trailed across the water to the north-west. The taste of salt fell upon the youth's tongue.

The fingers on his hand inside the pocket of his trousers rolled a pocket-knife over and over – Henry's parting gift to him last night. Moisture filled Smiley's eyes as he silently whispered goodbye to his friend of many years. According to Henry, they met in 1874 and it was now 1882. More than once over the past few months, Henry had explained to Smiley how, as he was now fifteen years of age, he must travel to London to attend University to become a doctor like his Uncle George. Smiley did not really understand the way Henry counted his years, but he understood it was similar to how his people counted the seasons passing. According to Henry, the university was like the Cooktown school, only in a building bigger than anything he was able to imagine, with young men more numerous than the stars in the sky. Just as Smiley went with his father to the tribe's initiation corroboree to make him a man, Henry must go to the university.

Smiley's sharp eyes caught the colour of Miss Abigail's dress as it fluttered in the breeze sweeping along the ship's deck. Henry's mother travelled with him to visit her family in the land on the other side of the water. Smiley swallowed and gritted his teeth. Henry did not expect to be back for at least nine or ten wet seasons. An impatient hand flung the tears from his eyes.

When the sails dipped below the horizon, Smiley stirred. He heard Doctor George's call from the back gate of the property, where he cared for sick patients on the verandah below his house. Smiley rolled down the trouser legs, buttoned his shirt and broke into a run.

"There you are, Smiley. Can you harness the horse into the dray? They have an injured farmhand at the Chinese gardens."

White teeth flashed as the smile widened to cover Smiley's lower face.

"Yes, Doctor George, right away."

PART ONE

THE PEARL DIVERS

CHAPTER ONE

Darwin

1892

A burning sun beat down upon the green waters of Port Darwin dotted with a handful of schooners, numerous pearl luggers, ketches and smaller vessels. Lines from two steamships reached out to loop the bollards on either side of the wharf.

Doctor Henry George Carson Baldwin almost stumbled as his feet landed on the timber jetty at the Port Darwin harbour. Henry threw his hand up to grab at his dark, felt hat when the wind caught it and threatened to send it sailing down to the water at low tide, fifteen feet below them. Auburn hair in need of a haircut blew around his freckled face.

"Steady on there, Red. Have you lost your land-lubber's legs or did you have one too many of the captain's fine rums at dinner last night?" A deep laugh accompanied a strong arm as Doctor Edward Benton reached out to steady his friend. The brown eyes danced with merriment. "I've only ever seen you down one glass of rum a night in all these past ten years that I've known you – or any alcohol for that matter. No wonder those Londoners called you 'Sober-sides'."

Henry's mouth opened to return a sharp retort when both men swung about to where a fellow rowing a little dingy towards the end of the jetty called loudly.

"Hey, Squid! Squid! Here!"

"Do you know that chap, Ed?" But Henry's words were caught by the breeze and swept out over the waves – unheard by his athletic friend who now raced over the unevenness of the timber planks and lifted over the railway lines with the grace of a dancer on any ballroom floor. A squashed hat held in a tight fist waved back and forth above Ed's longish brown hair as it flopped up and down to the unheard music.

"Hey, Diver Bird, Birdie! What're you doing here? Is Dad with you?"

A sagging straw hat hid Diver Bird's face as he secured the dinghy to a pylon. Unencumbered by any clothing except a pair of worn knee-length shorts, he ran up the ladder to the top of the jetty. Salt coated his sun-hardened, muscled body. The two men threw themselves into a warm embrace both talking at once, asking questions and offering answers.

Once the excitement of their reunion calmed, Ed turned towards Henry who had wandered up to find out what was happening.

"Oh, Henry, I'd like you to meet Diver Bird or Birdie. He owns the schooner out there." Ed pointed to a two-masted sailing ship anchored a short distance away. "Diver Bird is contracted to my father's fleet to gather pearl shells here in the north." Ed's hand waved between his doctor friend and his pearling mate who appeared to be anywhere between thirty and forty years of age.

Henry attempted to hide the grimace as his fingers disappeared within the strong hand of Diver Bird. He had grown soft while away in a country not familiar with the enthusiastic Australian handshake.

"G'day, Henry, is it?" Diver Bird's head bounced up and down.

"Doctor Henry Baldwin, actually, Diver," Ed explained.

"Two new doctors in the north. We won't know what to do with ourselves having all these medical people." Laughter lines crunched across Diver Bird's face.

With the greetings attended, Ed was pressed to ask his earlier unanswered question.

"Is Dad with you, Diver?"

"No, son, your dad has taken his *Mary Anne* and the rest of the fleet east to Princess Charlotte Bay to finish off the last few weeks of the pearling season before the monsoons hit. We've been over in the Broome area for the past two years, but your dad wanted to return to the Torres Straits. We'll anchor at Thursday Island, as usual, for repairs during the wet season."

"How come you're here at Darwin then? Don't tell me a woman has tempted you away from the water?"

A raucous laugh rang out over the waves. "Not likely, lad. Who'd have an old salt like me? No, I just had a bit of maintenance needed doing. I picked up another air pump and collected a new diving suit for the *Pink Pearl,* while here."

Ed looked over to where the anchored *Pink Pearl* gently rose and fell with the waves of the turning tide. "So, do I take it pearling was profitable over in the west, then?"

"Not bad. Not bad. There're some fine specimens to be found over that way, I can tell you."

"And now you've spent all your money in Palmerston and Port Darwin, and must get back to work?"

Diver Bird's laugh lifted a flock of seagulls squabbling over some fish remnants on the jetty.

"Something like that, lad. Something like that."

"Well, the other option could be that you are hiding out in the *Pink Pearl* evading a jealous husband or an amorous lady."

Once more Birdie's infectious laughter filled the air. Ed and Henry joined in.

Henry's gaze fixed on the *Pink Pearl* for long moments. The schooner looked tired and ready for a good strip down during the approaching off-season. Four men, all with bare torsos and wearing faded shorts, were visible on the deck.

"If you're putting another air pump on board, how many diving teams are you running off the schooner these days?" Ed's curiosity had been aroused.

"Only two teams on board at the moment. The two Thursday Island divers have gone on with your father. There's just me and Curley – you remember Curley – he's been my tender and backup diver since before you left us. Then there're two Japanese boys, Hikaru and Anago, The Eel. They've been with the *Pink Pearl* for about two or three years now. Of course, we have the four other deck-hands and cook." Diver Bird grinned at Ed. "There's always room for another on board. Do you two want to leave the comforts of your steamship and join us on the *Pink Pearl?* After we go out to the nearest pearl reef to test the new gear, I'm heading east to catch up with your father at either Thursday Island or Princess Charlotte Bay."

Ed swung around to look askance at Henry who did not miss the excitement flashing in his friend's eyes.

"Whaddaya say, Red? There's barely enough room for another cockroach to find a sleeping mat on that vessel, but we only need the clothes we stand up in. The rest of our gear can be sent on to Cooktown."

Henry chuckled. "Sounds pretty good to me. We did say we wanted to spend a few months with the pearling fleet before settling down to work. You've got three months before you're due at the Cooktown hospital and I'm sure my Uncle George won't mind if I'm a day or three late."

The burning sun brought an end to the men's conversation. With the fast-rising tide, Diver Bird climbed down to adjust the line securing his dinghy to the jetty. On his return, he headed over to where men were loading the train they called the *Sandfly* with the newly arrived supplies for the township of Palmerston. Steam rose out of its funnel to drift across the water towards the mangrove-lined banks of the coast.

Henry and Ed went to speak to the Purser of the ship they had travelled on from England. It was time to organize for their luggage to be forwarded to Cooktown.

"Squid?" Henry's green eyes sparkled with amusement. "You kept that quiet, Eddie boy. Are you going to tell me why your pearler friends call you Squid?"

"I can't remember. They've called me that since I spent my first school holidays on Dad's boat. I was only a young fellow."

Henry welcomed the wash of the salt spray over his body every time the bow of the *Pink Pearl* knifed through the waves. His tongue savoured the sea water on his lips. He did not attempt to seek a more sheltered position than here near the bow. The cool water provided relief from the burning rays of the midday sun. Even with his hat, long-sleeved shirt, and long trousers, he felt the heat on his arms and neck. Canvas shoes not only protected his feet from the rays reflected off the deck but helped him grip the timbers as the schooner breached the waves. Henry found the whistle of the wind through the sails a pleasant accompaniment to the harmonized singing voices of the Torres Islander deckhands as they manipulated the two sails on the main mast and the one sail on the mizzen mast.

Ed stood up on the platform with Birdie whose strong arms guided the helm which in turn operated the rudder to maintain their course. Curley and the two Japanese divers inspected and checked the air pumps, hoses, diving suits, and the webbed-roped containers in which they placed the pearl shells after their removal from the sea bed. Along the deck, four huge cane-woven baskets were filled to overflowing with pearl shells. Beside each basket lay further untidy heaps of unbroken shells waiting to be examined. These had been pushed back against the bulwarks on the deck. Henry's curiosity had been aroused at the one similar basket with a lid attached. When asked, Ed lifted the lid to expose four large marker-floats tied to the inside frame, along with several bundles of rope. Three of these floats were empty converted five-gallon kerosene tins. Gum from tropical trees sealed the caps. The fourth float was a similar-sized, sealed wooden cask. A layer of fishing net encased each float. Ed explained how Birdie liked to set out the floats around his chosen diving area, wherever he might be at the time. They provided the underwater divers with a navigation guide back to the ship. Henry looked down the length of the deck to where several of the wooden cask floats lay attached to lengths of rolled ropes.

As the sun closed in upon the western horizon, Diver Bird's bellow sent the crew rushing to furl the sails and to drop anchor. In the distance, Henry noticed two low-waisted, slim-lined pearl luggers making their way back to their home base of Port Darwin. After the schooner spun around on her anchor and settled to the rise and fall of a gentle sea, Birdie and his crew gathered for an evening meal of fish stew, prepared in the galley by the cook. The men ate their food whilst sitting outside on either the hold-cover astern of the main mast or the roof of the galley forward of the main mast. They began to entertain Diver Bird's guests with funny, frightening and terrifying tales which may or may not have had some element of truth at their first telling. As the stars appeared and the moon rose to lighten the night's darkness, the men wandered off to find their bunks or sleeping mats.

After the excitement of his first day on a pearling boat, Henry found it hard to drop off to sleep. He slapped at those mosquitoes left trapped inside the cabin during the boat's anchorage at Port Darwin. In the heat and humidity runnels of perspiration dripped from his body. He tossed and turned until Ed's voice distracted him.

"Come on, Red. This is impossible. It's too hot in here. Let's camp out on deck. It'll be much cooler and there'll be no mosquitoes in the breeze. Bring your blanket to lie on."

To Henry's surprise, it was pleasant sleeping outside even with the aroma of fish and salt radiating from every timber slab of the deck.

Despite the earliness of the day, perspiration saturated Henry's body within a few minutes of the sun making an appearance. Not a breath of air moved. Curiosity opened Henry's eyes at the clunk-whoosh, clunk-whoosh of the two air pumps being worked by the deck crew. One of the Japanese divers – the shorter one of the two with muscular, bowed legs, thickset torso and receding hair – the one they called Hikaru – guided a diving hose and a hemp rope with an ease of long practice over the port side of the vessel. Henry realized Hikaru's mate Anago, The Eel, the taller of the two, must be over the side of the boat working on the pearl beds.

On the starboard side of the *Pink Pearl*, Diver Bird tended the air hose and rope for the tall, well-built Curley whose head and body, encased in the shiny new diving helmet and suit, stood on the ship's Jacob's ladder almost ready to descend.

"You give the rope a good tug if you encounter the smallest problem with the new suit or air delivery, Curley," the captain instructed his diving mate. Any verbal answer was lost inside the helmet. An awkward thumbs-up signalled the message was received.

A rough hand on his thigh and a cheeky voice in his ear motivated Henry.

"Come on, Red, the men have had their breakfast. There's boiled fish awaiting you. Birdie's already been down on the reef testing out his recent purchase. Curley's just trying it out now."

On his way to the galley, Henry stopped to watch two deck-hands, under the watchful eye of Birdie, as they shucked the pearl shells. Down-turned lips and deep frowns heralded disappointment in the contents.

While Henry ate in the galley, Ed explained how each of the piles of pearl shells he had seen belonged to each of the separate divers. The individual diver would be credited with the money for the shells he collected, less his board and keep. The deckhands and cook were paid the going rates.

The morning passed rapidly with the divers returning after twenty-minute intervals to empty the shell containers of their contents and to undress. They assisted their diving mate into the cumbersome suit and helmet before taking over the tendering duties of caring for the umbilical cords for the other one going below.

"Not much pearl shell here, Boss," Hikaru spoke to Birdie.

"Nah, mate. You're right there, but we had to come and test the new suit. When The Eel comes up next time, you can call it quits if you want." Diver Bird turned to where Ed and Henry sat sheltering in the shade of the bulwark. "Hey Squid, you want to give this a go when Curley pop's up next time?"

"I sure would."

"Do you remember how?"

"I remember everything you taught me, Birdie. Do you mind if I wear the cut-off suit rather than the new full suit?"

"Hmmm." Birdie grinned. His head swung in Henry's direction. "You want a go, Henry?"

Henry looked dubious. His stomach churned at the excitement of diving great depths under the water but he was not ignorant of the number of deaths encountered in the pearl diving industry. He swallowed.

"I'd like that very much, Birdie, if you don't mind handling an absolute novice."

Henry envied the confidence displayed by Ed as he donned the alternate diving suit consisting of only a helmet attached to a corselet around his neck. Weights dangled from a short attachment to the front and back of the corselet. At his waist, he wore the belt and knife Birdie produced last night. It was Ed's own knife left with Diver Bird by Mr. Benton, knowing Birdie would likely see his son first. Without a glance behind him and listening to Birdie's last instructions, Ed backed down the short ladder attached to the ship's side and into the water.

Once Birdie was satisfied Ed was coping well down below, he handed the tender chore to Curley before disappearing below deck. When he returned, he had a well-worn belt with a ten-inch bladed knife attached in a tied-down pouch.

"Here, Henry, you can have this if you want. It's an old one been hanging around here, taking up space for ages."

"What do I want that for?"

"You might find it easier to remove the pearl shell from the reef with this. Or if a big mouth comes along and wants to chew you up, you can cut out its tongue." Birdie's roar ran along the decks causing grins to light up the faces of the crew.

A tremor of fear ran down Henry's body, but he managed to grin. His imagination filled his head with the horrors of what might have happened to the original owner of this knife, as he attached the belt to his waist. He decided not to ask Birdie. He did not want to know the answer.

When the time arrived for the helmet to be connected to the corselet now over his shoulders, Henry bit his lip. Now was his last chance to change his mind about this mad escapade. As Birdie lowered the helmet over his head and began to fasten the bolts, Henry felt overwhelming claustrophobia crushing his soul. The wave of panic roared in his ears. It tightened an invisible steel band around his throat. It rolled through his body and punched him in the stomach. He forced himself to resist the powerful demands of panic and sucked the air slowly into his lungs. With every controlled exhalation, dread leaked from his mind. Comfort arrived in a small way when the sound of the air pump being worked a few feet away from where he stood, filtered into the helmet.

Later, when Henry's canvas-shoed feet touched the reef, he was amazed at how easy the descent had been. Diver Bird's calm guidance soothed his trembling hands and the whirlpool inside his belly. He tested the limitations of his head movements inside the helmet. With inquisitive hands, he stroked the air pipe and the rope within his reach. It struck Henry just how vulnerable he was down here – totally dependent for his very life on the tender operator above.

Ten minutes, Birdie said he allocated to the dive. Henry tried to convince himself it would be over in a flash. He turned his attention to the reef. Small coloured fish darted in and out of crustaceans of all shapes and sizes lying in a bed of seagrasses – some fresh and many destroyed. In this murky world, peace and quietness surrounded him reducing his anxiety. Within the limitations of his helmet, his vision took in the degradation resulting from frequent pearl shell extractions. His heart rolled over when his foot slipped. Henry felt the fear drag inside his chest at the perceived depletion of his air supply. With determination, he concentrated on slow shallow breathing until he felt more comfortable. After he regained his balance, he took tentative steps, ducking as a large tropical fish flipped beside his face. The jerk of the rope at his waist called the five-minute signal. He replied in a similar mode.

Seeing what he thought might be an untouched pearl shell, Henry withdrew Birdie's knife from its scabbard. Unsteady feet shuffled to his goal. Apprehension seeped into his bloodstream. There seemed to be no apparent reason for this, except imagination. His fingers curled more tightly around the handle of his knife. The airflow continued. The silence continued. No warning signals were felt in his rope. Then he noticed. Where only a short moment ago a curtain of coloured fish fluttered within the reef, now there were none. All the fish had disappeared.

A dark long tail gliding left and right entered the perimeter of his vision. Moving his body ever so slowly, Henry viewed the head and main body of the shark cruising about twenty yards above him and off to his left. A silent curse escaped into the headpiece. He froze. Wide eyes followed the killer as best he could. Heartbeats – his own – deafened him. It became a struggle to control his breathing. The air pumping into the helmet seemed feeble. Had they forgotten him and stopped pumping? The predator disappeared into the shadow of the *Pink Pearl* above. A groan rolled around inside his helmet. Was there no way he could rip this headpiece off and have a proper look at his attacker? The urge to retain the enemy within his sights at all times overwhelmed him. Henry struggled to focus on his breathing. The shark came into view once more. It seemed much closer. Was it spiralling towards him? Henry could see a long scar on the nearside of the tough hide – maybe the outcome of a fight with another monster of the deep. Imagined oxygen deprivation weakened his legs. His arms felt as if they had no strength left. When he felt the knife begin to slip from his hold, he willed his fingers to tighten their grip. The pounding of blood through the carotid arteries in his neck threatened to choke him. Was this how he was going to die?

CHAPTER TWO

Cooktown

Abigail raked her fingers through the auburn hair now streaked with grey as it hung limp and moist around her face in the heat and humidity of another approaching monsoon season. She reached over to open the wooden louvres to their extremity in the hope of accessing a breath of cool air. Sharp green eyes examined the dirt stain on her fingertips. Along with the frown which marred her forehead, lines sprung out from the edges of her intelligent eyes. She sighed and mentally bemoaned the failure of her current housekeeper's attention to her cleaning duties. The canvas, which had protected the patients' beds lined up around the downstairs verandah of her home, had been replaced with these louvres nearly twelve years ago – two years before her only son Henry had left for an education in London, and her short visit at that time, to her family in the old country. Her fingernail flicked at the peeling paint, but her thoughts weren't really on the paintwork or the poor housekeeping. Her thoughts concentrated on the expected arrival of her son and his triumphant return with his medical qualifications from St. Bartholomew's Hospital. If his sea journey went as planned, he should be entering Port Darwin any day soon, if he had not already reached that point.

"Miss Abigail! Miss Abigail!"

Abigail Baldwin moved to the rear of the building. Her heart lifted. Eve Jones, no, Eve Dougall now – Abigail shook her head. How quickly the time had passed. And yet, when thinking about her son and the ten years he had been away studying, the time had dragged more slowly than the healing of a chronic leg ulcer. As she had witnessed over all the years assisting her brother at his surgery, they too seemed to take forever to resolve. Abigail remembered the day she rescued Eve, a child, from a fearful life on the streets of London all those years ago – shortly after her husband had died in eighteen sixty-five. Now her one-time maid, housekeeper, helper, nurse, and friend, was married to Gus Dougall, engineer and part-owner, with his brother Josh, of the coastal trader *The Northern Orchid* – since the demise of their mentor, Captain William Sloan.

Three young children scampered about Eve's legs while an eight-year-old child pushed a well-used perambulator with a babe asleep inside. Eve and Gus's oldest daughter Gina, at fifteen years of age, worked as a nurse in the surgery. Abigail and her twin brother, Doctor George Goldfinch, had delivered each of their five offspring. They now lived next door in the house long since vacated by Abigail's one-time companion Jane, and her husband, Ewen MacGregor – the previous Mate of *The Northern Orchid.* Jane and Ewen had moved back to Brisbane to offer improved education for their children.

"Hello, Eve, how are you today? How are the troops?"

Eve's smile widened. Her brown plaits tied loosely up near her ears, bounced.

"Oh, Miss Abigail, they are bursting with health as usual. This heat never bothers them at all, whereas I feel myself flagging before nine o'clock each morning." Holding a small biscuit tin in one hand, Eve walked up and held Abigail's hand in her other. Her sharp eyes did not miss the beginning of wrinkles in her saviour's once flawless skin. "You're looking tired yourself this morning. Has the excitement of Henry's imminent arrival been keeping you awake at night?"

Abigail's smile shamed the sun. "Oh, Eve, I cannot believe it will be only a short time before my Henry is standing here on Cooktown soil." Tears sparkled upon her eyelashes. She retrieved her hand from Eve's grasp and flung the tears away. "Come, my dear, into the kitchen. You must be thirsty." Abigail lifted her voice. "Would the children like a cool drink of cordial and a biscuit?"

"Yes, please, Miss Abigail." Those that could speak replied in unison.

With the children sent outside to drink their cordial in the shade, cups rattled in the saucers as Eve prepared the tea and opened the tin of biscuits.

"I'm sorry I have not been over for a few days, Miss Abigail. The baby has a tooth rising and there is little sleep for either of us. Gina is a wonderful help and my eight-year-old looks after her siblings like a little mother. How have you and Doctor George been managing? Are the patient numbers still down?"

Abigail poured the tea from the smaller of her two tea pots, before speaking. "With the gold at Palmer River dwindling and the Cooktown hospital growing, you can count on one hand the new cases we see at our surgery each day." She sipped from her cup and chewed her biscuit before going on, "We received a letter from our cousin who has been running the practice in Brisbane. He wants to leave the colonies and return to England. George and I must return to Brisbane within three months."

"Oh, Miss Abigail, that is wonderful news. My Gus has been hinting for months he should pack me and the children up and follow Miss Jane and Mr. Ewen to Brisbane. *The Northern Orchid* is in port there more than it is here in Cooktown. We would see each other more often."

Abigail smiled. Her gaze through the window took in the children playing tiggy around the mango tree. The smile turned to a grin.

"Perhaps *The Northern Orchid* might be in Brisbane too often, Eve. How many children are you planning on having?"

Eve dropped her eyes and chuckled softly. "I know, I know. I mentioned that to Gus myself, but he only laughed. He loves kids and he loves making them too." Her hand rubbed at her swollen abdomen.

Abigail's smile held a world of love but a little envy as well. "I will be so glad if you do decide to return to Brisbane. I would be bereft if you and the children were so far away."

"Have you and Doctor George decided on when you will be leaving, Miss Abigail?"

Abigail reached over to refill their teacups. "Henry will be at Thursday Island soon and in the latest correspondence from him, he plans to holiday there for a few weeks with his doctor friend Edward Benton, and family. When Henry eventually arrives here, he will help us with the move and join us as George's partner at the surgery in Brisbane. Apparently, it has been very busy and will need two doctors."

CHAPTER THREE

Pink Pearl

"Devil's eyeballs! Diver! Birdie, will you look out here?"

Diver Bird's head lifted at the sound of Curley's call from the stern of the vessel. His hands never left their hold on the rope and air hoses snaking their way down to Henry below as his eyes opened wide in horror.

"God forbid, that's one big shark. Hopefully, Henry hasn't seen it. It'll frighten the bejesus out of him." At that moment, Birdie felt the stillness of the man underwater. "I think he may have seen the shark." Diver Bird's gaze moved to Ed who stood beside Curley staring into the sea. "You know this fella, Squid. Is he likely to panic?"

Ed shook his head. "In all the years I worked in St. Bart's hospital with Red, I've never seen him flinch at whatever is thrown his way. He spent his early years helping his doctor uncle in the surgery at Cooktown during the height of the gold rush. But a shark wanting to feast on him, I don't know."

Birdie next addressed the deckhand now swinging the air pump handle.

"You just keep pumping that air, Teak. Don't you go watching the bloody shark."

His gaze returned to Ed whose eyes followed the shark. "Well, you can say a few Hail Marys or just pray Henry keeps perfectly still in the hope the monster isn't hungry or hasn't smelt him out yet."

Curley walked over to where Birdie held the umbilical cords loosely in his fingers straining to sense what may be happening below.

"How long's he been down there? You said you'd only give him ten minutes. That can be extended if needed as long as we keep the air up to him."

"Take the rifle up onto the helm deck and watch the bloody shark will you, Curley. Let me know the moment it shifts in any direction. I don't want to shoot it unless we have to – the blood will start a feeding frenzy with every shark in the ocean inviting themselves along." Birdie whispered. "Ask Ed and The Eel to come over here in case I have to rush Henry up and he needs medical attention. Quietly, Curley, we don't want to set everyone on edge."

But it was a bit late for that. The remainder of the divers and the crew, including the cook from the galley, hung over the side of the ship.

Henry struggled to draw air into his starving lungs. How was the shark going to make its move? Was the hungry marauder of the deep, going to swoop in one violent strike and remove his entire midriff in one crunch? He felt a tremor run through his body. All breathing stopped for a moment at the thought of his demise. Or was this devil-of-the-sea planning to play with him – like a cat torments a mouse? There was no doubt in his mind the hunter circling above had seen him and was undecided on how hungry he really felt, or how best to enjoy this tasty morsel.

And then it happened. A wall of water swirled around him. He felt himself stagger on the uneven surface of the reef. With his eyes clenched shut, Henry's body stiffened as he waited for the strike. His fist clenched on the knife.

And waited.

Something pulled at his waist. It tugged. Henry's paralysed fingers of his left hand felt the rope slip away. Curiosity, or was it masochism, opened his eyes. There was nothing to see in the small circle of his vision. Vainly he tried to rotate his head to locate the attacker. And there it was. The strong tail propelled the body forward – mouth opened wide. Evil eye partly opened.

Did he pass out? Henry's arms thrashed at the water. The pearling knife remained firmly clenched in his right hand. His left hand sought the rope. Relief of a kind rushed into him as the taut rough hemp contacted his fingertips. Henry's hand gripped the one of his two lifelines. He sucked at the feeble airflow from the other. Where was that damned overgrown fish? The water current flowed against his shoulders. Tugs were felt along the rope in his hand. Did it have the rope in its teeth pulling him along? Worse still, was the air hose in those same teeth? He sucked at the air in his helmet. Nothing. Or maybe just a little.

"Ooh." The soft sound whispered inside the headgear. His eyes caught the sight of his tormentor now a distance away with a large broken turtle in its mouth. Two other turtles paddled furiously away from the scene.

And then Henry felt something grabbing at his body; it dragged at his arms. Were there two hunters in this sea with him?

"Come on, you silly bugger. You've had enough of playing with the shark. Can you make those feet climb the ladder?"

Ed's anxious voice drifted into Henry as if from afar. Muscles trembled in his legs. His limbs felt as though they did not belong to him.

Diver Bird helped Ed with the last heave to lift Henry from the ladder and into the boat. With the diver out of the water, Birdie's hands immediately began to release the fasteners securing the helmet to the corselet. When Henry's head emerged, Diver joined him in sucking in a long deep breath.

"Geez, Henry, lad, you're one lucky son-of-a-gun. Not too many divers have lived to tell the tale after being that close to a prowling shark."

The auburn hair released from its confines framed the fear-whitened face, where even the freckles appeared faded. Henry stood unmoving. His gaze followed Ed's hands as they unfolded each of his fingers one by one, releasing the grip he had on the haft of the pearling knife.

With the *Pink Pearl* restored to order and the sun creeping down the western horizon, the conversation around the evening meal erupted into shark stories and lost divers. Henry slunk off to his sleeping rug on the fo'c's'le and tried to shut out their voices.

The next day, everyone was up at the first hint of light. Diver Bird's orders calling for action seeped into every nook and cranny on board the ship before rippling out across the waves of the sea. The *Pink Pearl's* sails billowed in a following breeze.

At Henry's query, Ed explained. "Birdie doesn't want to waste too much time getting to Thursday Island. He'll keep travelling day and night if the conditions are favourable. It'll take a week or so."

While the *Pink Pearl* made headway in an easterly direction, Henry watched Hikaru and The Eel sorting through their heaps of pearl shells gathered on the deck. His mesmerised green eyes fixated on the speed of the divers' hands as they manipulated their knives without any waste of energy or time. Shells were opened and gently examined. On the odd occasion, when a pearl was found in residence, it was removed with the delicacy and skill of the best surgeons he had ever seen at work. The few pearls collected were stored in a wooden box, kept locked in the safe in Birdie's cabin below deck. Open shells were stored in each diver's large cane-woven basket on the deck. He had seen more of these storage baskets full of shells in the hold below.

"That's a lot of work for a few pearls, Birdie," Henry remarked later. "What will happen to the shells now?"

"Most of our money is made from the pearl shell itself. Sometimes we strike it lucky and get some perfect pearls to grace a lady's lovely neck."

To speed up their travel, Diver Bird sailed his ship with two teams. He and two deck hands in one team and Curley, Teak and Teak's brother in the second team. Each team worked six-hour shifts. Birdie and Curley each led a team. They guided the ship while the deck-hands answered the instructions to maintain sails and kept each other awake. Ed was usually found refreshing his seamanship skills under Diver Bird's tutelage.

On the fourth morning, the whispered patter of busy feet first registered on Henry's tired brain. He remained recumbent with his eyes shut. The boat was still – absolutely still. A quiet mumble of voices fell upon his ears. At the sound of Diver Bird's laughter, which entered his brain, not unlike the St. Bartholomew's bells in London on a Sunday morning, Henry's head snapped up.

Birdie's voice, flavoured with mirth, danced around the deck. "I'll take your money, you fellas. I tell you we're going to see a storm before this day is done."

During the day, the sails moped from the masts with only an occasional tickle of wind and the sea current to propel the *Pink Pearl* forward. Irritation became an almost tangible thing. Birdie fretted at this delay to his planned schedule. His nagging of the crew along with the brooding heat and humidity had the men grumbling among themselves – when out of sight of the captain. Henry and Ed – even Curley – gave Diver Bird a wide berth. The cook's temperament did not change. Cook was always a sullen, unhappy sod, but he did produce edible food, which was more than the crews of most pearl ships could say of their cooks.

For one hour before the sun approached the horizon, the wind lifted and the sails billowed. Birdie's raucous laughter flowed across the decks on the breeze. Everyone cheered, but the revelry was short-lived. At dusk, the ship lay still in the water once again. Only the current from the Arafura Sea behind them pushed them closer to its rival current driven by the Pacific Ocean on the other side of the Torres Strait.

"Damn, we may as well light a lantern and have a bite to eat." Birdie turned his head to face the galley. "Cook! Have you anything in your dungeon down there to fill an empty stomach?"

Cook's answer came in the repeated ringing of the gong stationed at his doorway. This gong was seldom used, given Cook's voice covered the length and breadth of the ship, when called to do so.

Birdie next instructed the crew to furl and secure the sails. "We'll be in for a blow before the new day. You may as well come and eat."

The meal was barely served when the storm hit without any further warning. In a frightening suddenness, dark clouds blackened out any light from the moon or stars above. The ship rose and fell upon the roughening swell. Fast approaching lightning emanated in the north-west. Each strike illuminated the wide-eyed faces of the crew surprised at the sudden squall. Claps of thunder united into an unbroken drumroll.

"Ed! Henry! That mizzen-mast yardarm is rattling around like my grandmother's teeth in her head. You've finished eating, go and tie it down more securely, will you." Birdie turned his attention to the crew members. "Teak, gobble up your food, I want the sea anchors released."

Ed and Henry proceeded to the stern of the ship to do as they had been asked. The others stood at the entrance to the galley listening to Birdie's litany of further orders.

Ed found the loose tie and asked Henry to put his weight into pulling the rope taut, while he attempted to make it more secure.

"Whatever you do, don't let the tension on the rope go," Ed told Henry. "This damn yardarm isn't too happy about being corralled."

Both men jumped and swore as a streak of lightning struck the sea only several hundred yards away from the ship. They shook their heads at the force of the immediate thunderclap to follow. The light and noise, now a solid wall, enclosed the small stage with its unfolding drama. Birdie and the crew stood at the base of the main mast, frozen in time, staring for what proved to be fateful seconds.

Within moments, the next lightning strike split the main mast. The accompanying clap of thunder silenced the crack of the thick timber as it tore asunder from top to bottom before it burst into a blaze of fire at the upper deck level, engulfing every man gathered around the galley entrance. The parting of the timber ripped down through the decks and opened up a large hole in the ship's hull. Water thundered into the holds which in turn quenched the fires as it dragged the *Pink Pearl* to a watery grave.

Neither Ed nor Henry registered the destruction of their shipmates nor their ship. The power of the strike flung the mizzen mast yardarm, with the sail unravelling like a kite, out into the ocean, until it landed with a splash in the water. Following the shock of the fatal lightning strike and the crash of thunder, the men's eyes burnt, their ears clanged and their minds froze.

Within the blackness of his head, Henry felt the rope on his fingertips. Ed's last words returned to him.

"Don't let the rope go."

He clenched the hemp. His body became the tail of the sail kite as he flew out over the sea for thirty yards or more. A powerful odour of smoke filled his nostrils before a wall of pain erupted in his rib cage as he landed across something in the water.

At the other end of the spar, Ed's left foot had been caught up between the sail lanyard and the yardarm. Both his canvas shoes had disappeared into the darkness. His body flapped in the air unnoticed by a mind trying to comprehend the red heat of pain in one ankle. Ed's head landed with a thud on the yardarm settling on the water. Unconsciousness rushed over him along with the wild sea as instinct wrapped his arms and legs around the timber.

Sea water swallowed the smouldering fires in the timbers, the ropes and the sail edges now cast upon the ocean. Debris from the *Pink Pearl* dispersed on the turbulent waters. Larger pieces of the ship's broken body drifted off into the distance with flickering fires lighting the way until drenched by the waters of the sea. Unrecognizable charred human remains sank slowly into the depths. Lightning and thunder took their destructive forces further east-south-east. A calmness returned to the seas of the burial site.

Through breaking dark clouds, a piccaninny dawn tinted the east. Henry groaned. His eyes remained closed. Light rain fell upon him. A breeze sent a shiver through his body. What the hell was digging into his ribs? The sound of waves lapping close at hand aroused his curiosity. He struggled to roll over and nearly fell from his perilous perch. A louder moan greeted the passing waves.

What on earth was he doing here? Had they been drinking last night – heavily? The presence of seawater all about him sent him into a sudden movement, which once again, nearly upset his delicate floating raft.

Henry's feeble hands patted under his body to identify this uncomfortable mat upon which he slept. His eyes opened. A wave of nausea washed over him along with a crest of seawater. He spat. His exploring fingers revealed his tangled body sprawled out upon a sail canvas draped across something floating on the sea beneath him. Pain ripped along his side as he tried to move. He sank lower on this sail into what he realized was the container of marker-floats Birdie kept on the deck of his *Pink Pearl*.

The deck! The ship! Once more nausea set him gagging when he tried to lift his head. The lightning strike and the scene of the erupting fire around the crew on the ship in the night flashed across his memory. This cannot be. He looked more closely at his raft. A coughing sound came from close by. With his head raised, Henry stared in the direction from whence it came. In the poor light of the predawn, he discovered the sail still attached to the long wooden yardarm. Snorts and movement were heard and felt from the other end of the timber spar. A pounding heartbeat in his chest stole his breath as the vision of his recent encounter with the shark returned to fill his head. Panic threatened to engulf him. Common-sense returned. The shadow he stared at was not a shark.

"Devil's blood, what the hell's happened?" Sharp coughs filled the early morning. Water splashed as whoever it was attempted to secure his hold on the floating timber of Henry's sail-raft.

"Ed! Eddie, is that you?"

"Red, is that you? What happened?" Ed coughed, shook his head, and spat saltwater from his mouth when a wave washed over his face. He inhaled noisily. "I've got half the bloody ocean in my lungs. And the rain's saturating the little bit of air I'm trying to breathe. What's going on? Where's the *Pink Pearl*?" Another cough interrupted a long groan.

"Hang on, Ed. I'm coming to help you." At that moment, Henry realized he was shoeless, but suddenly it did not seem important.

"Where are you, Red? I'm spreadeagled across a log of some sort."

Henry endeavoured to ignore his pain as he manoeuvred that part of his body partially inside the oversized hamper, up and over the wooden frame digging into his ribs. A sigh of relief was drowned in a splash of seawater breaking against the raft. He slipped down to float in the arms of the partially submerged sail. Both he and the sail began to sink further into the water. Henry's moisture-wrinkled hands grabbed frantically at the ridged edge of the canvas which he then used to drag himself up to the floating yardarm and towards Ed's voice. When Henry did this, the basket threatened to wriggle out from under the edge of the sail. A sudden thought interrupted Henry's rescue mission.

"Hang on a second, Ed. Can you hang on a bit?"

Sea water splashed over him as he about-turned and caught the basket before it popped out from under the restricting sail. Threading his fingers through the dangling lanyards along the top edge of the container, he hauled the floating basket with its imprisoned markers, towards the timber spar. The stiffness in Henry's cold fingers hindered his attempt to anchor the prize. To add to the difficult exercise, Henry's head repeatedly sank below the surface of the sea as the weight of his body dragged the sail deeper into the water. Once he had his legs astride the floating yardarm, he wrapped the lanyard, attached at one end to the basket, around the spar, and tied a knot. A vague thought swam on the periphery of his mind on how he planned to use this basket of floats.

Henry slithered his way to the other end of the timber pole. A shiver of fear ran through his body at the sight of the wound on Ed's forehead. Blood in the water was not an ideal environment for them to be in. But then floating on a pole with an attached sail drifting in the open sea was not a situation he would choose to be in either.

"It seems, Red, we're in a bit of a pickle." Ed's fear-clenched throat attempted to keep his voice light-hearted. Having spent most of his younger life at sea, Ed struggled to cope with the dread in his mind, when he discovered the open wound – blood and sharks a demonic pair.

"Right, the first thing to do is cover your wound as best we can." Henry pushed his own fear aside and concentrated on medical practicalities.

"Yeah, Doc, I already thought of that. Can you tear a strip off my shirt tails?"

Henry heaved Ed up into a more secure position on the spar with his arms clinging to the timber and both his legs lying along the sail fanning out under the water.

"I think I'll use my shirt tails. It'll be easier." Henry heaved his own body upright with his legs wrapped around the yardarm. He reached down and lifted the corner hem of his shirt and drew it up to his teeth.

"You know you still have Birdie's knife on your belt – it might be easier."

Surprise brightened Henry's eyes. "I'd forgotten all about it." Numb fingers fumbled with the flap of the pouch as he dragged the knife out of its nesting place.

Ed's warning, "Don't drop that knife, Red, it might come in handy if we hope to ever get out of this predicament," did not in any way add confidence to Henry's attempts as he dressed the wound. He tied the knot of cotton material firmly.

With his teeth clenched on the knife, Henry slithered back into the water, paddled around Ed's legs, and across to the fire-blackened point of the sail which undulated in the waves and tide. His mind clamped down upon his memory of the cruising shark of days before as he trod water with his legs. With the edge of the sail wrapped around his wrist, he attempted to cut off a piece of the canvas near the fire damage. By the time he returned to the patient, Henry was exhausted. With the knife back in its pouch, he clung to the yardarm drawing deep breaths between each wave washing over him.

Ed freed one hand and assisted Henry to reinforce the dressing on his head with the sail remnant.

"What's happened to Birdie and the others do you think, Red?"

Henry tried not to think about Ed's query.

Lying along the spar, they each dropped their head onto a folded arm in an attempt to keep their faces above the wavelets washing over them.

It was only a short time later, when Henry's head snapped up. He felt Ed's body slipping from the timber.

"Ed! Ed, wake up."

"Yeah, I'm awake."

"Wake up properly. You nearly slipped into the water." Henry reached over to help his friend return to his previous position lying astride the timber. "Now don't go back to sleep for a minute. Stay awake. Can you do that? I'm going to get some rope out of the basket of floats and tie us both to this log."

"Hmmmm."

"Ed, wake up properly."

"Will you drop the noise, I'm awake."

"Well, don't go back to sleep until I tie you with the rope."

"When I was a kid, my mother used to say I was fit to be tied."

"Keep talking to me about when you were a kid, while I get the ropes. I want to know you're still awake."

"How can I talk? My throat is red raw from all this salt. I would kill for a dram of whiskey."

"Yeah, well I might even join you in that. Will some fresh water do? I've an idea."

"Sweet saints, yes."

Henry slithered back along the yardarm to the other end, where the attached oversized hamper floated. He stretched to reach inside and past the marker-floats, to collect the rolls of rope at the bottom. With much of his body now over the top frame and his head under water well inside the basket, his fingers grabbed what rolls of ropes he touched. His lungs burnt for air when he found himself unable to extricate his body from the confines of the container. Just when he felt he was done for, his flailing feet hooked around the yardarm. This gave him enough leverage to haul his head and torso into the open air. His lungs dragged in torturous breaths.

With his equilibrium restored somewhat, Henry's water-wrinkled fingers sorted amongst the five coils of rope he had rescued. He selected two, each about fifteen feet in length, and the remaining three he tied to the yardarm beside the basket.

He stopped and swung his head around. "Ed, are you still awake? I can't hear you talking." But the shape of his friend's body lying along the timber reassured him despite the lack of a response. Henry's hands and fingers, now numb with cold, fumbled as he secured one length of rope to his waist and belt and the other to the yardarm.

On the journey back to Ed, he pondered on the issue of their drinking-water predicament. If the light scuds of rain of this morning continued, thirst did not pose an immediate problem, but once the sun erupted with a vengeance, thirst promised to be a frightening concept.

Another thought niggled inside Henry's head. What were they going to do, when their bodies did not have the strength left to lift their heads and allow them to breathe between the bigger waves? If another storm followed, and there was everything to suggest it might with the thickening clouds above them, this could become a very significant complication.

Anxiety caused Henry to draw a sharp breath when he reached out to touch Ed's unmoving form lying along the yardarm. He thought his friend was dead. A snort and a cough followed by creative curses reassured him his companion was still definitely conscious, if not particularly alert.

With Ed's safety rope secured, Henry returned to the basket of floats. He sat staring at it for what seemed hours, but was possibly only minutes. He needed to get the basket back under the sail, but first, he had something he wanted to do. Reaching into the basket he untied a lanyard securing one of the markers to the basket frame. This proved to be not as difficult as diving into the depths of the basket for the ropes, had been earlier. This float's lanyard became another item tied to the end of the timber spar without any sail attached. He repeated the process with another float. Satisfaction gleamed in his salt-reddened eyes at his success. Now he had two marker-floats tied to the spar and two still attached inside the basket.

Once more Henry sat in thought planning what he had in mind. If he could lift the sail back over the basket and secure it under the canvas, was there some way the sail might be manoeuvred, folded, or pleated, to form a receptacle inside the space from where the two marker-floats had been removed? A receptacle that might hold rainwater – or even dew moisture.

"Red, what are you doing up there? You've got this damn yardarm bouncing like a schoolyard of girls dancing around a maypole."

"I see you're better then – grumbling once more. I'm tidying my office."

"Saints above, I'm not going to ask." Ed wriggled his body in an attempt to gain a more comfortable position. He dragged his hand over his face to remove the sea and rainwater. "What time will you be serving breakfast then?"

Relief filled Henry's smile. "I'm the office sorter, you're the hunter."

"Poor service on this cruise, I say."

"I was thinking, if I tied one of these floats up short under the sail near you, it should hold the sail up a little more and give you something to lie your head and chest over – to lift you out of the water a bit." Henry pointed to his two rescued marker-floats.

"Dare I ask what role the other marker has to play in your dreams?"

"I plan on tying it under the far point of the sail to help keep it from sagging deep into the water."

Silence rose loud and long from Ed's end of the yardarm.

"Red, I'm glad to see you so positive, but I don't want you to build up your hopes too high. You do realize the chance of us being found out here is next to nothing. No one will even know we're missing for at least a fortnight. This flimsy raft offers little hope. We can't live without food and water for too long – you know that. I'm truly sorry I got you into this fix."

Henry hung his head. He did not speak. Inside, he knew Ed was right. He knew Ed was only trying to prepare him for what would undoubtedly follow. His mind took him back to his mother and his uncle in Cooktown. A grin lifted his downturned mouth as a picture of his friend Smiley's face filled his mind.

NO! I may not survive this, but until that time comes, I will do everything possible to stay alive.

He did not answer Ed's warning. Fear and determination struggled for prime position in his gut, as he bent to the task of diving into the water and struggling with the basket and the sail to achieve the earlier vision in his head. With two floats less in the basket, it now lifted itself and the sail covering it, no more than a couple of feet above sea level. Henry found he had to use small lengths of lanyards to tie the sail to the upper frame of the basket to prevent the weight of the outside sail from dragging the bowl-shaped canvas from within the basket. He utilized the point of Birdie's knife to make slots in the canvas.

Now to secure the final marker-float to the other end of the sail. It took a conscious effort of willpower to force himself to drop into the sea and paddle himself and the float to the site he had chosen. A lanyard hung from his mouth. Weariness gnawed away at his determination. But determination won out and the float lifted the tail of the sail to the surface of the sea.

Pain screamed from the muscles of Henry's arms and legs by the time he sat his butt on the spar, and rested his head on his arms crossed along the rim of the basket to watch the light raindrops fall into his water receptacle. His tired smile held a shade of satisfaction. Henry's eyes closed.

Without the sun to indicate how long he had slept, Henry was unsure of the time of day, when he felt the spar bouncing under his hips. A glance at the water level inside the canvas water bowl lifted his spirits. His grin returned.

"Hey, Ed, want a drink of water?"

Ed smiled. "I don't suppose you've a crystal glass to be drinking from then, Red?"

Henry moved over to allow Ed access to the freshwater.

Ed shook the salt water from his hands before dipping inside to scoop up a little of the contents.

"Wow, that's nectar of the gods. You're not just a dumb doctor then, are you?"

They both laughed at Ed's reference to one of their previous lecturers not flush with kind remarks to his pupils.

Henry followed suit in tasting his rewards. "It has a hint of salt in it, but what can we expect? No doubt, the sailcloth has been saturated in salt spray over the years."

"I guess it's now up to me to find something to eat." Ed grinned.

But hunting food in the middle of a sea from a flimsy craft with no tools, other than their pearling knives, presented what appeared to be impossible challenges.

CHAPTER FOUR

Cooktown

The lap of waves against the hulls of the two large ships and the numerous smaller vessels anchored on the Endeavour River hummed a lullaby for the folk asleep in their beds at Cooktown. An insistent call of a mopoke in the trees on Grassy Hill kept harmony. Wails of a curlew echoed across the cemetery. The murmur of voices from the hotel in Charlotte Street had been silenced some three hours since. The protest of hunger from a young baby split the hot and humid air of the sleeping township.

In the stables at the bottom of the garden of Doctor George Goldfinch's medical surgery, the body of the young black man they called Smiley, asleep on his bunk, stiffened. His head and torso snapped upwards as he woke from his dream. His dark eyes glistened in the moonlight beaming in through the open doorway. This was not the first time his father appeared to him in his sleep. A tremor ran through his body. The horse resting under the awning outside stamped a nervous foot. Smiley's gaze burnt into the night. As if sleepwalking, he stood beside his bunk when another spasm shook his body. His head cleared – his plan now a distinct vision in his mind. The sound of his tortured breath filled the shed as he moved on silent feet to collect his things for travel. He must go to the place where the lagoons sing, when the skies fall open – to where the land becomes a sea of water during the wet season. Such a journey, for any adult man travelling on his own, promised to be an arduous one. For his friend Henry's sake, Smiley knew he had no choice.

Smiley took up his satchel inside of which were his tin of pencils, a sketching pad wrapped in oilskin and a honing stone. This bag he slung across his body. He wore a cut-off pair of Doctor George's old black trousers. After patting the fold-up knife in his pocket, he slipped out of the shed with a soft word to the horse watching his every move. Having disappeared years before on walkabout, Smiley promised an anxious Doctor George never to leave again without telling him he was going. On silent feet, Smiley walked down to where the doctor slept on one of the empty patient beds on the downstairs verandah.

"Doctor, Doctor George," Smiley spoke softly so as not to disturb the man at the other end of the line of beds.

George's eyes opened on the first whisper. "Yes, Smiley, what's wrong?"

"I go walkabout, Doctor George. I must go bring Henry home."

"Botheration, Smiley, why do you always have to go haring off in the middle of the night? What do you mean – bring Henry home?"

But, like a silent wraith, the black body of Smiley disappeared into the night. Dingoes howled from the hills across the river. Despite his limping gait, Smiley's feet did not disturb the ground upon which he walked. Domestic dogs gave no warning of his presence. The narrow bush track cut down to the river bank, where his people kept a canoe hidden in the mangroves. The smell of saltwater, mangrove vegetation and river mud blended in the air whispering over his body. His feet sank into the muddy silt, while he stood still on the bank listening and sensing for the presence of a crocodile in the vicinity. When all seemed at peace, he recovered his two boomerangs, one light and one heavier, and his long and short spears, from where they were kept hidden in the timber. After throwing the bark camouflage covering aside, he turned the small canoe over and placed his hunting tools in, beside the single oar. Out on the water, he knelt awkwardly – handicapped by the limited movement of his scarred legs. With strong strokes, his muscled arms worked the paddle driving the fragile vessel across the water, avoiding the raised sandbank on the far side, where the crocodiles gathered to feast on the waste from any vessels in the harbour.

Smiley left behind a very puzzled George Goldfinch who struggled to fathom what his native friend had meant; 'to bring Henry home'. Henry was a passenger on an overseas steamship that should currently be anchored at Port Kennedy on Thursday Island. They expected the arrival of his nephew at Cooktown in a matter of weeks. Should he mention this strange comment from Smiley to his sister Abigail? To do so might only worry her unnecessarily about her son. But then, he and his twin never kept anything from each other. Besides, he knew Abigail to be an observant woman who would know immediately if he tried to withhold anything of interest. She always managed to wheedle out his secrets. Maybe first thing in the morning, he should go to the post office and telegraph the ship to assure himself there was nothing amiss and Henry was quite safe. Yes, that's what he would do, first thing.

CHAPTER FIVE

Henry and Edward

Neither man slept soundly on this, their second night at sea on their flimsy raft. Waves washed with irregular frequency over their floating yardarm. On the first morning, hunger had caused nothing more than a minor irritant as they had eaten just prior to the shipwreck, but by the second morning, their stomachs announced, with determination, their shrunken state. Henry's improvised water tank, constructed the day before, held thirst at bay. Both men avoided sitting astride the yardarm and stretched their legs along the trailing sail in the hope of going unnoticed by any prowling shark. Sometimes they sat with their butts on the log. In Ed's case, he faced the one marker-float, now secured under the sail in front of him, on which he lay his upper body and arms. In the case of Henry, he draped his arms across the frame of the cane-woven basket containing the last remaining floats, ropes and the drinking water – the rainwater with its strengthening hint of salt.

As the second day wore on, the weather deteriorated into heavy showers of rain. Wavelets turned into breaking wave crests. A cool wind whistled through their summer attire. The men shivered. Unseen in the dullness cast across the sea, their faces and extremities turned blue. Intermittent calls from one to the other competed with the noise of the wind and the waves.

"You alright, Ed?"

"You alright, Red?"

Both accepted grunts of reply.

"We have company, Red. Best you don't move a muscle."

Sunk in his deep thoughts of a not-too-hopeful future, Henry did not, at first, register Ed's warning. When the words penetrated his mind, he struggled not to jump up or move in any way. He felt the heartbeats in his throat strangle his breath. *What now?*

Ed continued his warning, "A frigate bird is sitting on your water collector. Its bum's hanging the wrong way around. If you scare the thing, it's sure to explode up into the air leaving its droppings behind in our drinking water."

The bird's head twisted towards the voice from the other end of the log. Its beak pecked at the sleeve on the arm over Henry's head.

"What's it doing?"

The bird hopped around the basket's frame. The glossy dark feathers shone in the fleeting streaks of sunshine. The head, with its long knob-ended beak, rocked from one side to the other side. Its orange bib below its chin flashed with each movement of the head.

"Just investigating a strange being in his world. At least his bum's over sea water now. Oh, no, it's off. Something frightened it." Ed's head swung left and right. "What the devil's that? Look, Red, look – you don't get to see that too often this far east."

To the west of them, nearly one hundred yards out, the sea churned. Flying fish rose into the air and flew above the surface of the water before they landed back in the sea again.

"Something hungry is on their tail." Flying fish landed in the shallow pool made by their canvas raft – within arm's distance. Ed's hands flashed out. In seconds a fish flapped from each clenched fist.

Their recent visitor, the frigate bird, joined the hunting melee. It dived into the midst of the flying fish.

Henry's eyes scanned the waters towards the rear of the school of fish. "Ed, can you see what's chasing these fish?"

Both men searched the waters. Ed pointed one of his fish-holding arms. "See over there, Red, a large bonito fish, a predator fond of flying fish. There'll be a few of them for sure. Oh, is that … no, saints preserve us, those fins are not sharks' fins, they're dolphins' fins – another hunter of the flying fish."

When the entertainment dispersed and calm returned to the raft, Henry watched Ed cutting fillets off the two fish. Even though the answer was obvious, he found it difficult to come to terms with.

"How do we cook your fish?"

"Sorry, Red, raw fish only is on the menu. I understand flying fish don't taste too bad – here" he passed a fish over to Henry.

The slippery flesh curdled Henry's stomach. He gagged at the feel of it in his mouth. But hunger soon killed off his fussy attitude. He began to chew little bites.

As the third dawn fought its way through the clouds, the twisted bodies of the two exhausted men slept – all-be-it lightly.

Henry opened his red, swollen eyes. He sat up to look around him. The sight of an overflowing water storage brought a smile of satisfaction, but curious anxiety soon filled his expression.

"Ed, Ed."

A grunt rolled back along the yardarm in reply.

"Ed, wake up. Look, we've changed direction. The sun is on our left. We must be going south."

Ed's bandaged head lifted, but it was sometime before the dark, sticky eyes opened. Gradually comprehension dawned along with the sun.

"You're right, Red; we've turned to the south. The currents in the Gulf of Carpentaria travel clockwise. If we're lucky, this mixing bowl of the gulf waters will drop us off on the west coast of Cape York Peninsula." His mouth dropped. "On the other hand, if these accursed currents decide to haul us up into going-nowhere-circles and refuse to spew us out, things might become grim."

"Assuming the current gods are in our favour, how long do you think it might be until we reach a shoreline?"

"With everything in our favour, maybe a few days. Hopefully, later today we'll get a sighting of the land on the horizon."

The brief flash of hope in Henry's eyes faded. "A few days? We'll be damn weak and hungry by then. My stomach already thinks my throat's been cut."

"With any luck, a fish may come up and jump into our laps. It's possible. Look at the flying fish yesterday …, or was that the day before?" Ed's voice carried no element of confidence.

"What about a turtle? I saw several of them pass by yesterday."

"Devil's tongue – hush your mouth. Whatever we do, we don't eat any turtles while we're sitting here on a narrow log and a thin sheet of canvas. Sharks can smell turtle flesh from miles away. Most pearling boats won't allow their divers to eat any turtle before diving."

Even under the layer of sunburn, Henry's face appeared to fade at his memory of the shark's attack on the turtle rather than himself only days before.

Both men buried their faces in their arms once again and dozed. The sunburnt skin of his face as it rubbed on his shirt stirred Henry. Having reddish hair had always been a curse for him, when in the Australian sun. The problem to find some type of cover for his face held his attention. A rueful smile brightened his eyes at a fleeting thought. He wouldn't sneer at one of his mother's fancy parasols if it was offered right now. In his mind, his singlet offered itself up as a sacrifice, but Henry recalled how cold he had been during the night. That experience would have been much worse without his singlet, despite its saturated state. He loosened several top buttons of his shirt, hunched his shoulders then dragged the shirt up over the unruly auburn hair leaving the collar open over his forehead. Relief from the sun on his red face was short-lived as his back and shoulders began to ache and the wind and waves cooled the exposed back over his kidneys, where the shirt tails had been removed to make Ed's head bandage.

It seemed inevitable he was going to have to make another paddling trip to the trailing end of the sail to remove another remnant of canvas to wrap around his head. Nausea triggered by fear swirled in his empty gut. The talk of sharks earlier hung in his memory. Henry appreciated their partly submerged canvas sail held little protection, but it felt so much safer paddling above it than swimming in the open water.

"Red, what on earth are you doing now? You're bouncing the damn log again."

"Sorry, Ed, I have to get more sail to cover my head. This sunburn's killing me."

"Stop worrying, if you can feel the pain, you must still be alive."

But Henry continued on his endeavour. With the strip of canvas in his teeth and the knife back in its pouch, he followed his umbilical cord of rope to his original seat. As he pulled himself up onto the yardarm, the aftermath of his fear heaved his stomach into a spasm of dry retching. Another half-hour or so was spent as he patterned the cover to protect his head and face. A flap hung over his forehead and another over the back of his neck. Extensions wrapped around the side of his face and under his chin to be tied.

"I presume you won't be wearing that to the Ascot track then, Red."

"It does the job and that's all I'm worried about."

"Can we stop wriggling the log now?"

Both men settled into a doze.

Henry woke with a start. "Ed, are you alright? You reckoned I bounced the log, what are you doing?"

He looked over to find Ed now astride the spar holding an impaled fish flapping on the blade of his knife.

"Hungry?" Was the laughing reply.

"You betcha," But a cloud of doubt drifted across Henry's face. "Raw fish again, isn't it?"

"Don't be choosy now. The boys on the little pearl luggers with limited cooking facilities eat raw fish every day."

Ed removed the fillets with the scales still attached, from either side of the fish and handed one to Henry. Ed placed the other fillet on his lap, while he tossed the head and bones as far from their raft as he was able.

"Scrape off the scales, Henry, then cut off little pieces at a time. You'll find them a bit chewy, but it's that or starvation."

Disgust filled every line on Henry's face as he struggled to chew and swallow the first few bites of their small offering. Sticky fingers removed the occasional scale stuck on his lip or face. The gratitude messages received from his stomach dissolved the facial disgust and replaced it with a satisfied smile.

"Not too bad at all, Ed."

"Hunger does improve one's appreciation."

Only their rainwater added to their intake for the remainder of the day.

The night slipped over them leaving both men with the gentle sound of the sea lapping against the log and their individual dark thoughts lapping on the periphery of their minds. Henry's thoughts drifted back to his home in Cooktown, where his mother, uncle and his native friend Smiley, were all kept busy running the medical practice. Was he ever to see them again?

The morning sun burst upon them. The material of their clothing posed little resistance to its scorching rays. Lassitude and the ache of empty stomachs haunted both men. Ed lay floating across the sail with his head on one folded arm anchoring him to their one solid stay. In the hand of his other arm resting on the yardarm wrinkled fingers saturated with seawater held his pearling knife. His eyes stared out over the waters of the gulf.

Henry, now twisted sideways between the timber and his adapted water vessel, watched with little interest until he sensed rather than recognized the stiffening of Ed's body. His friend's quiet words fell like a sword blade across his ears.

"Henry, do not move – not an inch."

Henry's body froze and his eyes roved around their sockets searching for whatever it was Ed had seen. Inside his head, he once again visualized the cruising shark at the reef near Darwin. He bit his lip and struggled not to move his head. When the flash of the long thin pale body with its brown dots and blotched gold spots zipped onto the log, over Ed's shoulders and back into the sea, Henry could not prevent the grunt of surprise. He shuddered. Ed cursed. The sea snake whipped its way across the water.

"Fuck, I hate them things."

Ed's expletive surprised Henry almost as much as the appearance of the reptile. Ed may have spent most of his childhood living a harsh life on board ship with the pearlers, but having a father of strict religious beliefs, Ed's curses were usually mild and came in moderation. Henry did not have much time to ponder this thought before Ed's next warning turned his head out to sea.

"Look, Red, a bait ball of fish."

Henry followed Ed's gaze to where a large dark cloud of fish just below the surface of the water swarmed towards their floating refuge.

Fear challenged his empty stomach when Ed's frown relayed the message – there might be every reason to be fearful.

"This might mean breakfast for us, or it could be we might be breakfast for the inevitable predator following this lot."

Ed's words still hung in the air, when his arm holding the knife flashed out. Within a blink of Henry's eyes, a sizeable fish fluttered on Ed's blade once again. But this time Ed did not wave his prize in the air. He dug the point of the knife with the fish dangling from its blade into the timber spar.

"Keep down! Stay still!"

Like a speeding train, the large circling ball of fish raced towards their raft. Flashes of reflected sunlight in their scales lit up the dark curtain of swimming bodies. It appeared their raft was to be swamped. At the last minute, as if on a driver's command, the thousands of fish swung off at a sharp right angle away to their left. Frozen to his seat on the log, the ache of hunger in Henry's stomach was quickly forgotten, when fear turned to terror in his gut. He did not need Ed's next warning as the familiar triangle of a shark's fin flashed amongst the tide of fish. Then there were two fins making random charges into the prey. The tail of one shark hit the edge of the yardarm. It almost unseated Henry as the predator dived into the swirling bait ball. The two sharks followed the fish without further bothering the men.

Erratic heartbeats and strangled breaths almost suffocated both observers, as they struggled to bring their emotions under control.

Ed's broken laugh accompanied his words. "I can remember once saying, I'd rather face a shark head-on than Matron Ferguson of St. Bart's on one of her bad days, but I've changed my mind on that point. I'd rather face Matron Fergie on her very worst of worst days rather than a bloody hungry shark."

Henry did not answer immediately. He drew in slow deep breaths.

"Twice I've avoided the appetite of a shark. It's doubtful I'll be so lucky the third time." His voice shook.

"The gods are with us, Red. It's not a forgone conclusion the shark will be lucky the third time. It could be you who is the lucky one at a third encounter." Ed struggled to put enthusiasm into his words of hope. He unwedged his knife and began to fillet their meal.

Both men chewed in silence. Henry, usually the optimist, began to feel the effort seemed such a waste of time. Why attempt to sustain a body which was destined to nourish the sea? The lassitude of the early morning dragged once more at his failing optimism. The men dozed and chewed at their raw fish on and off during the day.

Henry's eyes opened as the sun hung low on the horizon. His head, draped over his arms, faced east. While he readjusted his makeshift canvas hat, Henry stared through swollen eyes. He raised his head and upper body. He willed his eyes to focus.

"Ed," his tired voice lifted just a fraction louder than the lapping of the water on their frail raft.

"Hmmm."

"Are those clouds I see on the eastern horizon, or am I looking at land?"

Ed lifted his head. He stared eastwards. "If those are storm clouds, we're in no fit state to survive another tossing about on this sea, but there's every chance you're looking at land."

Darkness took away their vision of hope, but enthusiasm stirred in their blood. As the moon glided across the heavens, Henry and Ed made their plans.

"Ed, have you thought about what we're going to face if that was the land we saw at sunset?"

"Yes, Red, we're not out of the woods yet, not by a long shot."

"What is the west coast of Cape York Peninsula like, do you know?"

Ed sat silent for some moments. His memories included several landings his father had made on the west coast of Cape York Peninsula. His father had more than one site he liked to stop at to cook and dry the bêche-de-mer when they had abundant supplies. The landing near the Mitchell River, with his father and crew, when he was about ten years of age, had been unforgettable for the number of crocodiles. As he recalled the event, his ears echoed again with the sound of gunfire. He remembered how his feet burnt on the hot sands through which they ran, desperate to reach the dinghy. A memory he tried to forget. Now fifteen years later, in the darkness of pale moonlight, he rubbed at the softened, wrinkled skin of his hands and his feet.

"When we reach the shore …," Ed paused for a second, while the devil in his head suggested, *If we reach the shore …*, "We'll need to wrap our feet in canvas bandages. The rough hot sands will make mincemeat of our bare feet." Ed fell silent for a moment, as his thoughts continued. "We'll need to make a satchel of sorts to carry your water-bag – something resembling those the stockmen carry. You'll have to tie a lanyard around the neck of the water bag. We can't carry the basket."

The yardarm wobbled as Henry wriggled into a more comfortable position. His voice gained some enthusiasm.

"Ed, how about we cut two large pieces of canvas, one for a shelter and the other to build another collection point for drinking water? We'd better take some ropes and the smaller lanyards."

"With the monsoons not too far away, we might be lucky to catch some rain. If not, there should be morning dew to trap. This west coast doesn't see much, if any, rain in the dry season."

Silence returned as the men's hopes and thoughts and plans burrowed into their brains.

"You know, Red, we won't be in any fit state to carry too much. Loops of rope may rip the skin from our shoulders even with our shirts as protection."

"I'll cut more canvas to use as pads."

Ed chuckled, which in turn made Henry laugh.

"We'll be as right as rain, Ed, you'll see. I'll be damned glad to feel solid land under my feet again instead of this continual bathtub of water."

"Just remember, Red, this canvas is a mizzen sail and not nearly as big as the main sail. There'll be a limit to what we can cut from it." Ed did not mention the challenges awaiting them at the beach.

Henry's bowel rumbled as anxiety returned to torment him. How close they were and yet how many dangers lay in wait to deny them their first goal.

CHAPTER SIX

Cooktown

"George, what was Smiley wearing when he left?" Abigail stopped pacing the kitchen floor and returned to sit in her chair beside the large table taking centre place in the room surrounded by the wood stove, workbench, crockery and utensil cupboard. Kitchen pots and the larger utensils hung from the wall hooks above the fireplace. She twisted her tea cup around on her saucer.

"I'm sorry, Sis. To be honest I cannot be sure I even noticed. It was the middle of the night and I did not really see much in the dark except the whites of Smiley's eyes and his white teeth when he smiled." Clunk, clunk, clunk went the bread-and-butter knife beside his plate, with every turn, as Doctor George Goldfinch fiddled. "I think he had on a pair of those old trousers I gave him."

Abigail stood upright again. Her fingers destroyed the harmony of her once tidy hair as she raked at the tendrils now infiltrated by silver strands dangling at the side of her face.

"Tell me once again, what exactly did he say?"

"Oh, I remember that quite well because I couldn't go back to sleep trying to figure out what he meant." George sipped from his cup looking up to the ceiling as if the words might be written there. "Smiley said, 'I go walkabout, Doctor George. I must go bring Henry home.'"

"But what did he mean, do you think?"

"Abigail, I've told you all I know. I have wired the captain of the steamship Henry and his friend were travelling on. Depending on how long it takes the ship to reach Port Kennedy and the upkeep of the telegraph line, we should hear back in six or seven days at the latest, I'd think."

"Doctor Benton is the new fellow coming to the Cooktown Hospital, isn't he? I'm sure that's what Henry said in his last letter. The man starts in a couple of months."

George nodded. "And Henry did say they hoped to join this Benton fellow's father who runs a pearling fleet up north, remember. So really, I don't know what all the fuss is about. If Henry and his friend join the pearling fleet, they may be weeks before they arrive in Cooktown."

"That may be, but why would Smiley go off on walkabout to 'bring Henry home', then?"

"I am as much at a loss on that point as you are, Abby."

It was the turn of the teacup and saucer to rattle a protest as Abigail fiddled.

"George, do you remember how Thomas said Smiley was something like an American witch doctor to his tribe? Thomas believed Smiley knew all about the ancestors of his people, and the healing properties of many plants in the forest. According to Thomas, 'Smiley had been unable to go hunting with the men of his tribe due to the damage to his leg muscles after the fire burns, when he was a child. As he grew older, he concentrated on healing others and directing their spiritual followings.'"

George sat silent. His hand, holding a spoon above the jar of bush honey provided by Smiley, stilled. His blank gaze passed out through the open window. Black flies began to gather around the rim of the honey jar.

Abigail reached over and shooshed them away.

"You still miss Thomas don't you, George? I'm sorry."

George shuddered and returned his attention to his sister.

"Oh, Abigail, he was a good friend to us all. It seems unbelievable he's dead – especially after being thrown from a spooked horse. I didn't think there was a horse able to throw Thomas." With his spare hand, George reached over and patted his sister's forearm. "I wish he was here now. He understood Smiley. Thomas enjoyed nothing more than helping Smiley improve his artistic talent. Over the years, they talked a lot. I think Smiley looked upon Thomas as a whitefella father." George stirred the honey into his tea. He paused. Curiosity filled his eyes, when he looked up at his sister again. "Abigail, what are you saying? Do you think Smiley knows something through his spirit world involving Henry, that we don't?"

Abigail pushed the crockery aside and jumped up again. "Oh, I don't know what I'm saying; only they were strange words for Smiley to say and yet so simple."

CHAPTER SEVEN

Henry and Edward

The sound of the waves as they crashed onto a nearby shoreline fell like music upon Henry and Ed's ears, filling the darkness after the moon disappeared beyond the horizon. Both men spent the passing hours alert on their timber perch straining their eyes to see ahead. In the muted light, when the morning sun struggled to penetrate the thickening cloud cover, Ed's gaze alternated between the approaching outline of land to the east and the activity of his friend.

"Red, what are you trying to do with our water container?"

Henry looked up from his self-imposed task. "I was thinking on what you said last night about the water-bag. I imagine we'll be in for a rough landing. There'll be no guarantee of fresh water, where we'll end up. I figured I should seal up what water we have in the hope it may survive our arrival on dry land." Wrinkled white fingers threaded one of the lanyards dangling from the inside of the basket through the holes now along the top edge to make a drawstring. With his tongue held between his teeth, Henry made the final slash of his knife extracting the canvas water holder from the basket. He pulled it tight as if strangling a turkey, before tying another lanyard around the neck for security. "Do you know any of this coastline, Ed? Are we likely to end up as scrambled eggs on a rocky beach?" Henry's activity with the preservation of their water supply was not only intended to be productive, but it kept him from anticipating what form the end of their sea journey might take.

"You're right about the dubious availability of fresh water. As to where we are, I can only say with any certainty we are on the west coast of Cape York Peninsula. I don't think we've come far enough south to run into any of the islands in the gulf. When I was a boy, my father brought the fleet into several areas on this coast. He'd anchor the *Mary Anne* off the shore, while the smaller luggers beached and set up camp for a few days to process the trepang. I'd feel a little easier if I could pick out a landmark."

Henry readjusted his head cover, and with the blade beginning to dull, he cut into the scraggly canvas around the basket area. From this and the few lanyards remaining, he fashioned a carry-bag with a strap to sling over his head and shoulder. Using his knife, fingers and teeth, he cut and tore strips of canvas for feet wrappings leaving the larger area of the canvas to be converted into their shelter and ground mat, once they were on the sand – hopefully. The feet wrappings, he stuffed into the carry-bag.

Henry lifted his head just as Ed called the warning. Their log swung longways on, caught up by a rolling wave rushing them into what appeared to be a sandy shore. With no chance to offer up thanks for this piece of luck, he felt the sudden jar, when the end of the yardarm dug deep into the sand under the crashing waves. His one arm held tightly to the improvised water-bag, while the other clung desperately to their timber beam as it was upended, somersaulted and bounced across the sand. Sea water swamped him. It seemed an age before it fell away and Henry felt himself thrown forward; not unlike those times he fell from a horse, which insisted on pig-rooting. All he could think of was his precious rainwater storage, but when his senses cleared the water-bag was gone. At his attempt to sit up, he felt the strap of the carry-bag pull tight against his larynx. His improvised hat now covered his face and nose. On the verge of panic, his hands tore at the canvas hat to clear his breathing. He shuffled the bag out from under his body to release the pressure on his throat.

A frantic search for the water-bag in the sand around his body followed, while all the time he called, "Ed, are you alright? Ed?"

"I'm in one piece at least. Don't know about alright. Does this belong to you?" Ed coughed and spluttered from where he lay sprawled face-down. Their timber spar, lying across his lower legs partly buried in the sand, anchored him. In the hand raised above his head, he held the water-bag. "There's still some water inside, at least. Whether it's saltwater or fresh water I'm not going to hazard a guess."

"What about your legs? Have you been hurt?" Having yet to regain his land legs, Henry wobbled across to help Ed assess the damage.

When he strained to lift the spar, Henry's groans accompanied those of Ed. From his upside-down position, Ed was of little help. The yardarm was too heavy for one man. Henry began digging around Ed's legs to make a hollow.

"Stop!"

Henry's head snapped up. He glanced left and right. "What's wrong?"

"If you dig like that, the water-softened skin on your hands will peel off. Firstly, I want you to wrap those canvas bandages around your feet. Once the sun breaks through those clouds, the sand will roast the soles of your tender feet down to the bone. Then go search up on the high tide mark. Look for a large shell or maybe a solid digging stick."

At the tide mark, Henry paused in surprise at the collection of shells, large and small, some broken and some intact, amongst the debris of sticks, leaves, sea grass, small stones and mangrove seeds. He chose a large rippled-walled shell. Armed with this, he did not take long to scoop out the sand from around Ed's lower legs. Ed slithered out from his confinement. Both men sighed with relief when he wiggled his toes.

"Not broken at least, it would seem." Ed grinned and then groaned as he rubbed his left ankle. "That smarts a bit." He handed the water-bag to Henry who stashed it safely against the upside-down cane-woven basket.

Henry knelt beside his companion and began to move and palpate the ankle joints, calf muscles, knee, thigh muscles and hips before giving instructions.

"Let's have you upright and see if you really are still in one piece."

Once again, a groan lifted into the air when Ed's limbs took the weight of his body.

"The spar bounced off my right thigh and knee." Holding on to Henry's shoulder, he swung his right leg gently back and forward bending his knee. "No, not broken only bruised, I would think. The left ankle's going to have me limping for a bit. We'll see in a couple of days."

Ed stretched his neck. His gaze took in the undulating sand dunes on which the sparse covering of green grasses lay flattened by a wind, which rustled the foliage of the line of casuarina trees. A large kangaroo returned the human gaze.

"How fast can you run, Red."

But Henry had also caught sight of the animal. "Not that fast, Ed." He smiled ruefully. "And if I did catch it, how am I to kill it do you think?"

"We could do with a solid waddy to throw at it. Never mind, where there's a big animal there must be smaller ones of some kind. I really need a feed of meat."

"Well, great hunter, you had best sit down and allow me to bandage those wrinkly white feet."

With his feet protected, Ed hobbled along the beachfront for a short distance. "Red, would you like some good news?"

"It's been a while, remind me again, what is good news?"

Using his hands to help him scramble up the sandbank, Ed moved up to the tree line.

"Yessirree! I know exactly where we are. Come have a look." When Henry joined him, Ed pointed at what appeared to be an old campsite. No coverings were in evidence, but cut tree saplings stood in an arranged plan, even if a bit distorted. Some horizontal limbs were still tied together with twine, while others either hung with only one end attached or lay on the ground.

"So, what am I looking at?"

Ed selected one of the fallen saplings and tested its strength before he measured it up beside himself as he explained. "This was one of my father's bêche-de-mer processing camps." Ed pointed eastwards through a gap in the casuarinas to where a huge tree dominated the landscape. "I recognize that large tree back there." Ed forgot the pain in his leg as he twisted around to point along the shoreline to a thicker grouping of trees to the south. He grimaced. "See along there, those are pandanus trees. Diver Bird, Curley and Teak used to love eating the fruit when it was in season. They made themselves sick on unripe fruit one time we were here." Ed stopped talking.

Henry noticed how Ed's eyes glazed over when talking about his friends. Henry was not immune to the pain and horror of their experience and loss himself. How much worse it must be for Ed who had lost close lifetime friends? He reached over and touched Ed's shoulder.

"Come, Ed, we've got a long way to go ourselves, yet."

"As usual, you're right, Henry."

"What's on the coast beyond your pandanus trees?"

"About five miles further south, three rivers all come together in one large mouth with islands and swamps before they exit into the ocean. Birdie caught some great fish down there – when he wasn't being chased by crocodiles."

Henry rolled his eyes. "You're telling me I've escaped the sharks to be eaten by crocodiles?"

"Now don't you worry none. You're all bones, they'd spit you out." Ed laughed. "Be thankful we're not further south at the Mitchell River. There were so many crocodiles there when I was a kid, one couldn't even count them." Wrinkly white fingers pointed east across the sand dunes. "One of the three rivers runs parallel behind us over there. That's the one Diver Bird named the Crabby River. He reckoned it was like a woman – always moody."

Ed watched Henry as he paced back and forth across the dry sand with his head down swinging left and right.

"What on earth are you doing? I'm not sure you'll find any gold here."

"I'm more interested in looking for any evidence of the presence of those overgrown lizards."

"Crocodiles? I can't remember us ever seeing them at this spot, when I was a boy."

"I'm more interested in today, not years ago."

Ed's gaze fell towards the sand also. "Nothing here, see, not even human footsteps. Come on, let's go to the mouth of the three rivers and see what we can find amongst the mangroves there."

"How're the legs? Will you be okay walking that far?"

"Yeah, I'll give it a go. If I only make it to the pandanus trees, there should be a feed to be had at this time of year."

"Will I bring the water-bag?"

"Nah, it's only extra weight. There's no one here to steal it. Besides, there's always plenty of juice in the pandanus fruit. Take your bag up to where the tide won't wash it away." Ed leant heavily upon his improvised walking crutch as he hobbled off in the direction of the pandanus trees.

By the time they arrived at the pandanus trees, both men fell into the welcome shade of the wide-leafed branches. Henry's green eyes filled with concern, when he noticed the pain and exhaustion written in the lines and pallor on his friend's face. Their sighs joined those of the sea breezes whispering through the trees. Neither spoke. They lay on their backs watching the clouds sailing across the sky above.

It was Ed who broke the silence. "I see at least three ripe fruits waiting for us to eat."

Henry lifted himself onto his elbow and searched the trees himself. "Can they be eaten raw?"

"Either raw or cooked, but I guess it's going to be raw today – unless you can start a fire as the natives do."

Henry never answered as he stood up. He took his knife from its scabbard and cut down one large orange cone-shaped fruit. He held it to his face and sniffed. His nose screwed up in distaste.

"Don't be too quick to judge," Ed advised with a grin. "I have to admit when eaten raw the fruit smells a bit and it has small fibres which stick on the tongue for ages; but, it's food. When the nuts are baked in the coals, they're not half bad. Here, pass it over and I'll show you how to divide it into segments." As Ed dissected the fruit, he pointed to the base of a small section. "You'll find it soft and sweet. Just suck at it." Ed passed it over and watched the fleeting expressions of indecisiveness and finally satisfaction on Henry's face. He offered a warning. "Don't do this unless the fruit's very ripe or you'll end up with sore lips."

"You won't be travelling far for a day or two with that ankle, Ed, so maybe we'll learn how to make a fire and really enjoy your pandanus fruit."

"If you can get a fire going, we can bash the nuts into a meal and make flat cakes on a hot rock. There's not a lot we can't eat from a pandanus tree. And as a bonus, if you suck on the stems, you can relieve your thirst."

Exhaustion captured both men.

"What are you looking for, Ed?" From his somnolent state, having just opened his eyes, Henry questioned his friend from where he lay in the shade of the pandanus trees.

Ed knelt on the ground at the base of a tree. With his hands, he manipulated a heavy shell to shovel the sand away. He looked up at Henry's question.

"Curley often drank from the water he found near the base of the tree. He always made it look so easy to find the water, but I'm not so sure. In the meantime, you can suck on this root and tell me if it tastes like drinking water." Ed sawed off a piece of a root with his knife and passed it over.

Henry sucked and chewed at the offering. His eyes sparkled. "It's not as good as a brewed ale, but I've tasted worse water in the heart of London."

Both men laughed.

It was late afternoon when they returned along the beach to their canvas raft. Almost one hundred and fifty yards away from their destination, Ed's curse drew Henry's attention from his search of the tide mark seeking suitable stones on which to sharpen their knives.

"Hang back a bit, Red. Looks like a croc has stumbled upon our raft."

And then Henry saw the blunt snout emerging from under the moving sail as the animal swung left and right to dislodge Henry's self-designed carry-bag. The long tail of the crocodile flung the marker-float basket rolling across the sand. The crocodile wound the remaining length of sail into a canvas knot. One of the hemp ropes, dislodged from its tie on the yardarm, dragged from the rear left foot of the reptile.

"Ed, where's the water-bag? Can you see the water-bag?"

Ed watched the action for some moments before answering. "Sorry, Red, I can't see it, but it will be there somewhere."

Leaving the sand-covered remains of the raft behind, the reptile turned for the water, still doing its best to remove the carry-bag and length of rope from its stubby limbs. As it disappeared beneath the waves, the two men approached the debris site with extreme caution. They searched for the precious water-bag, which could not be found for some time. Eventually, Ed discovered it wrapped up in the knotted sailcloth.

"Maybe a mouthful each," Ed's expression grim as he shook their precious drinking water.

Dejection sat alongside Henry as he tried to come to terms with this new difficulty. Suddenly he jumped up and ran to the water's edge.

"Careful, Red, the blighter's probably still nearby, watching."

His call went unheeded as Henry ran into the shallows reached down into the waves and retreated rapidly with his carry-bag and the length of rope."

"I hope that's not still attached to our visitor, Red."

Henry did not answer. He was too busy making a hasty run up the beach.

The men sat in a bath of disillusionment for five minutes before they spoke together.

"This won't do …." They started to laugh. Their laughter became louder and louder until tears ran down their cheeks.

"Come on," It was Ed who sobered up first. "We'll have enough light to set up a bit of roof canvas over part of the frame at the old campsite. We'll direct any runoff water to flow into the remaining canvas set out over a hollowed-out area of sand. If it rains tonight, we'll recover what drinking water we lost today."

In the fading light, they took the time to collect as much brushwood as they could find nearby to build a feeble fort around their sleeping site.

"If the croc returns tonight and breaks through this brushwood, we'll at least hear the approach and hopefully have time to escape," Ed explained his plan.

Both men curled up tightly under their small roof when towards dawn the rain fell in heavy gusts. Neither complained. This was better than sleeping in a water bed at sea, and the thought of fresh drinking water in the morning appealed.

Clouds challenged the morning sun. Henry's squeals drew Ed from his slumber. A smile lit up Henry's face as he approached the camp at full tilt with a large fish on the end of his knife. Raucous squawks of disapproval rose in the air along with the rush of wings of a flock of seagulls scavenging at the water's edge.

"How'd you catch that? Better still, where did you catch that? Not in the sea with that croc, I hope."

"In a bit of a tidal pool just north – about half a mile from here."

While Ed went to relieve himself behind some bushes, Henry selected two of the sticks he had chosen when collecting the brushwood, the previous evening. From inside his shirt, Henry removed a small bundle of dry grass retrieved on his exploration walk this morning. His fingers tore at the itch it had left on the skin of his torso.

"Alright, Smiley, I hope you can hear me. I'm going to need your help here." He mumbled as he used his knife to shape the ends of the two sticks into the pattern he desired. He squatted down with one foot splayed over one stick, while his hands set the pointed end of the second stick upright in the groove made in the first stick. He sprinkled a thin layer of dry grass where the two sticks met. Taking the upright stick between his two hands, he began to roll it back and forth, slowly at first before building up the speed. Sweat poured down his face from under his canvas hat. The skin on his hardening hands burnt. The muscles of his back and neck burnt. After what seemed like ages with no sign of smoke smouldering the grass, Henry's hopes faded. *How typical,* he thought. *Every part of my body burns, but not a sign of any damn fire. Smiley always made it look so easy.*

He was just about to throw the sticks aside when a wisp of smoke rose from the swirling point. Before Henry could reach down to feed the spark, Ed fed in the dead grass little by little. Henry continued rolling the stick until the flame rose up from the grasses. Ed crunched up fine twigs to enlarge the fire.

"Thank you, Smiley." Henry laughed.

"Smiley? Isn't that the native boy you grew up with in Cooktown?"

"Yes, he taught me to make fire, but I was never very good."

"Well, you're good enough when it matters." After killing the fish with a whack across the head with the handle of his knife, Ed scraped the blade against the sides to remove most of the scales before he tossed their breakfast onto the cooking fire.

While Henry and Ed ate their fill of cooked fish, the sun emerged from behind the clouds sending both men into the shelter of their canvas roof. Like a pair of snakes with their appetites sated, they slumbered. Midday heat and sweaty bodies awoke them both with a raging thirst. With his feet wrappings secured, Henry went searching for two drinking vessels amongst the numerous shells of choice on the high-tide mark. They both agreed that no drink on earth compared with their fresh rainwater.

"Do you think your ankle will tolerate another hike to the pandanus trees later this afternoon, Ed? We can bring the fruit back here and cook it over the fire."

"Good idea – besides I have to get my legs working soon. We can't waste time here for too long or the monsoon weather will beat us. We'll be bogged on the flooding plains in a few weeks."

"I presume there's little chance of a boat finding us here given the lack of footprints in the sand."

"No, it's too late in the season to be processing any bêche-de-mer. The pearling fleets will be making their way back to Port Kennedy soon."

Henry paused to accept the truth of what Ed said. He sat looking across what he could see of the flat country to the east. It seemed to go on forever.

"What do you know of our journey east of here? Have you any idea in what direction we should go, Ed?"

"I think so. I spent time last night trying to recall the maps my dad had of this place. I know if we keep direct east, we'll arrive at the telegraph line. Dad wrote a letter to me about its construction, while I was in London. It was when the line was nearly completed a couple of years ago. He said they built it to run north/south over the Cape. I'm guessing we'll meet the line at a place called Mein, about eighty miles away. As I understand it, there's a telegraph station and a police camp there." Ed shut his eyes once more examining the map in his head. "I think there are several rivers and creeks between here and there. You have to remember that was ten years back, and the map was a bit outdated even then. It had all my father's scribble marks in the seas and oceans but he did not take much notice of the land in between." While he told Henry what he knew, Ed accompanied his words with a map in the sand drawn with a small stick. "Anyway, we'll give this ankle a run this afternoon and hopefully begin the trek tomorrow."

Henry enjoyed eating the pandanus fruit after it had been roasted. He even tried grinding the nuts into flour using a hand-sized rock and one of the stronger shells to hold the nuts. Tediousness almost had him give up on this project but he persisted. He dribbled some of their precious water into his coarse flour before rolling his mixture into two balls. These he squashed onto a flat rock he had heating up on the fireplace.

"Bit crunchy," Ed commented with a grin. "Fills the hollow spaces though."

"My mother's friend, Eve, could have done a much better job, I'm sure. My mother never won any prizes for her cooking. I guess it's her I take after." Henry laughed.

"How are your hands after making the fire yesterday?"

Henry spread the palms of both hands out in front of him. "They're fine. All dried up now and only a little red. Not a blister in sight." He proceeded to unbind the canvas coverings on his feet. The flesh on his soles had also returned to normal even if the skin tingled a little when placed in contact with the sand. "I'll bring our bandages with us tomorrow in case."

Ed and Henry settled themselves within their wooden fort. Their sporadic short conversations relating to the plans for the following day came to a full stop. Contented sighs and snorts of deep breathing heralded the arrival of sleep.

PART TWO

THE TREK

CHAPTER EIGHT

Smiley

Even with his hoppity gait, due to the damage to the muscles and tendons in his legs sustained after a fall onto a campfire as a child, Smiley's feet covered many miles along the animal pads within the forest each day. Perspiration shone on his black skin. Wishing to avoid the known areas of concentrated police presence at Normanby, Battle Camp, Boralga and Laura, he swept north of Cooktown for many miles until he angled the morning sun further onto his back and moved in a more westerly direction. When he reached the higher ground, the timbered terrain thinned out somewhat. He slowed the pace to allow his eyes to examine the area about him in more detail. To fall into the hands of the Native Mounted Police was not something he wanted to contemplate – not without the protection of Doctor George Goldfinch. From the stories related around his family's campfires, he knew full well how a young black man carrying a spear and boomerang presented a threat and provided target practice for many of their numbers.

Most days it was the simple foods – those easiest to collect without wasting time – kept his hunger at bay. Many of the trees passed during his day provided sweet gum to be chewed or flowers with honeyed nectars. In the sunny glades beside running water, bush tomatoes sated his appetite. In the heat and humidity of the midday sun, he took a short reprieve while raiding fruits in the wild fig trees. A digging stick made short work of the search for the witchetty grubs within rotting timbers. Regret caused him to pause at the sight of a bee's nest dripping with honey, high in a tree overhead. He licked his lips at the sight of his favourite treat, but shook his head. To retrieve the treasure safely meant time he did not have to spare. On more than one afternoon, when Smiley sought a protected site to spend the night, a large lizard sunning itself on a fallen branch fell victim to his silent approach and the accuracy of the blow with his boomerang.

Smiley set his night camps back from the usual sites along the banks of the rivers and creeks – regular search areas for the police patrols. He chose the protection of rough terrain with thick bushes and shrubs to burrow into. Smiley became almost impossible to see in the fading light of day. As the distance between the patrol routes and himself increased, he began to light a fire to cook his evening meals. In a matter of several minutes, heat ignited the small layers of dried grass lying beside the one firestick twirling upon another held under a calloused foot. Long black fingers eked out the tinder fuel until the fire took hold and he was able to add small twigs. When satisfied with his fire, Smiley dragged out the pocket knife from his trousers. Grubby fingers with chipped nails opened the blade before they reached into the satchel and retrieved the sharpening stone given to him by Doctor George, not long after Henry had left on the big ship, such a long time ago. Pride and the glint of the firelight shone from his eyes at each smooth sweep of the blade against the stone. His mind contemplated the reason for this journey. Since his father's death three wet seasons previously, Smiley had dreamt of him occasionally, but never with such clarity as occurred before his departure from Cooktown on this perilous journey.

The clouds, sailing in the increasing wind of the early evening, reminded him the wet season was nearly upon them again.

On the fifth evening, his step slowed further. He felt the restless presence of many of the ancestors dispersed by the patrol troopers in years gone by. In his head, he heard their murmurs as he sliced open the goanna at his feet. The goanna's guts were removed before he threw the kill upon the flames to singe. He shrugged at a brief vision of his father who never bothered removing the lizard's guts when out hunting. The wide smile, which had prompted his nickname, split his face at the recollection of Henry who refused to eat a small lizard with the guts still intact. There were some things Smiley had learnt from spending so much time with the white people. After adding more wood to the fire, he reached over to hook the lizard out by its tail. He grunted softly as the aromas of cooking flesh filled his nostrils. It took several attempts to pick up the hot animal before he turned it over and relocated it into the coals. He sucked at his burnt fingertips.

Having eaten his fill, Smiley sat cross-legged staring into the glowing coals of the fire. A soft tuneless hum drifted up in the air to add to the soft music of the night as he sang with his unseen people of long gone. All about him leaves soughed in the canopy of the trees, night birds called to other feathered friends, koala bears grunted their challenge for their right to food or a mate, and the grasses rustled as ground animals foraged – all undisturbed by this presence in their midst.

The moon sat long in the west before Smiley settled to sleep. Tomorrow his journey must take him around the white man settlement of Musgrave, where the recent addition of what Doctor George called a telegraph station, had been built near the Native troopers' compound.

CHAPTER NINE

Henry and Edward

"Edward," Henry's tentative call from the inside edge of their brushwood fortress induced Edward to grunt and roll over.

"Hmmm," he replied.

"We had a visitor last night." Henry stood staring at the marks in the sand outside their fragile fortress. A long wide smooth stretch of sand where the body of the crocodile had slithered along the outside edge of the brushwood with regular cup holes on either side where the four feet had sought purchase. "A crocodile – it didn't breach our defences which is a blessing."

Ed flew up off the canvas groundsheet and walked over to investigate. "You're right, it is a croc and it's heading inland." Ed's gaze followed the spoor until it disappeared within the longer grasses amongst the she-oak trees. He scratched his head. "Maybe a female returning to her nest or maybe just a croc heading for the small lake at the mouth of the river."

"Isn't that where you said we're heading?"

"Yes, Red. If I recall and remember this is going back over ten years since I camped in this area, it's about two miles or more from here to the lake."

The two men contained their sobering thoughts relating to the similarity between the crocodile's travel plans and their own. Henry guided more water, caught up in some folds of their canvas shelter during the overnight rain shower, into the open neck of their water-bag. He dipped their saucer-shaped shell into the solution and gulped down the fluid.

"You want a drink, Ed, before I tie this up?"

"Thanks, my tongue is drier than Professor Blink's humour." Ed referred to another tutor during their training years.

After Ed finished drinking, Henry secured the drawstring at the neck of their water-bag.

Both men wrapped their bandages around their feet in anticipation of a hot day and hot sands ahead. Henry shook the sand out of his canvas hat and re-covered his head against the burning rays of a sun already venting its spleen upon them. Sand flew away in the wind when they lifted the groundsheet and folded it into a tight ball. Ed took up one of the two rolls of rope they had chosen to carry on this journey. He wrapped one end of one rope around the one canvas roll and made a sling to go around his neck and shoulders with the remainder of that rope. They both caught up the shelter roof and rolled it into a tight ball before it too became an attachment for the second rope sling around Ed's torso. Each man checked the knife in the scabbard at his waist.

Henry picked up his satchel and placed the drinking shell, the honing stone and several small lanyards rescued from their marker-float basket, inside, before he lifted the water-bag and eased it into the carry-bag also – for support and protection.

"I could go a plate of bacon and eggs and a good cup of tea, but I guess my stomach will have to go on wishing for a bit longer yet. With any luck, we might catch something at the lake. We should find more pandanus trees over that way if I remember correctly." Ed lifted some branches away from their fortress and stepped outside its meagre protection. His gaze turned to the west. Waves of an incoming tide crashed upon the sandy shore. He swung to face the east. "No good procrastinating anymore. All journeys begin with one step."

Both men trudged on their bandaged feet through the soft dry sand as they walked towards the rising sun. Ed led them off on a path twenty yards further south than that of the crocodile track.

Within a mile, the forest of trees became dense. They followed the animal pads winding through the brush and trees. Henry examined the prints in the dirt, when any became visible to his untrained eye. A particular question filled his mind.

Do the natives live out here in this area and how inhospitable might they be? He recalled Smiley's advice. Some of his tribesmen had been treated badly by the white men. They harboured revenge in their hearts. Others, not having experienced the cruelty, tended to be either wary or even easy-going.

Wide areas of long grass challenged the calves of their legs already trembling with lack of sustenance. After what had seemed like a hundred miles to Henry, even though he knew full well it could only have been no more than two miles, a sandy tidal flat spread out before them. Saltwater gushed onto it through a line of mangrove trees. It filled the narrow snake-like shallow channels within the flats before overflowing and becoming one with the river on the other side of the mangroves.

"What's on the other side of those mangroves, do you think, Ed?"

"That's the lake I was telling you about. We'll have to divert north for two or three miles before we can cross the river at the other end of these tidal flats."

In silence with his uneasy thoughts, Henry plodded along behind Ed. Eventually, he spoke. "Ed, how many crocodiles live in this river do you think?"

"What, you're not keen on being a tasty morsel? The poor croc needs to eat, you know."

"Yes, well I need to eat too, but that's not looking very hopeful. The damn croc can also do without."

Ed chuckled.

The men took a convoluted track around the edge of the river flats. As the tide rose the water pushed them back against the tree line. Surprise and no little amount of fear snapped Henry's gaze from the area immediately in front of his feet, when the water erupted ahead of him. Ed's body dived forward into the water with his arms outstretched. Henry's eyes felt like they were spinning as he sought to find the perceived hungry crocodile. But there was no crocodile. Ed rose from the shallows with a large crab held firmly by the back legs in his strong hands.

"Lucifer's whore, Ed, what do you think you're doing? Can't you warn me, when you want to go swimming with the wildlife? I was sure you were done for then, but I couldn't see what had you." Henry's heart rate gradually returned to normal.

Ed laughed. "This, my friend, is our lunch. Do you think you could make a fire again? See ahead," he pointed his hand holding the crab. "This sand ends in those trees. We'll eat there, I think."

Henry moved higher up the bank and began collecting dry grass and twigs as he moved forward.

"How far do you think we've come this morning?"

Ed's face crunched up in thought. "Maybe four or five miles, no further."

When they reached their target point both men made a beeline for the shade of the trees. Unrelenting sun rays cooked everything on their way to the earth, and then again as they reflected back up from the sand. Here in the basin wall of gum trees on the west bank of the tidal flats and the mangroves lining the river bank on the east, not a breath of sea breeze reached the men. Humidity smothered them in an impenetrable blanket.

As they divested themselves of their loads, Ed asked, "Pass me one of the lanyards in your satchel, Red – I need to tie this crab's legs before it latches onto a finger."

Henry reached gently into the satchel beside the water-bag to recover a lanyard for Ed. He brought out the saucer shell at the same time.

"Want a drink, Ed?"

"Thanks, I'm parched."

With the crab secured and while Ed drank, Henry searched for a good site to start his fire. As he swept aside the debris from his chosen area, he scrambled backwards.

"What the devil …. Ed, will you look at this." He pointed to evidence of a previous fireplace hidden beneath a light covering of sand.

"Is it fresh?"

"No, it's stone cold."

"It's probably one used by the natives who come this way on their walkabout. Let's hope they're not planning any walkabouts while we're in the area."

Henry pondered these words for some moments before he made a further comment – one full of hope and limited knowledge.

"It's most unlikely they'd consider travelling in this direction with the monsoon season almost upon us. Surely, they'd be heading for the higher country." He dragged his collection of grass and sticks from inside his shirt.

"Hmmm, I guess so." Ed watched fascinated as Henry took two sticks and cut notches out of both. "I'll go and see what timber we have for your fire."

Henry laughed. "I've still to get a fire going, Ed. And keep your eyes out for that croc."

Sweat ran down his face, his body and his arms. It threatened to wash out his minuscule fire before it grew into anything more substantial, but by the time Ed returned with one arm full of wood and the other carrying a very ripe pandanus fruit, the fire was ready for the larger sticks.

"How are you going to cook your crab, Ed?"

"Well, we don't have a pot to boil it in, so I suppose we chuck it on the coals and see how it goes. I don't want to burn the lanyard though. Who knows what we might want that for further on?"

"Have you seen any big rocks in your travels? We could put one under the crab and one on top of it to hold it on the fire."

"Nothing big enough, but I do have an idea." Ed selected a stout stick from his wood pile and used his pearling knife to sharpen one end. He lifted part of the underbody shell of the crab with the tip of his knife. He then pushed the sharp end of his stick through the crab's body. After several attempts, he released the lanyard. Dancing hands avoided the crab's claws desperate to clamp down on anything within its grasp. Once the crab was upside-down on the coals, he hammered the stick, using the rear end of his knife handle, through the upper shell and further into the ground. When the heat first reached the crab's senses its legs thrashed the air. Some legs and one nipper fell off into the coals.

Henry watched fascinated until a flurry of branches in the mangroves nearby distracted him.

"What's that?"

Ed laughed when they discovered two mangrove herons with wildly beating wings navigating their way out of the mangrove trees.

"Don't you laugh, my friend, ask yourself the question; what chased the birds out of there?"

When Ed returned from a scavenge amongst the trees holding another ripe pandanus fruit, Henry laughed.

"A meal and dessert, no less."

Henry removed nuts from the pandanus fruit and threw them onto the coals of their fire.

Ed's curse erupted from somewhere to his left. "Red, there are miles of vines in the bush here. I nearly broke my leg falling over them." It was at least ten or fifteen minutes before he returned with rolled-up lengths of vine hanging from his shoulders. "These should come in handy."

When the meal was cool enough for them to eat, the clunk, clunk of the back of their knives breaking the crab shell echoed through the trees. The pair dissected the crab and sucked up every bit of meat within its body and limbs.

"You don't get food like this at the lords' and ladies' tables in London, I bet," Ed laughed.

After chewing on the flesh of the pandanus fruits both men sighed with contentment. They began to plan their crossing of the river. Ed had been down near the river's edge earlier, when gathering his firewood.

"Did you notice how far it was across the river, Ed?"

"About two to three hundred yards, I'd hazard a guess."

"I know we can both swim that far but I don't like the idea of crocodiles keeping us company. Should we follow the river further north until it becomes narrower or shallower?"

"Maybe." Ed lay back and stared up into the tree branches above their heads.

At the fireplace, Henry dragged their roasted pandanus nuts from the hot coals. He lay them out on a piece of tree bark to cool.

Ed jumped up. He removed the wraps from his feet. "With those clouds overhead, the sand's not too hot this afternoon. Come on, Red, let's have a better look amongst the mangroves – we've a couple of hours of light left, yet. The tide will have left them high and dry by now. Surely, we'll find something there to use to get across the river. Even if it's only a log."

"A log … to float on … over those dark murky waters?" Henry's face was devoid of any hint of confidence as he too removed his feet wrappings. With his now-tattered head-covering still in place, he rose and followed his more adventurous friend.

The men wandered in and out of the tracks within the mangroves. A blue-feathered kingfisher darted back and forth out of their reach. They noticed the mangroves upstream were growing in thick muddy soil and those downstream from their mid-day camp contained a much higher level of sand content. Other than a thick layer of mud on their feet, the only thing of note was a long strip of tree bark fashioned into what may have once been a native canoe, but now harboured a slit along half its length.

"The native people probably used this to cross the river. I'm sure, once upon a time, it floated alright. I'm not sure how many people it carried."

As they made their way back to their fireplace, Ed examined fallen logs, large branches and any other possible raft-building materials. He dragged them up above the tide mark.

Henry arrived with a log he had found. "Will this do, Ed?"

Ed laughed. "Not unless you're planning on going straight to the bottom. You'd be lucky if it floated at all. That particular timber is not known for its floating ability." Ed spent some time showing Henry the difference in the types of timber. "We'll store these above the tide line until morning when we'll construct our raft. With a bit of luck, we'll catch the tide going out later in the day. If we depart here, I reckon we'll be carried across to land before the next river bend. In the meantime, we'd better move back higher into the forest to sleep tonight – away from the riverbank."

As the night crept in around them, they chewed on the roasted pandanus nuts and made their plans.

Henry woke to the sound of water dripping from the roof canvas into their water-bag braced within the branches of a shrub near his head. Vaguely, he recalled rain falling in the night. He and Ed slept crossways on the groundsheet canvas with their torsos in the shelter of the roof canvas – their legs out on the ground and in the weather. His muscles creaked with stiffness, cold and dampness as he stretched. A breeze rustled the tree branches above their camp. His senses told him he was alone. He opened one eye. There was barely enough morning light to see past the shelter, but he confirmed he was indeed alone. A recollection of the crocodile's spoor, seen on their first morning back on land, lifted him to his feet. He looked more closely for spoor in the soil around him. If any crocodile had taken his friend, it had done so without leaving any evidence. He rubbed his eyes and ran his fingers through the now thick, long, red mop of hair on his head. Ed's voice coming from the east swung him around.

"Stir those bones, you landlubber. I've got the raft half-built and our breakfast – assuming you can stir up any hot coals from yesterday's fire." A dark muddy-looking fish dangled from his knife attached to the end of a long stick. Even in the dim light, Ed noticed the dubious glance Henry threw at his catch. "The Japanese divers love these mud skippers. I've never braved a taste myself but hunger will toughen up anyone's motivation."

"Hmmm," Henry doubted his hunger had reached such a point just yet.

"I thought it was your snoring that woke me earlier, but it was two koala bears fighting somewhere nearby. And I see we've had a possum visit us in the night. It finished off the remains of our evening meal."

Henry found the saucer shell and drank several helpings from the full water-bag.

"Can you take your fish thing down to the water and wash the mud off it? I'll see if I can get a fire going."

"Tide's on the way in." Ed's words went unheeded.

Henry collected any dry grass and twigs protected from the earlier rain as he made his way to check last night's campfire. Ed followed him towards the water.

"Ed, you said you had the raft half-finished. How long have you been up?" Henry bent to search around the stump of a tree now dead – snapped off and lying on its side. A result of a storm some time ago, Henry assumed. He reached in and drew out a few strands of browned grass. Ed's voice at his shoulder caused him to jump back.

"Red, what are you doing scratching around the log like that? Have you forgotten about the snakes in this country? You've been living in London too long. With this weather heating up they'll be starting to stir and at their most irritable."

"You're right – I must have left my brains back on the ship, I think. Anyway, how are you going with the raft?"

"I've lined up a few logs of similar length and laid them out in a plan. After we eat, I want to work on a rudder. I thought we might find the leaf branches of the pandanus useful. They are quite strong and if weaved onto a timber frame of some sort they might work a treat."

Henry's face fell as he uncovered the old fireplace to discover the coals quite cold. With a sigh, he lifted from his haunches and went looking for two suitable dry sticks to use to start another fire.

"We can eat these fish raw; you know."

Henry made an ugly face. "I remember telling Smiley one day, I'd try many of his food ideas but raw mudskippers were past my curiosity. Just watching them slurping and squirting mud as they do is enough to put me off chewing on their flesh. I'll get this fire going or go hungry."

Ed had given up waiting to see a flame produced under Henry's amateur hands and had returned to his raft design. He smiled as the curses and excuses drifted down to where he worked near the mangrove trees. His knife blunted quickly when cutting the lengths of vines required. Struggling not to laugh at Henry's frustration, Ed retreated to the fireplace to sit in the shade and hone his knife on their stone from the satchel.

Henry ground his teeth together as he stood up from his efforts and stomped back to the water-bag. He scooped up and drank several full shells of water.

"Sorry, Ed, yesterday's fire must have been a fluke. Damned if I can do it again."

"I did think you were being ambitious with everything dripping wet after last night's rain."

"You get to eat all that fish. I'll take a walk back to the nearest grove of pandanus trees and see if I can find any ripe fruit. What is it you want me to look for in the leaves for your rudder?"

Ed explained his plan for the pandanus leaves before he walked down to the cleaner water where the river tide overflowed onto the sand flat to clean his catch.

Henry returned to find Ed tying the last of the raft's mainstays together with his unending lengths of the vine. With the rough skin of the pandanus fruit clenched against his side with one elbow, Henry used his two hands to drag several separate branches of the pandanus tree.

"Is this what you were talking about this morning for your paddle?"

"Yes, that's a beginning. How did you manage to cut them off the tree with that little knife?"

"It wasn't easy, I can tell you. I'll need to sharpen my knife before we go much further."

Ed pointed to a long stout branch lying on the ground beside the raft. One end of the branch was divided into four solid branches jutting out in almost a three-quarter circle each to a length of about two feet six inches.

"There's our rudder. I've got to weave and tie those pandanus leaves over the frame provided by the four small branches at the end."

Disbelief filled the expression on Henry's face. "Will those leaves be strong enough? Won't the current just rip them off?"

"Those leaves are quite durable. When I was a kid, the boys on the Torres wove the pandanus leaves into long ropes, with which they used to tie up their stock. In one case they kept a crocodile until it became too big and had to be released before it pulled their hut down around their ears."

"You exaggerate." A smile accompanied the accusation.

"Would I tell you a lie? Anyway, the river is only a couple of hundred yards wide. We'll be on the other side before you even get time to feel lonely for this side."

"Hmmm. I'll play the Doubting Thomas if you don't mind."

"I can't insert the rudder pole until we carry this base to the water's edge. Once I pull it through the gap here …," Ed pointed to a gap in the base of the raft at one end, "I have another bar to tie on the top side of the base to steady the rudder and one more tie holding the pole itself so it doesn't drop. I'm hoping the knots in the timber there …," this time Ed pointed to the two bumps in the timber a third of the way along his pole, "will help keep it in place." Ed stood with his hand on his chin. "I was thinking I could utilize the split canoe we found. If I tied the two halves as a mat across the raft it might stop us losing a leg through the gaps in the timber."

Henry placed his fruit on the ground. Curiosity sent him to examine the raft more closely.

"Have you built one of these before, Ed?"

"Well, no, not exactly, but I did watch my father build something similar."

"Did it float?"

"You are a sceptic, Henry Baldwin."

"When do you plan on leaving, I see the tide is running out now?"

"I'm thinking the water will be on the other side of the mangroves in about another hour or so."

"Will I try again to light a fire and cook this fruit? What we don't eat we can take in the satchel with us."

"Sounds good. I'm hungry again. In the meantime, I'll pack up our things ready to leave as soon as we can."

With the sun leaning to the west, Henry held the raft steady as Ed made his last adjustments to the craft bobbing up and down in the water on the river side of the mangrove trees. The satchel with the water-bag, drinking shell and honing stone along with the cooled nuts of the pandanus fruit hung across Henry's torso. His now-sharpened knife held snug in its scabbard on his belt.

Ed had his two slings of rope with their rolls of canvas near at hand on the raft logs to throw over his shoulders when they were ready to shove off into the outgoing current.

"You look worried, Red. You're not still frightened of the crocodiles, are you?"

"Not at all. No self-respecting croc would risk his life and limb jumping on this thing."

"Humph! Well, we're ready. On you get."

Henry scrambled onto the wobbly raft and sat down supporting his precious water-bag.

Ed tossed his rope slings over his torso and pushed off from the shore, grabbing the rudder pole as he did so. With the balance of a seaman, he planted his feet on the uneven raft base and bent his knees a fraction. Concentration lines added to the peeling skin covering his face as he began to test the feel of the rudder. He did not mention his thoughts to Henry. *It's no good looking backwards. It's forward or sink."*

Two grey and white terns spread their wings and lifted out of the mangroves.

CHAPTER TEN

Cooktown

When the man with the work-hardened hands removed the stockman's hat, he revealed a tanned face with a strong jawline and piercing blue eyes. His grey hair may have disclosed his age, but his stature bespoke of a younger man with his broad shoulders and narrow hips. He knocked at the front door of the small private hospital.

"Are you there, Doctor Goldfinch?"

One of the two patients playing cards on the verandah ward answered.

"You'll find the good doctor out the back near the kitchen."

Max Young nodded thanks and turned to make his way around the building to where the kitchen was situated near the back door. He found George Goldfinch stretched out on a canvas chair almost hidden by an array of medical journals which lay open across his body. A recently added awning sheltered him from the afternoon sun.

"Doctor Goldfinch, sorry to barge in like this."

George jumped up in surprise, extending his right hand while sending medical magazines raining in all directions.

"Max, Max Young, since when do you need to call me Doctor? I thought we'd agreed long ago you'd call me George. How have you been? When did you arrive in town? Abigail was only saying this morning, to expect you in town any day now with the school holidays approaching. She said you'd never miss collecting young Victoria from the boarding school."

The men clasped hands enthusiastically.

"Just got into town this morning – had some business to attend to. I'll pick Victoria up tomorrow. We'll need to make a hasty retreat to Lavinia Downs before the wet settles in."

"How's your brother been lately? Has the prescription I made for David pepped him up a bit?"

Worry lines appeared on the visitor's face. "I don't know, George, he seems listless all the time and the weight is falling from his frame. You remember what a big man he used to be?"

"I wish you'd convince him to come into town and see me."

"Fat chance of that. He's more stubborn than our Pa was in his time. Can't stand to be around strangers. I promised him I'd bring home more of your mixture."

"Of course, no trouble – I'm sorry to hear David's still unwell, Max. You mustn't let yourself feel guilty. It's very true, you can't help those who won't help themselves, I'm afraid."

Max fiddled with his hat struggling to choose his words.

"George, I mentioned to you before how David has had a liaison with our native cook Summer, an aboriginal woman. This was after his wife died – shortly after we arrived on the Cape. This country took both our wives eventually. They have a daughter Velvet, a few months older than my Victoria. Things haven't been too peaceful between them in recent times since Summer demanded he should marry her and David refused." Max took a big breath and cleared the perspiration from his face with a sweep of his hand. "I'm just wondering if our David may have … well you know how they say natives can cast spells upon their enemies, and point bones and things to kill them. Do you think there's a possibility Summer may have got someone to do this to David as punishment?"

At that moment, the conversation came to an abrupt halt when Abigail Baldwin, twin sister to Doctor George, appeared from around the corner of their house-cum-hospital. The sparkle in her green eyes was reflected two-fold in the blue eyes of their visitor. The young woman at her side carrying the bulk of their parcels moved on into the kitchen area.

"Mister Young, this is a lovely surprise."

"The pleasure is all mine," Max stepped back and offered a small bow.

"Has George organized a cup of tea for you?"

"Now, Abigail, don't rush me. I was just on my way to fetch something a little stronger."

Abigail turned to their guest. "Are you in town to collect Victoria?"

"Yes, Miss Abigail. Victoria would never forgive me if I didn't get her home before the monsoons arrive."

At this point, George disappeared towards the dispensary room within the hospital area which occupied the ground floor of his home. Max Young spun the felt hat in his hands. He alternated his weight from one foot to the other. Abigail drew her eyes away from the bulging muscles moving under Max Young's khaki shirt and discovered her errant gaze glued to the shape of the muscled thighs threatening the integrity of his trouser pants. Her freckles stood out within the blush of her cheeks. Restless fingers tidied her auburn hair. A faint stutter coloured her words when she next spoke.

"I think I've told you before, Mister Young, if ever the road to Lavinia Downs is flooded and you are unable to collect Victoria, you must get word to me and I'll bring her here to spend the holidays with us. No doubt it will be a poor second to her own home, but she would be most welcome. Maybe she'd feel a little more comfortable than if she stayed in the school with the nuns over Christmas."

A red flush swept across Max Young's face. It had been fifteen years since his beloved wife Marigold died of the Gulf fever, and he missed her so much, yet for some reason, the vision of this red-headed beauty exploded into his thoughts at some time on most days.

"I appreciate your offer, Miss Abigail."

"It's my pleasure, Mister Young. Following our talk last time we met in June, Victoria and I have enjoyed a few outings to morning tea this term, as you suggested. We find each other good company."

"Thank you for taking the time out of your busy days"

"I'm more than happy to do so. It passes the time while we wait for the return of my son from London." Abigail's eyes sparkled even more as she spoke of the imminent return of Henry to the Australian shores.

George arrived with a tray of drinks. He directed his words with his head.

"Max, can you bring over those other chairs and the small table from up the end there?"

Abigail turned her head away from the magnetism of those wonderful muscles in action. Her eyes remained downcast as Max Young held the chair for her to sit. She placed her basket on the grass at her side and listened attentively while Max spoke of the workings on his property. His two sons, Gordon and Peter, now performed most of the daily chores, while Max's duties were mostly those of an accountant and supervisor.

The approach of a young lad walking across the lawn from the street went unnoticed until he spoke.

"Excuse me, Mrs. Baldwin," the young telegraph boy drew Abigail's attention from the conversation. "I have a telegram here for you."

"For me?" All the colour drained from her face. Telegrams normally meant bad news, particularly at this time, when Henry was on a ship bound for home. Only a faint tremble of her hand revealed her thoughts as she reached out to take the envelope.

"Thank you, son."

"Will there be an answer, Missus?" The boy stood taking in his surroundings with little empathy for the epistle he might deliver. He'd seen it all before.

Abigail's hands smoothed the envelope out on her thigh while she struggled to contain her emotions and fears. She lifted her head and straightened her back. Reaching down into her basket she removed a small pair of nail scissors from her purse. The envelope split open in one quick swipe before Abigail removed the paper inside and spread it flat on the table in front of her.

Her eyes read the words before her brain took in the meaning. When they both reached the same conclusion, she sighed loudly.

"Oh, George, this is from the captain of the steamship Henry and his friend Ed were travelling on. They have reached Darwin. The two boys have disembarked and joined one of the ships in Ed's father's pearling fleet. They will make their way home after a couple of weeks on a pearling adventure. They have both forwarded their luggage on to Cooktown." Abigail turned to their visitor. "Henry and Ed are now qualified doctors and Henry will join us in George's practice while Ed has a position waiting for him at the Cooktown hospital."

"When and from where, was the telegram sent, Abigail?"

Abigail's gaze returned to the top of the page. "Today's the fifteenth, so that makes it five days ago, George. It was sent from Port Kennedy on Thursday Island."

Abigail's attention returned to the telegram boy. She reached into her purse again and retrieved a threepenny bit.

"Thanks, sonny, there will be no reply."

Abigail sat quietly trying to understand her feeling of despondency. She had been so looking forward to Henry's return.

Each day was marked off on the calendar as she counted the days to his anticipated arrival at the Endeavour River. Giving herself a mental shake, Abigail noted, *Henry is not fifteen anymore. He is a man. Heaven forbid, my father's dictatorial character lurks inside me.* Her mind vaguely took in the discussion flowing back and forth between her brother and Max Young.

"I'm thinking seriously of retiring from Lavinia Downs after Christmas. Gordon and Peter manage the property quite well these days without me."

"Whatever will you do?"

"I thought it might be good for David if I got him away – maybe we could live on a small holding outside of Brisbane. And of course, I have to think of young Victoria. Sometimes I worry she's living like a wild woman on Lavinia Downs, and I know my wife wouldn't have wanted that."

Abigail's attention lifted when George spoke.

"Well, in that case, we might run into each other down there. I'll be returning to my old practice within the next few months."

"Max, what will you do with Victoria?"

"I plan to enter her into a boarding school in Brisbane, Miss Abigail. Do you happen to know of one you might recommend?"

"I certainly know several people I might ask. Maybe the Girl's Grammar School comes to mind, but I think they are a day school only. Victoria would be welcome to live with us and go to school from there if you thought it might work." Abigail paused as she thought. "I'll let you know what else I can find out." The clanging of a pan in the kitchen drew her attention. "That will be Mrs. Burton ready to do the evening meals." She glanced up at their guest. "Mister Young, you will join us, won't you? I'm sure you'll find Mrs. Burton's meal a step or two up on the hotel fare."

George joined in with his sister's invitation. "Please, Max, you really must."

Max paused, trying to calm his racing pulse. "Thanks, Miss Abigail, George, that will be lovely."

CHAPTER ELEVEN

Henry and Edward

The raft's impetus forward instilled by Ed before he jumped on board, began to wane. With a shudder and a jerk, the tide caught the craft and dipped its nose below the water. It swung the timber frame first left then right before hauling it off downstream. Henry's eyes opened wide along with his mouth when a wash of water rolled across the timber and over his legs. He grasped at the precious cargo in the satchel hanging across his torso. The wind whistled in his ears. One glance in Ed's direction convinced him to remain quiet. Ed's muscles bulged; his face reddened with the effort. He strained to push the rudder against the flow of the water and ease the frail raft in the direction of the opposite bank.

In small increments, their vessel altered its focus and the nose pointed to where they planned on landing. To Henry, the once thought-to-be only two hundred or so yards distance to their destination seemed to grow further and further. He again looked up at his friend when a grunt reached his hearing.

"Need a hand?" He had to yell to be heard over the breeze, the wash of water, the creaking timbers and his pounding heartbeat.

Ed shook his head in reply. His gaze was fixated on the proposed landing site. Strain distorted his face. Henry imagined he heard Ed's teeth grinding together. When Ed's frown deepened with concern, Henry's gaze turned towards their target. His heart skipped a beat. Surely, they had no chance of bringing the craft into the bank before the bend of the creek, as hoped. They were still too far out in the middle of the river. Their craft hurtled downstream on the current.

A vine knot snapped on one log in their raft. A neighbouring knot prevented a destructive domino effect. The end of the log shifted a fraction with the pressure of the current. Water splashed Henry's face. His attention lifted to his companion once more when Ed growled. Pain added to the worry and strain on Ed's face.

The thought of the rudder frame wrapped in the woven pandanus leaves set Henry's worries off in a different direction. He visualized the leaves shredding under the pressure. The fingers of his spare hand turned white as he gripped even more tightly to the edge of the raft. Thoughts of marauding crocodiles had long been forgotten in his litany of other worries. Horror washed over him along with river water, when the second log-end shuddered and its vine attachment snapped.

The race to the bank versus the race past the bank engaged all their attention. Inch by inch they made headway towards the new line of mangroves. With surprising suddenness, the loss of resistance, as the river current spat them out into the quiet waters near the bank, sent Ed flying forward. An imminent dunking seemed inevitable. Ed dropped the rudder and grabbed Henry's shoulder. Henry reached over and held onto Ed's leg. Laughing and whooping with excitement, Ed regained his balance and began to swing the rudder back and forth, gently pushing the tortured vessel into the bank.

Their feet disappeared into the mud as it squelched up over their ankles.

"Red, help me wedge our raft into the mangroves. It's better hidden here where it might never be seen than floating down the river advertising our presence in the area."

Slurps and squelches of their feet accompanied their activity as they concealed the craft and made their way through the thick mangroves. Their legs ached with the drag of the mud. Anxiety filled both men's eyes as they scanned their immediate vicinity.

"I'll be glad when we're out of these thick mangroves where we can't even see a croc coming for us."

"Now, Red, any crocodiles in the area will be sunbaking on the nearest mud or sand bank, while the tide is out. They won't be too interested in our passing."

The heavy breathing of both men filled the air by the time, and without warning, a long and wide tidal flat appeared through the foliage. Thick clouds gathered behind them to hasten the fading of the late afternoon sun. Ed and Henry threw themselves onto the welcome sand as they struggled to catch their breath.

"I think my legs are a ton heavier with all this mud. How is your ankle coping with this extra work?"

"Good." The word returned as little more than a grunt.

"How far from the river do you think we are, Ed?"

Ed's hands came away muddy as he massaged the calves of his legs. His breathing returned to normal. "I cannot be sure we haven't ended up in a curl of the river. I suggest we make use of the one and only tall tree over there," he pointed to the only obvious tree one hundred yards away, "and sleep on a high branch."

Henry's gaze followed the direction of Ed's finger. A frown ran across his brow. He looked at his friend.

"You're serious, aren't you?"

"Nevermore, Red. We can't be sure how close we might be to your friendly crocodiles and I don't want to wake up to one chewing on my leg for breakfast."

Henry delved into the satchel to recover the drinking shell and loosen the drawstring of the water-bag.

"Want a drink?" He offered the shell full of water to Ed.

"A bottle of rum never tasted as good as this water, even with its hint of salt. I'll have another." With their thirsts quenched they dragged themselves to their feet. "Come on, Red. We'll set up the roof canvas to catch more water in your bag before we find our roosts."

The lowest branch on their tree hung fifteen feet from the ground. A similar branch matched it on the other side of the tree trunk. Ed utilized the spare rope, previously used to carry the roof canvas, to climb up onto the branch. He threw the end down to Henry.

"Put your feet in the loop and I'll help haul you up."

They perched on the separate branches like oversized, ungroomed, dirty members of the monkey family seen in picture books. Rising winds of the approaching rains thrashed the lightweight branches about them.

"Ed, do you think our water collector will be alright?"

"Are you going down to check?"

"Maybe not."

"Me either. Now, have you got any of those pandanus nuts in your magic bag of tricks there?"

"I hope you don't walk in your sleep, Ed." Henry laughed as he passed over a large handful of nuts.

Lightning lit up the pale sands of the flats nearby. Crashing thunder covered the sound of Henry and Ed chewing their pandanus nuts and savouring the seeds inside.

"Red, do you want this other canvas as a pillow?"

"I'll be the martyr – you use it."

Despite the uncomfortable circumstances, neither man took long to drape themselves over their branch and fall asleep. Henry's last thought as he drifted off vaguely registered. *At least this sleeping log is dry and not in the middle of the sea.* At that moment, the rain showers commenced, *or maybe not,* his thoughts continued. During the night, the rain fell in torrents but failed to disturb the travellers.

A glimmer of morning light draped everything in pale gold when the cool of his wet clothes lifted Henry from his semi-comatose state. He rubbed at his reddened eyes and raked the long hair from his face. His eyes snapped open when the tree trembled. His mind struggled to understand the cause. The wind had dropped in the night. He peered over the side of his branch. To his relief, a crocodile was not seeking to climb the tree to reach its breakfast. With great caution, he rolled himself over to peer into the branches above him. Ed's feet and legs crossed his vision.

"What's going on, Ed?"

"You're awake. I was beginning to wonder if you'd died."

"Not yet, Ed, nearly, but not yet." They both laughed.

"I've been up to the top of the tree – or as high as I could get – to look over the countryside. By the way, your water-bag is full. If we can't find food today, at least we'll have water to drink."

"What did you see from the top of the tree?"

"This tidal flat is long and wide. We'll have to go a little north or a little south before we continue east. I'm a bit concerned we might run into quicksand near the middle of the flats and I want to keep closer to the timbered edge."

"It was a bit much for us to hope for, to be able to go direct east, I guess."

"You'll be pleased to know, there was not a croc to be seen." Ed threw down the ropes and groundsheet before he swung to the ground.

Henry groaned and followed Ed to the sand, where the men drank their fill before he removed the water-bag from its supporting frame of sticks. He pulled the drawstring tight and replaced the bag into the satchel.

"Any ideas on food, Ed?"

But Ed was off searching for something on the ground at the base of nearby trees. He returned with a slim, strong branch about four feet long.

"Red, can you pass me one of our lanyards?" He began to bind his knife firmly to one end of the timber. He waved the finished weapon in the air. "My spear," he informed Henry.

Henry looked up from where he had been scraping away at a rotting timber stump near their sleeping tree. His hand rose, holding something in his thumb and forefinger. He angled his head backwards and dropped the prize down his gullet.

"Good Lord, Red, was that what I think it was?"

Henry grinned.

"You're the one who turned up your nose at my mudskipper, and here you are eating grubs."

Henry laughed. "Who's got the weak stomach, now? Here, try one. They're not too bad – just don't let them touch the sides going down." Henry's dirt-ingrained fingers passed a grub to Ed.

Ed frowned. He went to refuse, but thought better of it – *was it to be said he had a weak stomach?* He angled his head, as he had seen Henry do, and tossed the breakfast down.

Between them both they finished off a dozen grubs for the morning meal before drinking copious scoops of water.

"Those grubs are full of goodness, my Uncle George said."

"I'd be much happier getting my goodness from a big juicy side of meat on the fire, thank you."

Sizzling juicy beef filled the imagination of both men as they collected their gear and took the first step ahead for the day.

Henry only half noticed Ed place the wooden end of his contrived spear into the sand and then lean his weight on it at each step, as they made their way across a narrow strip of the tidal flat. Following behind in Ed's footsteps, his thoughts were filled with enjoyable meals he had eaten as a child in Cooktown. It was some time before Ed's actions registered. Henry looked up in surprise when Ed stumbled forward. Henry reached out and grabbed the back of his shirt.

"Whoa there, Ed, what are you doing?"

"Nearly lost my spear and myself in that soggy hole. We'll move closer to the tree line."

By the time they left the flat behind them and travelled along the animal pads within a scant forest, the sun punished them despite many drifting grey clouds above. They ran into small creeks running a banker following the previous night's rain. Henry dropped to the ground under the branches of a low tree. He unslung the satchel and loosened the drawstring on the water-bag. He handed the first scoop of water to Ed.

"Drink?"

Ed took the shell and swallowed the contents in one long gulp.

"Again?"

Once both their thirsts were satisfied, Henry dug around in the bottom of his satchel for his canvas hat. The raggedy piece of canvas was drawn taut over his wild hair.

"Ed, do you want your feet wrappings?"

"No thanks, the rain last night has left water puddles everywhere." Ed's body froze. Softly he whispered. "Henry, don't move."

With movements barely noticeable, Ed lifted the spear. He aimed and threw. The whoosh in his ears almost raised Henry off his feet. He turned at the thud followed by a twang as the spear shaft vibrated against the blade through the lizard and into the driftwood on which it had been sunning itself.

"Lunch," Ed grinned. "Hope you're feeling up to making a fire later."

As they proceeded east, the tall, wet grasses thickened on the forest floor. Trees grew closer together. When the sun reached its zenith above them, they stopped in the shade to eat and rest. Henry began his rote of making the fire using the scant dry grass he had rescued along their morning hike. Ed gutted his prize ready to throw it onto the coals.

"Where do you think we are now, Ed?" Henry asked later, as they chewed on the tough charred flesh.

"Who really knows? We've been going in an easterly direction. I'm guessing we won't be too far off the next big river. I can remember it on Dad's map, but cannot remember the name."

But they did not reach the river that night. At their camp near a grove of big trees, the sky dropped only light rains to disturb them. Before the sun lifted above the horizon, Ed managed to lure a grey duck paddling in one of the bigger puddles of rainwater using pandanus seeds retrieved from his pockets. Before the bird knew what happened, Ed managed to knock it out with a large stone thrown from a sling contrived from one of the foot wrappings the previous evening.

"Where did you learn to do that?" Henry sat amazed at the newly-discovered skill of his friend.

"Too many idle hours as a kid during the off-seasons on Thursday Island – we all called the island Waiben, then. The local Kaurareg people called it Waiben. They say it means a place with no water. Some of my friends were much better than I ever was with a sling."

$$\approx$$

CHAPTER TWELVE

Smiley

Smiley groaned as he rubbed at the sunken scars on his aching legs. His body had never been asked to maintain persistent speed over a long journey before now. When able to join his family on those walkabouts, the group travelled at a comfortable speed for adults, young and old, and children of all ages. As far as he remembered he had only made this trip four times – usually when the family celebrated the draining of the flood waters at the end of the wet season: the regeneration of grasses, return of animals to hunt, fruit and plants to enjoy, and rivers alive with fish to catch.

This was a journey to rescue his boyhood friend.

He had foregone the pleasure of a fire and a more substantial meal this afternoon and settled for the morsels recovered on the track during the day. Having left the town, which the white fellas named Coen, well behind him, Smiley lay under the bushes on the hill away from the river. With the sun still above the horizon, he gave in to his body's needs. He allowed himself this one luxury. He curled into a ball and slept – a sound sleep – a dangerous sleep. The arrival of the police patrol on the sandy river bank below went unnoticed. The troopers' soft voices interspersed with the orders from the white constable failed to arouse Smiley from his slumber.

$$\approx$$

In the last light of day, Constable Hetherington's sharp eyes caught a movement in the bushes on the rise behind them. Weariness, after the troop's hurried journey from the Coen Police Patrol Camp, fell from his shoulders. With languid movements, he squatted near the fire to drink the pannikin of tea served by one of the troopers. The stiffened part-brim of his cap shaded the eyelids hung low over the blue eyes, which never shifted their focus away from the point of movement on the hill. Most likely it had only been a wallaby. Yet, he knew from experience, it may have been something else. Many good men he once knew were now long dead because they had underestimated their enemies.

The shout of a trooper returning from the deep pool of water waving a large barramundi fish in his hands caused some commotion but did not distract Constable Hetherington's focus. His gaze never left the bush, now stilled. While the men chattered amongst themselves in the preparation of their fire and fish baking, Constable Hetherington rose and moved away. He patted the revolver in its holster on his right hip.

"I'm going for a walk," he called back to the men who barely lifted their eyes from their tasks.

Constable Hetherington moved out in a wide circle to approach his target from the side. His keen eyesight noted the absence of footprints, neither animal nor human, on the narrow pad leading to the bush holding his attention. He paused to look more closely and discovered faint traces in the dirt, where a handful of brush, or maybe a branch of leaves in human hands, had swept the path – something only a man would have thought to do. Not a whisper of sound announced the removal of his gun from its holster. Its light balance felt comfortable in his familiar grip. Strain as he might, his gaze was unable to penetrate the dark shadows within the foliage.

A long soft groan of pain rolled out of the thick bush.

"Right, fella, you'd better come out of there now, with your hands empty, if you know what's good for you." He issued the instruction in English followed by a brutalization of the Sugar-bag Bee language learnt when on duty at the Laura police patrol, and lastly, the Sandalwood English language picked up when working on Thursday Island. When only silence answered his request, he fired a bullet through the top branches of the bush.

CHAPTER THIRTEEN

Henry and Edward

The following day presented the two young doctors with a country no different from the previous afternoon – forest country with many animal pads through occasional areas of dense, tall grasses, which dragged at their legs. A shy sun appeared spasmodically between layers of clouds and provided a directional guide.

Henry felt he was ploughing through the humidity. With a stout stick for support, he led the way. His clothes dripped with moisture, but this time it was perspiration, not rain. When they arrived at a sandy-bottomed waterhole in a small creek, it became a competition to see who retained enough energy to safely stow the loads they carried and be first to scramble down the steep bank into the pond.

"It's freshwater!" Henry laughed before he ducked his head under the surface. His wet hand grabbed at the hat slipping from his head. He went to sink into the shallow depths when a thought flashed through his mind – his usual nemesis, *crocodiles*. A bow wave of water preceded his thrashing legs as he rushed out of the waterhole. After Henry climbed onto the bank, his gaze searched every inch of the perimeter but failed to find any evidence of their presence.

"No crocs then, Red?" Ed floated on his back, in the shallow pool.

"No crocs, Ed, but tell me, do you know how to catch freshwater crayfish?"

"I imagine they'd be something like crabs. As a kid, we used long sticks to prod those out of their mudbank holes. The offsider had the job of grabbing the bad-tempered tenant."

"I've seen Smiley do the same with crabs, too. So, where are we going to look for the front door of the crayfish home?"

Both men lay partially submerged in the shade of the overhanging gum trees searching the banks of their pool. Partial roots of one particularly high tree exposed in a darkened corner near a deep hole caught their attention.

"That looks a likely spot." Waterfalls poured from Ed's body when he stood to find a suitable prodding stick.

Henry paddled over to watch the process. Scepticism hung in his frown. Ed looked for likely holes within the tree roots and the bank. Eventually, Ed gave a hoy as a crayfish arrived at the surface gripping the prodder. His hand flashed down to rescue his catch.

Henry laughed. "That's what you call a fluke, my friend. Bet you can't do it again."

"Shouldn't you be matching my effort?" Ed attempted to fill his words with disdain, but his wide grin told a different tale.

"Well, come on then, come out. There's no room for two in there."

Ed backed out of the dark recess allowing Henry access. He handed over the prodder. On his first try, a crayfish burst out into the water. Henry shouted and dropped the prodder. He lashed out with grasping fingers reaching for the crustacean swimming in frantic circles to find another safe retreat. Water splashed up over Henry reducing his vision. By pure chance, his fingers clasped around the tail end of the crayfish as it strived to disappear into another hole. Henry held it aloft with a cheer.

Ed held his side as he laughed. "That doesn't count. The poor thing committed suicide." His laughter snapped off. "Devil's blood, Henry, back away from there – very slowly."

Henry did as Ed instructed, all the while his gaze darted left then right. A soft grunt escaped his open mouth when he saw what Ed espied. They had disturbed a large dark-patterned python snake, which gave every indication it had enough of the noisy intruders. What seemed like unending coils unwound around the tree roots. A reptilian head swung out of the dark space to hang suspended by its strong body over the lightened strip of water. With his heart pounding in his chest, Henry continued his slow retreat. The pendulum neck swayed the head back and forth. The tongue flickered in and out and the beady eyes watched Henry's every move. From the safe distance at the opposite side of the waterhole, the men watched the slithering body disappear back amongst the roots.

Henry gave a snort of laughter. He held up his prize crayfish and looked down at the similar specimen in Ed's hand. "It takes more than a damn good fright to make a man drop his dinner."

The flutter of fear still whispered inside Henry's gut as he searched amongst the grasses and debris timber to find the makings for his fire.

Ed and Henry laughed and joked as they climbed out of the creek bank near where they had left their damped-down fire and crayfish shells. The afternoon sun made its presence known. The men turned to face in an easterly direction. Free of the mud and filth, their clothes felt more comfortable. Clean hair and skin along with appetites somewhat satisfied, their spirits lifted further.

"Lead on, Ed, I'm right behind you." Henry readjusted his canvas head covering.

Little broke the boredom of the trek other than the increasing aches of tired unnourished limbs and the sudden retreat of kangaroos as they shot off in leaps and bounds at the sight of these strangers in their domain.

By late afternoon, both men were grateful to find the shade from the thickening forest canopy cooled their bodies a little. Animal pads led off in different directions at random. The men followed the ones heading east.

"I'm thinking we might be at the river I was expecting. I wish I could think of the name." Ed ducked his head below a large branch partly snapped off from its tree. "Look out low branch. Oh, I remember now, Weston … no … Watkins … no … Watson. Yes, I'm confident it is named Watson River. Dad mentioned it in a letter – maybe last year or the one before that. A pastoralist named it when he came to the area a few years back when the telegraph line was finished." When his feet slipped on the edge of the riverbank unseen within the thick foliage, Ed threw his arm out to grab the nearest tree trunk.

Henry joined Ed at the river's edge on the other side of the tree. He sucked in a deep breath. What he expected to be a bit of a creek appeared in front of them – all of one hundred yards wide, running with deep dark waters. The opposite bank looked imposing.

"Ed, hold my hand for a bit. I'll climb down and taste the water."

Gripping Ed's extended hand, he leaned down to catch a handful of water and scoop it into his mouth. His eyes narrowed under a slightly furrowed frown.

"Well, Red, how is it?"

"Not too bad, but it has a tainted taste to it. Not that much more than our water-bag."

"The forest is too thick here. All the animals we've seen must surely have a track down to the water along here somewhere. We need a cleared area to prepare a crossing of this waterway." Ed turned left then right. "Let's go downstream. The forest to the north here is almost impenetrable."

After an hour's pushing through low branches and bushes and darting down each break in the terrain leading back to the water, they came to a gap in the tree line where two enormous trees had been lifted from the bank by the forces of some previous storm. The dirt which had once held the root base together had partially washed away into a small bay eaten into the bank. The trees lay one across the other, stretching out into the water towards the far bank. Their leafless top branches lay buried in the river bed. Debris from earlier flooding had gathered against the trunks.

Using the protruding roots for a ladder, Henry climbed up to remove his satchel with the water-bag and hang it over a stubby root before he sat on the tree trunk. Ed followed, unslinging his two canvas rolls and hanging them beside the satchel. Exhaustion and hunger lined both their faces as they sat in silence taking in this new challenge. The lap of the peaceful waters below eased some of the aches from their bodies.

Ed scraped grimy hands down his face. "Red, we don't have much daylight left. Perhaps we should move – surely, we'll find somewhere suitable to make a night camp."

"You've had me sleeping in an upright tree, why can't we just sleep right here on this horizontal tree trunk? I'm beat. I'm hungry. I'm tired of walking." He sighed and then turned around towards Ed. "Ed, I'm sorry. Listen to me griping like a baby. I'm sure you're just as tired and hungry, and that ankle of yours must be giving you trouble."

"You're right, we both need a rest. We've been to sleep before with an empty stomach, I'm sure another night won't hurt."

Neither man moved. Silence descended upon them along with the evening shadows.

Clouds drifted across a half-moon casting interrupted light over the men stretched out on the wide timber trunk.

"Don't sleepwalk, Red." The last word of advice.

A watery sunrise greeted the travellers. Henry found Ed bent over the deep puddle of water at the exposed tree roots. One of the canvas rolls lay unwrapped, part in the water and part out of the water.

"There's a big bream in this muddy water. I saw it earlier when I went for a walk. I'm determined to have it to eat."

"Should I be calling you Squid, like your pearling friends do; seeing as you seem to have such an affinity with the fish society?" Henry laughed.

Henry knelt and watched Ed using the canvas as a fish trap. Both heads snapped up at the sound made by a large kangaroo when it landed with one spring onto their fallen tree. The timber echoed with the thud, thud, of its bouncing feet as it made its way along the wide trunk to the farther end.

"Is that roo planning on swimming from there to the other side of the river, Ed?"

"I've heard they can swim a bit, but I don't know about that far, and there will be a current out there."

Gasps exploded from their lips when the kangaroo lifted off the tree trunk and landed in shallow water. Water splashed up around the animal as it hopped to the far bank.

"There must be a sand bank at the end of the fallen trees, Ed. Maybe we can follow his example."

"Worth a try, I'm looking forward to this fish for breakfast. See the bit of cleared ground on the other bank. We should be able to get a fire going and eat there." Ed chuckled, "That's if you can get a fire going."

Ed yawned as he waited for the exhausted fish to settle over the canvas trap. The outcome of the competition did not, at first, appear obvious. Eventually, Ed sprang into action and dragged the catch onto the edge of the hole, where he tied it tightly within the canvas roll.

"Come on, Red, let's get over to the other bank and eat."

Loaded with their meagre supplies including the still wriggling fish wrapped in the canvas, the men began with tentative footsteps along the length of the tree trunk.

Ed pointed, "Look, this is where the roo leapt off. It is shallow I can see the bottom. You ready, Red?"

Ed braced himself ready to jump down when Henry grabbed his arm. "Stop!" he yelled.

Both men teetered on the log striving to regain their balance.

"Devil's horns, what do you think you're doing, Red? You nearly had me going in head first."

It was Henry's turn to point. "Who is the hungriest, you or the croc lying there in the mottled shadows beside the tree branches?"

"Devil's dinner, he nearly had me and my fish. What the hell's he doing this far upstream?"

Fear lurked in the depths of the eyes of both men. They shuffled about-face and returned along the tree trunk.

Still, on the west bank, they moved to the outer edge of the thicker timber line and used the music of the river water's current to guide them. When the animal pad they had been following turned west, they forged their own pathway in a north-easterly heading. The sun cleared the clouds and beat down onto the forest canopy, which sheltered the men from much of the heat, but exposed them to a suffocating hell-hole of humidity. Eventually, a cleared patch of river bank appeared. Both Henry and Ed paused to search for larger predators before they threw themselves down on the ground.

Henry smiled at his success once more in his fire-making. The option of raw fish motivated his efforts.

Impatience directed Ed's hands as he took up a stick and dragged the partially cooked fish from the coals.

"I'm starving, I can't wait a moment more." He cut off a fillet and shoved the remainder back onto the heat.

Henry's dislike of raw fish wrestled against the hunger within him. The sight of Ed's expression as the fish flesh went down his gullet became too much. Henry took his knife and retrieved the meal slicing a large fillet of his own. As he chewed the flesh, he wiped the sand from his lips.

When only the bones of their meal blackened in the heat, Ed stood up and walked to the riverbank. He found a bridge of flat rocks and banks of sand reaching across to the other side divided by threads of narrow deep channels filled with tumbling waters almost ready to overflow. He felt sure a grown man would have little difficulty jumping across each one. Search as he might he did not find any evidence of a crocodile waiting for its dinner.

Securing themselves with the two ropes joined together, Henry and Ed, one after another, jumped over each channel, waiting for the second jumper to find a safe footing before the first jumper moved on to the next channel.

The release of built-up tension following their morning's escapades, rang through the trees in their laughter, as the men scrambled up onto the far bank.

"Come on, Ed, let's put a few miles between those damn crocodiles and ourselves before we make a night camp."

CHAPTER FOURTEEN

Smiley

A black man with dirt-stained trousers rolled to the knees, crawled out of the thick bush. The constable was not surprised. He did raise his eyebrows at the white man's satchel hanging around the man's neck and shoulders. The man standing in front of him carried no weapons of any kind in his hands. He waved his revolver indicating the prisoner walk in front of him towards the river camp.

"What name, you?" He asked as he removed the satchel from Smiley's neck.

Smiley remained silent. He limped down the hill with the man holding the gun at his back.

Even in the darkening evening, the tangled scars snaking down the prisoner's legs below the trousers were obvious. Constable Hetherington's curiosity was only a passing thought. *How the devil did the beggar get those wicked scars?*

When they approached the camp, the six native troopers stood lined up with their firearms at the ready. They each wore the regulated distinctive pointed cap with its protective neck skirt, but their uniforms were at various stages of tidiness and completeness. However, the assortment of Snider and Martini-Henry rifles were held in steady hands.

"We thought you shot a brown snake, but you bring us black fella instead." One of the troopers laughed. "You want we shoot him too?"

"No, you can check his pockets, Boxer. And ask him his name, he might understand your lingo?"

Grey hair stuck out at all angles from under his cap as the man named Boxer approached the prisoner from behind, jabbering in several different dialects of the local languages. Smiley remained silent, while Boxer slipped his hands into his pants and retrieved the pocket knife and the honing stone. Boxer's white teeth shone in the firelight as he held up the trophies.

"I can keep these, Boss?"

Hetherington looked up from where he was going through the contents of the satchel in the light of the campfire.

"Er … no, Boxer. This is very strange. The bag only contains pencils and an art book wrapped in an oilskin. I'm wondering if this fella's killed a white man around here."

"You want I shoot him now, Boss? He only a bush myall. His twisted legs slow us down, much."

"No … no, I don't think so. We'll have to follow this up further. He'll have to come with us to meet the Mein patrol. Chain him to a tree." Constable Hetherington stood and made his way, with the evidence items, to his tent.

With his head down, Smiley went with Boxer to where he was to be secured, near where the troopers settled to sleep. A chain slung around the trunk of a solid tree linked into a pair of heavy biting handcuffs on the prisoner's wrists. He curled once more into his sleeping ball and began to hum a toneless tune seeking the strength of his father's presence. When the dark clouds blotted out the moon and dropped a heavy scud of rain during the night, he drew his legs up tighter against the shivers of his torso. He welcomed the warmth of the morning sunshine.

At the sound of the wakening camp, Smiley dragged himself into a sitting position. He shuffled his hands in an attempt to relieve the discomfort of the cuffs. The aroma of baking damper dough along with the hint of gum leaves in a boiling billy of tea teased his empty stomach. He held little hope of a drink or feed this morning. When Boxer approached with a ladle of water, surprise almost released an involuntary smile. He gulped greedily as Boxer poured the water down his throat. When the last bit of fluid ran out the sides of his mouth and down his chin and chest, Boxer laughed.

"Bush myalls all need bath."

Later the same trooper arrived at his side with a thick slice of damper, minus the treacle the others around the fire were enjoying. Boxer tossed it in Smiley's direction. The bread bounced off his head to land in the dirt between his legs. Pride urged Smiley to ignore the food offered in such a manner, but common-sense, and his father's presence prevailed. Without the use of his arms, he twisted his body to lie down and eat the offering from the sand. Sustenance was his prime concern at the moment.

As he ate, he felt the eyes of the white man burning into him. He took little notice and continued to chew the dry damper. The white man surprised him again when he spoke to Boxer.

"Give the prisoner another drink, Boxer."

Curiosity lifted his eyes to peer directly into the blue eyes of the policeman. *Was this a trick, this act of kindness?* He swallowed deeply again from the ladle of cool water.

When the troopers began to decamp and load their packhorses with the equipment, the white man walked over to Smiley and squatted near the tree to face his prisoner.

"What language you talk?"

Smiley remained mute with his eyes looking down at his toes.

"Can you speak? Can you nod your head?" With a sudden movement, he clapped his hands beside Smiley's right ear.

Smiley's gaze lifted briefly then dropped again to the dirt.

"So, you're not deaf then, boy. How did you come by those scars?" The white man's hand reached over and he ran his forefinger down one of the thick marks on the skin. "My name is Constable Hetherington."

But Smiley neither looked up again nor spoke.

"Did you kill the white man for his drawings?"

Smiley's mouth twitched at the urge to answer in the negative, but he bit his tongue. Horror tales of these men were part of his people's fireside talks. They were not to be trusted.

"Did the white man make those scars on your legs?"

Smiley clamped down on his reply.

"Who is the man named Smiley who signed the drawings in the book you carried?"

An involuntary grunt forced its way past his lips.

Intrigue filled Constable Hetherington, widening the eyes under his raised eyebrows.

"Who is the man, Henry Baldwin, engraved on the pocket knife you carried? Did you kill Henry Baldwin?"

Determination removed all expression from Smiley's face. Even the curious Constable Hetherington recognized the man was not going to talk this morning.

"We have to travel a long way today. You'll need to run to keep up. If you cannot keep up, I'll have to shoot you. We cannot be delayed. Can you run? You can hold my stirrup leather to help you." The constable rose and made his way over to where the mounted troopers leading the loaded packhorses, waited for his order to move out.

When Boxer came to undo his chains from around the tree, Smiley heard him speak to Constable Hetherington in a dialect of a tribe a long way from this country.

"Why we not shoot him, Boss."

"I'll tell you when to shoot, Boxer. I need to know who this Henry Baldwin is and if he's dead. Until then we keep the prisoner alive. Give me the chain; he can run at my side this morning."

"Yes, Boss."

Smiley gritted his teeth. Pain melded into a red haze in front of him. Blood dripped from the lacerations inflicted by the handcuffs. His hands clenched the stirrup leather behind Constable Hetherington's right knee. Tired legs felt as if they were on fire again. Dust from the horse's hooves filled his eyes. He discovered early in the day the danger of falling when his body dragged and bounced from the chain slung over the pommel of the policeman's saddle. Violent curses erupted from the man when the horse sidled away from the impediment in front of his feet.

After what seemed like a lifetime, Smiley felt the ground beneath his feet changing. Soft sand pulled at the depleted calves of his legs. The horses were not immune and slowed their pace, which brought a little relief. Smiley did not hear the constable call a break. He fell to the ground hanging by his wrists when the horse pulled up snorting and shaking its head.

Smiley did hear the annoyance in the constable's order. "Boxer, bring me the spare packhorse. No, better still, bring me the packhorse carrying the tent. Transfer everything, but the tent, onto the spare horse." He ran his gaze around the gathering. "A drink for everyone." Hetherington dismounted and released the chain from the pommel. Smiley's bloodied arms fell to the ground. Impatience filled the policeman's eyes, but he did call to the trooper measuring out the water from a waterbag. "Bring the prisoner a drink."

As Constable Hetherington drank from his canteen, he looked down at his prisoner. "Can you ride a horse?" But, as he expected, the prone prisoner did not answer. The captive lifted his hand to support the water ladle Boxer held at his mouth. "Well, you're still alive I see."

When the trooper brought up the packhorse with both sides of the animal wide with its canvas load, Hetherington walked over to examine the animal and its loading. He looked up and rapped out his orders to Boxer.

"Boxer, sit the prisoner on the horse with his two legs between each canvas roll and the horse. They should hold him on the animal. Let him grip the girth strap. Loop the chain between his handcuffs around the horse's neck. Give me the lead rope. We don't want this fella to die just yet, and we don't want him to slow us down either. I want to be at the Archer River tonight and at the Mein Reserve tomorrow sometime."

CHAPTER FIFTEEN

Henry and Edward

With fewer trees, the midday sun set the traveller's skin on fire through their worn clothing. Bare feet began to stumble. Their breathing laboured. Henry's lengthening hair sprouted between the ties on his self-designed head-covering like the uncombed tail of a chestnut horse.

"You need a hacksaw to cut through this humidity, Ed."

Ed yelped as his feet skidded down the bank of another dry tributary.

"Curses upon this heat and these unending gutters in this godforsaken land. Let's stop here, I need a drink. How is our water supply, by the way?"

Henry clung to the thick bushes on either side of the animal pad they had been following as he slid down into the dry creek bed.

A pleasant gurgle of fluid rewarded their ears and their thirst as Henry unhitched the waterbag from his shoulder.

"With those clouds coming again, we're almost guaranteed rain this evening. It may bring brief relief from the heat, but it means the monsoons are settling in and this country here will be nothing more than a flood plain once that happens."

"Hopefully these creek crossings we've traversed today are tributaries of the Archer River and we'll have almost reached our first goal, the telegraph line," Ed reassured Henry.

"Maybe they're from the Watson River behind us."

"Perhaps."

While the birds serenaded them from the trees above, Henry and Ed contemplated such a depressing thought in silence.

When back on the track, the heat took its toll on the two men and their conversations ceased. All their efforts were needed to keep placing one foot in front of the other.

The third tributary on their track appeared as dusk settled. They fell more than climbed down the bank to land in a small waterhole.

A halo of water sprayed around him when Henry ducked his body beneath the surface and came up tossing his head left and right. He laughed and began to drink.

"Freshwater tastes almost as good as a cold ale." Ed grinned.

On the other side of the water pool, stood an elevated rocky platform at least six feet high with its base in the creek bed. Time and water currents had worn this monument of stone into an almost perfect circle with a radius of six or seven yards.

"Here, Red." Ed held his hands with his fingers laced into a stirrup.

Henry slung the satchel around his body to hang from his back as he placed his right foot into the stirrup provided, with his hands pressed against the rocky face for balance. Ed hoisted him up onto the flat above. Knees and elbows scraped on the rock surface as Henry pulled himself into a safe position. After removing the satchel with the water-bag, he placed them in a shallow indent on the surface of his landing site. While lying on his belly, Henry swivelled his body around, stretched down his hand, and using his body weight with feet scratching for purchase, he helped Ed to scramble up beside him.

"I doubt if a croc would get us up here." Ed hoped to reassure.

"At least we'd hear its approach. Surely, we're too far inland by now to find any crocs – at least any saltwater crocodiles." Henry hoped he was right.

With nothing but the contents from their water bag in their stomachs since the feed of bream earlier in the day, their bellies rumbled as they settled to sleep on the hard surface. Each man folded a canvas under his body.

The moon appeared briefly before the rain began to pelt down. Both men dragged their small canvas sheet over their bodies, hunched up tighter and tried to ignore it.

Light showers greeted them as they awoke with the faint glow of morning light through the clouds above. The water beside their rock roared in their ears. The water level now ran from one creek bank to the other. Horror silenced them. They stared at the swirling torrent.

Henry was the first to shake himself. "Ed, that water seems only shallow and the current isn't too bad. With our staffs to steady us, we can walk across to the other side. We'll use a rope to help each other along if we get into trouble."

"This is from the man who believes crocodiles are hiding behind every ripple of water?"

"What do you suggest?"

"I'm tossing up whether we should go back to the closest bank and head further upstream to where the crossing may be narrower."

"The opposite bank doesn't seem all that far away."

"Not close enough I think, Red. I'm sure you'll find the current much stronger than you expect and neither of us is at full strength. I can guarantee our fear of the potential presence of crocs will weaken our strength and our resolve even further. Once you enter the waters there'll be no coming back. We have to keep going until we get to the other side or drown in the attempt."

The sound of the water churning around their rock base rose in volume to enter the silence between the men.

"Okay, Ed, I know you're right. Let's try to get back before we have no retreat at all."

Each man with his load around his neck and torso, a staff in one hand and the other arm hooked through a loop at either end of the one single rope, slipped from their stony haven – back the way they had come.

Ed led the way through the river trees into a more open area and moved forward with the sun on his right cheek. Thick wet clay soils clung to their legs from knee to toe. Anxiety frazzled the nerves of both Henry and Ed knowing a delay such as this could be dangerous. Their time was limited. The monsoons threatened an early arrival.

The country opened up into swamps for as far as the eye could see.

"Is that one swamp or lots of smaller swamps do you think, Red?" Ed fell flat on his face into the waters hidden within the lotus lilies, the bullrushes and the straggly fronds of the water ribbons. "Cursed water."

Louds squawks, swooshing wings and paddling feet exploded around the two men. A flock of ducks rose into the air. Many others of their number dived beneath the surface to find their way through the underwater forest.

Henry reached over and pulled Ed up from his knees.

"Ooh, look, Ed," Henry moved over to the water's edge where bush tomatoes shone yellow in the sun. His grasping fingers hauled a handful and shoved them into his mouth.

"Red, be careful. Are you sure they're safe to eat?"

"Yes, Ed. Besides bush honey, these tomatoes are Smiley's favourite tucker."

In a short time, a wide swathe of plants devoid of fruit remained. Juice and seeds dribbled down from the wide grins.

Henry began to take in the sight of other edible foods growing within the swamp.

"You know, Ed, if we feel down to the roots of those bulrushes and the water ribbons, we'll likely find edible tubers."

"And you want to paddle around here in this water, where you can't see an inch in front of you, digging for tubers?" Ed stretched upright. He flapped one hand at Henry while digging into his pocket with the other hand to remove the sling and his small collection of stones.

"Red, can you find any more stones? We'll have duck for dinner." One by one the heads of those ducks under the water began to surface.

Henry moved back, away from Ed's spinning weapon. The first stone ran true and the wings of a brown duck flapped uselessly at the water. The head lay bent backwards. The still-floating body rocked in the bow wave as Ed ran out to retrieve his meal. His yell of glee spun up into the air along with the wings of more frightened ducks.

With the immediate threat of starvation relieved, and the promise of a meal ahead, Henry and Ed retreated to the wide strip of almost bare clay soil interspersed with raised islands of thick grasses, through which the overflowing swamps drained into the nearby river. The occasional boggy patches posed some difficulty, but they were happy with the illusion of safety surrounded by the clearer ground which provided an early warning of any lurking crocodiles.

Henry readjusted his hat as the sun rose. None of the earlier clouds marred a sky of azure blue. Sweat ran freely off the men's bodies.

Ed bumped into a stilled Henry causing him to grunt.

"What's the matter, Red?"

The pounding inside his chest deafened Henry to the wind whistling across the plains and the cheeping of the small birds fossicking in the grass. He may not have heard Ed's words, but he understood the gist. Slowly his hand rose and pointed to the path thirty feet in front of them. A crocodile lay along the cleared track, the great, scaled body coated with mud. Belligerent eyes focused on the newcomers. Long-nailed, webbed feet propelled the unwieldy body in a rush forward half a dozen paces. A broken wallaby hanging from either side of the toothed jaws gave a feeble tremor of its hind legs. Henry and Ed retreated several paces with speed. The crocodile rushed again. The men retreated twice as far.

"Ed, what the hell are we going to do now?" A hushed whisper was almost blocked by the spasm of Henry's throat.

CHAPTER SIXTEEN

Cooktown

Blood dripped from the patient's head wound onto the surgical dressing-room floor. A long red stain appeared on Abigail's white apron.

"Damn."

George looked up from where he had been changing the dressing on a large burn wound on old Mister Gordon's back. The doctor's startled eyes shone out from under his permanently furrowed brow. He did not speak, but his mind had shifted from the dressing at hand to his sister's state of mind. *Abigail never swore ... well not since we were children together and practised the words overheard between our father and the gardener sometimes. Something has sure got her stirred up.*

He returned to his work and made a mental note to be more observant of his sister today.

Over at the surgical table, Abigail swabbed the large gash above Mister Norton's eye before taking up the recently sharpened suture needle clamped tightly in the jaws of the needle holder. Nimble fingers and the expertise of long practice guided the thread through the eye of the needle. In her other hand, she held a pair of toothed dissecting forceps. Lifting the skin on one side of the wound with the forceps, she pushed the needle point through the skin and angled it down and up through the flesh on the other side of the wound. She lay the forceps down and swabbed the leaking wound once again.

With her agile fingers and a flick of the wrist, she cast the first throw of her knot. This knot was repeated two more times before Abigail took up the suture scissors and snipped off the ends.

Thirteen more sutures were installed before the gash had been united in a tidy line and the flowing blood reduced to an occasional red swelling drop. Another swab of the wound and a firm bandage completed her chore.

At his twin's next words, George blinked but restrained from lifting his eyes.

"Mister Norton, do you think you might keep away from the bars and dens for a while? There is only a limited number of times the body can take this sort of punishment. If you want to stay alive, try to use a little bit more sense."

That's the first time I've heard Abigail talk to a patient so bluntly. Something, and I've a fair idea what, is eating her. All our lives our minds and feelings have ebbed and flowed in unison – a duet of bass and violin tossing about on the musical tide of life's symphony.

"Time for a cup of tea, Sis?" He sighed. The poetic flow of words and thoughts was something his greatest friend Thomas would sprout. How he missed his long-dead companion.

In the tub on the bench on the downstairs verandah of the house, surgical instruments clattered in the soapy water stained with the murky shadows of blood as Gina, the assistant nurse, scrubbed each one clean.

"We're going to the kitchen for a break, Gina. Please join us when you've finished what you're doing." Abigail invited her assistant.

George sat at the table with half a buttered scone devoured. The level of the tea in the cup sitting in front of him had lowered to half-mast. Behind him, Cook added water to a cauldron of stew simmering on the large wood stove before bending to lift a lump of timber from the box on the floor. She opened the fire door of the stove and shoved the wood inside. The door slammed shut.

"It's a bit hot in here, Abigail, how about we take our tea out under the awning?"

George's impatience became almost a tangible thing as he waited for his sister to settle.

"Abby, I've never heard you speak so sharply to a patient before. Want to talk about it?"

"Why shouldn't I? Mister Norton and his stupidity drive me insane." She threw up her right arm – palm forward. "Sorry, George, sorry. I shouldn't snap at you. The man has barely a square inch on his body which I haven't had to sew up at one time or another. I'll soon be sewing over my own mending. The man stinks of cheap grog and today the aroma of opium hung about him like a thick coat."

"Half the remaining fossickers turn up here in the same condition – frequently. Since when has that bothered you to this extreme? I have a distinct feeling it's not Mister Norton and his smelly coat that has you in such a humph."

Abigail opened and closed her mouth – twice – ready to throw out further excuses for her tantrum, but slowly her body slumped.

"You're right, George," she reached over and sipped her tea, and bit into a scone. Her gaze lifted to take in the boat-filled Endeavour River. Echoes of labour along the wharf drifted through the shady trees along the river banks. "I'm worried about Henry and his friend. It will be two weeks tomorrow since they left Darwin on the pearling ship – and nearly a week since we received the telegram sent by the captain of the steamship from Port Kennedy. I guess, since we collected their luggage from the harbour store yesterday, I'm thinking we should have heard something from them. I know Henry would be sure to send us a telegram at his first port of call."

"Abby, I know it's been such a long time since we've had Henry home with us, but he's not a boy anymore. He's a grown man. Obviously, he and his friend are enjoying their pearling lark. I've no doubt he'll send you a telegram as soon as they arrive on Thursday Island." The wide smile on George's face belied the black cloud of anxiety and disappointment, which fell like a cloak about his shoulders.

"It has been only two years since the "Quetta" sank in the Torres Strait. It's a treacherous stretch of sea. And what about the strange words from Smiley before he disappeared? I do hope he is safe also. I think of him as my son too."

"He has been with us a long time and I know how you feel, but this is his land. I'm sure he knows what he's doing." George jumped up brushing the crumbs from his shirt front. "Come on, Sis. Will you join me on a walk to the hospital? I need to see if Matron has everything under control. Since Basil collapsed, it has been quite an extra workload, although I have to admit Matron does a sterling job. She'll appreciate it when Henry's friend arrives to take over as superintendent. It can't have been easy on her – all the extra responsibility."

"You'd never know to look at her except for the dark shadows under her eyes and sometimes a few wrinkles in her uniform, but not once have I seen her flummoxed." Abigail rose from the table. "Can you wait a moment while I fetch my parasol? I'll bring your hat too. In the last few years, I've noticed how the sun is making your skin darker by the day. I won't be able to tell the difference between you and Smiley when he gets back."

CHAPTER SEVENTEEN

Henry and Edward

"I'm happy to give the crocodile all the track it wants, Red. It won't be interested in us with that meal between those teeth. I wonder if he'd share. I could make short work of a roast wallaby right about now."

Both men edged backwards giving a sharp yelp when the crocodile made a rapid movement sideways and forged a new pathway winding its way through the grassy islands.

Ed's voice wobbled, "Must have a nest in there somewhere."

"A long way from here, I hope."

Both men held their knives at the ready as they resumed their journey.

The slurp of their feet on the wet ground and the call of the birds in the high river gum trees was the only sound to interrupt the silence.

After almost an hour, Ed spoke. "Will this damn mud ever end? We must have come miles through this sludge. Should we make our way back to the river, Red? Maybe there'll be somewhere to cross by now."

"Suits me, I hate this feeling of crocs on both sides of us."

With drooping shoulders, Henry and Edward angled back towards the river bank. They struggled to breathe through the heat and humidity which threatened to steal all speech from them. Frequently Ed nudged Henry's shoulder when thirst overwhelmed him. Both drank greedily knowing freshwater was not too far away. When at last they stood in the shade of the river gum trees, they paused. The edge of the river here was steep, but at least only a narrow strip of water presented itself near the far bank. Leaning heavily on their wooden staffs they followed an animal pad downwards to land on a firm dry section of the creek bed.

"Hen …," but Ed found speech beyond him for a moment. He swallowed and tried again. "Red, let's look for crocodile tracks as we cross the river bed. We'll eat in the shade of the paperbark trees over there near the water. It will give us a chance to plan our crossing while we cook and eat this duck."

Relief shone in their eyes and wide grins when they found no evidence of fresh crocodile spoor. As he moved along, Henry scavenged for dry firesticks and kindling protected under rocks, logs, or undergrowth. With his legs crossed, he sat in the shade at the chosen site for quite some time before he moved to prepare a fireplace.

"You alright, Red?"

Henry sighed, unsure whether he had the energy to twirl the firesticks. His body ached in every muscle he could identify. In fact, he began to suspect he may have had a few more muscles than those found in the anatomy books swotted over so diligently at St. Bartholomew's Hospital in London. By the time the tinder caught and small twigs were added to the weak flame, Henry doubted he was going to have the energy to swallow a morsel of Ed's duck.

Having replenished the water in their waterbag from the clear stream, Ed cleaned the guts of the duck. He drove a stake through its body from end to end ready to hold the bird over the fire and soften the feathers for removal.

Both men dropped into a deep sleep while waiting for the duck to cook. The sun had shifted to the west when Ed's voice and the aromas of hot flesh burrowed into Henry's brain.

"Wake up, Red. Good grief, this bird looks like a meal old Poison fed us every day at college." He used his knife to drag the well-browned body from the coals. "Henry, come on, wake up. Eat; you'll feel a new man." He nudged Henry's leg with his foot. "Red, are you awake?"

With a grunt and a groan, Henry drew his knees up to his body and stretched his arms. "What's all the noise about, Ed?"

"I was beginning to think you'd died in your sleep."

"I wasn't asleep, I was just resting my eyelids."

"A likely tale." Ed passed half the simmering bird to Henry. "Here, will you have a go at this? It's pretty well cooked but a feed fit for a king."

Above the men savouring every morsel of their meal, golden breasts and blue wings flashed, as three kingfishers darted amongst the foliage of paperbark trees shaped by the whims of the annual monsoonal tides. The men tossed the meatless bones into the coals of a dying fire.

"While you were out to it, I found a place downstream, where we can cross quite easily. Rocks have been swept up into a weir by flooding waters at some time. They are now covered with about a foot of water – easy to negotiate."

Henry gave a feeble nod and pulled his body upright. He made his way to the creek. Cool water washed over him as he sank into the pool. Red hair spread out in a halo above his head as he disappeared. With a whoosh, he rose to the surface drawing in a deep breath and renewed energy.

"How many hours of daylight have we got left do you think?"

From where he sat sharpening his knife on a large rock, Ed looked up at the sky.

"Maybe two hours – but we need to keep moving. We can't have too much further to go now."

They travelled over low undulating terrain moving directly east between the trees. Several times, when they slid down the banks of dry gullies, pain ripped through the calf muscles of their legs. Audible groans accompanied their climb up the other side with both men leaning hard on their staffs to provide some semblance of balance.

A flicker of anxiety flared in Henry's belly when he noticed the return of a limp in Ed's left leg. From his position behind, he realized the swelling reached above and below the ankle even into the hardening edges of his foot sole. Henry slowed his own pace a fraction.

"Ed, can we rest a moment? I need to sit down."

Henry led them over to a large shady tree and dropped to the ground leaning back on the wide trunk. His gaze did not miss the lines of agony on his friend's face and the care taken as he lowered himself to the ground.

"Ed, you know what this tree is, don't you?" Henry's head swung around while he checked out three other similar trees. "We're in a grove of wild plum trees. The fruit ripens in summer."

"I see." Ed lifted his head.

"That's right, but …" But Henry's warning arrived too late. Ed's hand reached out and picked one of the luscious shiny rounded purple fruits. He slipped it into his mouth.

"No, Ed, don't eat the fruit straight off the tree."

Mangled fruit sprayed forth as Ed spat hard. "Why not, is it poisonous?"

"No, it isn't poisonous, but when eaten from the tree it leaves the membranes of your mouth totally dry. Drinking water will have little to no effect." Henry had risen and uncovered a short stick to scratch around the underground beneath the tree.

"What good is it then, if I can't eat it? And what are you doing with the stick?" Ed's cheeks sucked and stretched as he struggled to roll his tongue and encourage saliva back into his mouth.

"The natives bury the fruit in the sand for a fortnight before eating. I'm guessing there'll be lots of dropped fruit in the dirt around here."

In a short time, Henry had gathered a heap of wrinkled dark purple ripened and matured fruit.

"Red, you'll pardon me if I let you test one of those plums before I chance another. Each one has more wrinkles than my great-grandmother's face. She looked about that colour too, with her emphysema."

Henry smiled. He cleared away as much dirt as possible from one of several plums he dug out of the leaf litter. Grubby hands rubbed the fruit up and down on his shirt front before he chewed a mouthful of flesh from one side. When his small collection of fruit had been devoured, he explained to Ed.

"They only have a thin layer of flesh, but it tastes delightful if not a bit acidic." With his appetite sated, Henry rested back against the tree trunk and watched his companion.

Once his mouth returned to normal, Ed began to nibble at another piece of fruit he recovered from under the tree.

"I suppose your friend Smiley showed you the trick with these plums."

"Yes, he did. He showed my mother how to boil the peeled fruit and make a jam too."

"I think, Red, I'm too full to go another step today. The sun will be down behind the horizon shortly, how about we stop here tonight?"

"Ed, you took the words right out of my mouth."

As the night settled, Henry pondered the problem of the exacerbation of Ed's ankle sprain injury. Should he say something about his observations, and have Ed snap at him to mind his own business, or should he stay silent and take the risk of Ed's stubbornness being the cause of more tissue damage?

In his medical opinion, the latter wasn't an option.

"Ed, how's your ankle standing up to this marathon foot journey?"

Ed's silence dragged out. Henry thought he must be asleep already.

Ed rolled over and lay looking up to the starlit sky as the moon eased over the horizon.

"What, you want to practice your doctoring skills on me?"

Henry sighed waiting for a further taunt but was pleasantly surprised at Ed's next words, even though he would have preferred not to have his suspicions confirmed.

"I have to admit the fall into the last deep gully did not do it a lot of good."

"In the morning, how about you use both of the staffs? During the day I'll find another. That should keep most of the weight off the affected leg."

"I can't take your staff, Red, I see you leaning on it heavily at times yourself."

"Ed, we're in a bloody great forest. I'll find another staff in no time at all."

"Wow, you sound a bit fed up with forests."

"Sorry, yeah, you could say that."

"I know what you mean. I can't promise to get you out of the forested country, but if my calculations are right, we should be nearing the telegraph line in a day or two."

Even though not a cloud marred the sky tonight, they set up the top canvas in the hope condensation might drip into the second canvas spread to follow the contour over a hollow in the ground.

It was not the rain that woke the sleeping men on more than one occasion during the night, but several possums feeding on the plums.

After a sluggish start the following morning, Henry and Ed maintained a slow but steady pace. Now using two poles to lean upon, Ed was able to relieve his painful ankle of most of his body weight. After some protest, he agreed to hand over one of the ropes with its rolled canvas to Henry who slung it over the opposite shoulder supporting their precious satchel.

"Not far now, Henry," Ed offered hope.

CHAPTER EIGHTEEN

Henry, Edward and Smiley

From behind the boulder, the two emaciated men savoured, for some moments, the sight of clear running water only yards in front of them. They went to step out. Flaked layers of skin peeled from sunburn on areas of skin not covered by their clothing. Henry's red hair poked out of the canvas wrapping over his head. Ed's brown hair hung like a dirty mop on his skull. Henry grabbed the arm of his companion almost unbalancing Ed and the two stout branches he used for support.

"Wait, Ed, listen. I can hear horses and people – someone's coming."

"Well, Red, I hope they've enough food for an extra two at the table."

"Let's just see who they are before we go rushing out into the open."

Both men pulled back into the shelter of the rocks still hot from the sun earlier in the day. In the flickering shadows of the windblown clouds above, they watched as a mounted white constable and six native troopers rode out into the cleared sandy beach on the river. A prisoner rode a packhorse on a lead behind the constable. The two observers watched as the patrol halted and dismounted.

"Looks like a police patrol, Ed." Henry readjusted the remains of his canvas head covering. "It should be safe to join them. We need to know exactly where we are."

"You're right, Red. I just hope none of them have restless fingers on those rifles they're carrying. Let's give them a chance to settle in."

Henry and Ed watched the troopers remove the native man in handcuffs from the packhorse and secure him by chain to a tree trunk. The prisoner looked in poor shape as he limped from the horse to the tree. The constable stood for several minutes looking down at his captive. It was impossible for either Henry or Ed to see or hear if he spoke to the fellow.

"I wonder what the poor blighter has done?"

"At least they let him ride on the horse. I don't think I've heard of that happening before."

"Come on then, let's go and introduce ourselves."

The two dishevelled men stumbled down the rough track both supported by their improvised crutches. The sharp call from a native trooper echoed up the rise.

"Boss!"

The constable's head swung up. His hand held a revolver at the ready.

Henry and Ed almost tumbled as they pulled up at the sight of the weapon pointing their way.

"We mean you no harm. We need help. Please don't shoot." Ed's dry throat struggled to yell the words loud enough to be heard by the policeman.

"Come on down, mister, and no tricks I have this gun aimed at your chest and I don't usually miss."

With the aid of their timber sapling crutches, Henry and Ed shuffled over the last twenty yards. It was Ed who found his voice first.

"Sorry to barge in on you. I'm Doctor Edward Benton. My friend and I ...," Ed pointed at his companion, "... were shipwrecked in the Arafura Sea a few weeks back. We landed on the west coast and have been trying to reach the Mein Telegraph Station. I'm sorry, neither of us has any identification. We lost everything at sea."

"Constable Hetherington of the Mounted Native Police. We're headed to Mein. It's about a day's journey north of here. You've done well to make it this far." He lowered the gun and replaced it in the holster. "Come into the tent – or the beginning of a tent. You both look done in."

"Thanks, Captain, but do you mind if we drink at the river first?" Ed unslung the roll of canvas from his shoulder and dropped it on the ground, near where Henry had placed their remaining supplies against a tree trunk.

"Of course, come into the shade of my tent and one of my men will bring you water." Hetherington ushered the two arrivals towards the tent before turning his head. "Boxer, fill the water ladle."

As the native trooper offered the drink to the thirsty white men, his gaze took in the two strangers. "Plenty cool water, drink." He passed the ladle to Ed who passed it on to Henry.

"Here, Red, you first."

Constable Hetherington leant his back against a nearby sapling and drank from his canteen. "Who is your friend, Doctor Benton?"

"Sorry, of course. Doctor Henry Baldwin."

The captain's eyebrows shot up while capping the canteen. "Who did you say?"

Henry wiped his chin and handed the ladle back to Ed before he answered the policeman.

"I'm Henry Baldwin from Cooktown, recently on return from studying at Saint Bartholomew's in London. We were on our journey home when we ended up in the water."

"I haven't heard of any ships being sunk in the Gulf recently."

"No. You probably wouldn't through the normal channels. We left our steamship at Darwin to join a pearling boat belonging to Ed's friend. It's doubtful if anyone has heard of the *Pink Pearl's* demise yet. As far as we know we're the only survivors."

Hetherington turned back to Ed. "Didn't you say your name was Benton? Are you from the pearling fleet Benton family?"

Ed nodded.

The policeman then turned to Henry. "Henry Baldwin, you said?"

This time Henry nodded the affirmative.

"I have something I want to show you."

While Constable Hetherington moved over to his saddlebags, Henry looked askance at his friend, Ed, who shrugged in return. The policeman removed the satchel taken from his prisoner. His hand shuffled around inside before it exited holding the pocketknife. Before he could speak Henry jumped in.

"Where did you get that knife?"

"You recognize it, do you?"

"I certainly do. It was mine. I'm sure you can still see the name engraved on the edge and that miniature wooden pyramid hanging off the end was carved by my uncle's manservant, Thomas, who came from the middle east. Where did you get it?"

"It was taken from a fellow who carried this satchel with drawing books and pencils inside. We thought this Henry Baldwin must have been murdered. The sketches in the book are signed by someone …,"

Henry interrupted. "Called Smiley?"

"Yes, that's right. Do you know who he is – this painter named Smiley?"

Henry ignored the question and struggled to his feet. He held onto the tent pole and stared at the black man chained to the tree.

"Are there thick scars running down both your prisoner's legs?"

"Yes, there are. How do you know?"

"That man out there, your prisoner, Constable Hetherington, is the man named Smiley – the painter and my best friend. The pocketknife was given to him before I left for London and he should have a honing stone with him too."

"Yes, he did. He has refused to speak to me. He just hums some sort of lament all the time. I thought he did not understand. When I saw the name on the pocketknife and the books in the satchel, I thought he must have murdered this man named Henry Baldwin."

"Well, I'm still alive – just. And Smiley understands English very well. He can speak and write it quite well also. We had the same teacher when we were boys. As for his dirge, I don't fully comprehend it myself, but Smiley says he sings to his ancestors. It's something to do with the time, as a baby, he nearly died after falling into the campfire."

"He's not just a bush myall at all it would appear."

Henry gritted his teeth.

"No, he most certainly is not. He has worked with my uncle, at his medical surgery in Cooktown, for years. I can't guess what Smiley's doing up this way. Can I talk with him?"

"Yes, of course. If you vouch for him, I'm happy to release him from his bonds."

"Thanks. I will talk to the man first to make sure it is Smiley. I didn't recognize him when I came in. But then I was not too bright myself."

"I'll tell Boxer to go with you. If you confirm the man's identification and you're happy to take the man into your care, Boxer will release him." Constable Hetherington walked over to where Boxer was putting the finishing touches on the tent. He gave his orders before turning back to Ed and Henry. "Will you join our group to travel to Mein tomorrow? I can reorganize the horses and double up some of the men. We've enough food – plain though it will be."

Ed offered up thanks for the two of them. Henry was on his way to talk to his childhood friend.

Tears moistened Henry's eyelashes as he watched his friend sitting with his head bowed. Chains held his arms in position around a tree trunk. Blood dripped from lacerations under the handcuffs. As he approached, Henry caught the sound of the familiar tuneless hum Smiley used when distressed. He spoke in a version of Smiley's own language the pair had used as children.

"If my mother saw the filthy condition of you, she'd scrub you with soap and water in the tub."

The prisoner's face transformed as he swung his head up to look at this new arrival in the camp. To Henry, the wide smile felt like a familiar treasure returned.

"Henry, what you doing here? I come to take you home."

"I think it might be me taking you home, my friend. How did you know I was up in this country?"

"My father tells me."

Henry frowned. He recalled a letter from Uncle George reporting Smiley's father had died a few years back, but then his frown cleared. Henry only vaguely understood the connection Smiley had with his people's ancestors, but he offered Smiley full respect.

Fear clouded Smiley's eyes as a rifle shot rang through the clearing. Henry's head snapped up. He swung around to see what the constable made of the shot, but he had not moved.

"It's alright, the men are hunting meat to eat."

Reassured at this message, Henry nodded to Boxer who was in the process of releasing his prisoner. He did not miss the suspicion in the man's eyes. No doubt he did not really trust this stranger in tattered clothing and a canvas wrap over his head who received such respect from his boss.

"Thanks, Boxer." Henry smiled at the trooper before he leant heavily on his crutch to help Smiley to his feet. He returned to their childhood language. "Come on, Smiley, let's clean you up and we'll have a look at those hands."

"Have you looked at yourself, Henry? And you say I need cleaning up. Miss Abigail will have two in her tub."

Henry laughed.

Two distinct groups sat around the campfire eating fresh damper and roasted wallaby meat. Five of the six troopers chattered in their own tongue as they sat near the flickering fire attacking the remainder of the meat. Sitting in the glow of a kerosene lantern away from the fireplace, near the constable's tent, the three white men continued to discover information about each other, while they too sated their hunger.

Smiley sat at a respectful distance behind Henry eating from a bark plate with his attention divided between Henry's safety and the not-to-be-trusted native called Boxer. Smiley was not the only one displaying distrust within the group. Also sitting well back from the white men, Boxer's gaze alternated between a protective concern for his boss and surreptitious glances at the scarred man who only a short time ago hung off the handcuffs.

Ed turned to Henry. "As much as I'd like to hoe into that whole wallaby, I guess we'd better take it easy eating this rich food after having days of only eating raw fish and witchety grubs."

Hetherington looked up from the food on his tin plate. "I was going to ask what you lived on during the journey across the plains, and where did you learn the skills to survive?"

Ed took up the question. "We discovered a wide range of skills within each other not known before. My years as a youngster on the pearling ships with the Torres Straits' boys taught me many things, I had forgotten I knew. I think Red's … er … Henry's discovery about himself, and the lessons received from Smiley, when they were boys, followed a similar path." He swung his head to face Henry. "Which reminds me, I have to ask Smiley to spend more time teaching you to light a fire." He grinned and explained to their host. "Henry hasn't grasped the concept completely and there were some days we were hard put eating raw flesh."

"That's gratitude for you." Henry laughed. "It's thanks to Ed we knew what direction to make for. I'm sure if I had been on my own, I would have exhausted myself walking in circles."

Late in the night, when the rain hammered down on the heavy canvas of Constable Hetherington's tent, Henry felt glad he had offered one of their sail-canvas sheets to Smiley. He would not have liked to think of him sleeping in the rain. Henry knew he was in no position to invite his friend into the constable's tent. A smile in the darkness creased his lips as he wondered if the trooper named Boxer was still outside keeping his suspicious guard on the ex-prisoner or if he had returned to sleep with the troopers in their tent, further along the waterway they now knew as Archer River.

Henry's exhaustion soon dragged him away from his thoughts of the falling rain and into the depths of sleep. Hetherington's curses woke Henry in the pale glow of early morning. He wandered outside to find the native troopers rushing off into the bush. Only Boxer remained to explain to the constable how the horses, including the packhorses, had all gone walkabout in the rain. The only saving grace was the fact the horses all wore their hobbles, which gave the men a chance of retrieving them without great difficulty. Constable Hetherington left no doubt in anyone's mind, that the thought of a delay in their journey to the police camp at Mein today, left him in a sour mood.

Flour covered Boxer's lower arms as he blended the damper mixture in the cooking pot before placing the dough into the coals for baking. Hoping to keep out of the constable's sight, he then made his way to where a fish trap had been left in a likely spot in the river to catch freshwater crayfish. No one was more surprised than Henry to see Smiley accompany the trooper to check the trap. When the pair returned with a heavy catch, Smiley's grin had returned in full. They chattered at the fireside, while the water in the pot came to the boil in preparation to cook the tasty morsels for breakfast.

"Where is everyone?" Ed emerged from the tent rubbing the sleep from his eyes.

"They all gone fetch horses. Boss, he gone to shoo them up with his whip."

Henry and Ed looked at each other. Did the man mean, to whip the natives searching for the horses or whip the horses when found? They were left with no time to ponder as Boxer let them know a feed awaited them at the campfire, and they should hurry to finish before the constable returned. Henry and Ed returned from their ablutions to find Boxer standing over the constable's tent now dismantled and folded on the ground. Hetherington's jacket, saddle, horse blanket, and saddle bags sat in a tidy heap nearby. Their own meagre belongings lay close by.

"He not happy." Boxer referred to the constable. "Come, Smiley has food ready."

The heat reflected off the sand and the humidity suffocated everything and everyone in camp by the time the troopers arrived. Hetherington, in the lead, rode bareback with his whip twined within the halter.

While the men stuffed damper and crayfish into their pockets to eat on the day's journey, Boxer served Hetherington's breakfast leaving him to eat. Boxer went to help load the packhorses.

Within the hour, the procession made its way north. Henry and Ed doubled up on one horse. Two troopers rode double also. Smiley rode, with his satchel back around his neck and shoulder and minus the handcuffs, the same packhorse he had the previous day, with the captain in control of the lead rein again. High grass in some areas muffled the soft sound of the horses' hooves, but when they moved over the harder rocky tracks, the sound changed to a thunk-clunk, thunk-clunk. A dead silence hung over the group. Not that Constable Hetherington encouraged chatter when the troopers were supposed to be giving their attention to their surroundings, but compared to yesterday, the silence lay thick upon them all.

They had only been an hour on the track when Ed whispered in Henry's ear.

"Devil's blood, Red, I've been on some luggers in a thunderstorm smoother travelling than this horse. You sure all its legs are the same length?"

"When the policeman calls a halt, we'll swap around for a bit. You can ride up front and I'll hang on the rump." Henry, in turn, kept his voice to a whisper.

"We might be in for a long wait. If his face is anything to go by, he'll not be too concerned about the comforts of his fellow travellers. At least he's put your friend Smiley back on the packhorse." Ed stopped talking suddenly and pointed through the thinning trees to their left. "Will you look at the size of the ant hill over there? It must be all of twenty feet high."

Both men rode in silence as they admired nature's feat. It was Henry who next whispered.

"Did you hear what Boxer said as we left?"

"No, I don't think so. What did he say?"

"The troopers riding double-up were responsible for securing the rope used to keep two horses close to the camp at night. I bet they're regretting their knots right about now."

Ed shuffled his sore bum about and stretched and retracted his legs. "Hetherington was saying last night after you began snoring, he and the troopers have to collect a white man from the Mein police reserve. The fellow's to be transferred to Cooktown to face up to a court hearing."

"I don't suppose he'd want to take along a couple of ship-wrecked sailors for company."

"No, I hinted at that, but he'll not be able to do such a thing. The prisoner is a notorious criminal as I understand it. They won't want any distractions."

"Oh, well, to be honest, by the time we get to Mein, I'll be happy to sit in the one place for a bit." Henry looked up at the sky where the thickening clouds challenged the sun. "Looks like we'll get another wetting before we make it to Mein."

"Looking at that lot up there, I can tell you, I'm awful glad to be in country a little higher than those flood plains we just travelled over."

The sky was black with storm clouds when Constable Hetherington called a halt at a waterhole surrounded by fresh young grass. He called loudly down the line, "Only twenty minutes to stretch the legs and let the horses have a nibble. Boxer, a cup of tea with the stale damper will go down well. And don't take too long; that rain will be on us before we know it."

Boxer laced the dry bread with treacle. Henry was pleased to note that even Smiley rated the sweetener. Everyone added cool water to their pannikins knowing the captain would not wait for them to dawdle over hot tea.

No sooner had they remounted, when the rain began to fall. Lightning and thunder sounded in the distant east, but the riders on the Coen to Mein track that day only had to contend with heavy rain. It pummelled both horse and rider before pouring down their sides, exacerbating a slippery surface for the horses to lose their footing. One or two horses tossed their heads as the large drops thudded onto their faces or stung their rumps. The riders were kept alert, as they attempted to protect their own sensitive skin. It was not long before horses and men settled for moving forward with heads hung low, drawing on their inner strength to get through this challenge.

All hearts lifted along with the rain when a double rainbow arced over the tiny town of Mein. Without pausing, Constable Hetherington yelled to the procession.

"Keep to the worn track. Don't let your horses wander off. This place is full of melon holes. Your horse will break a leg if it falls into one of those."

Ed, now in the saddle, and Henry, riding on the horse's rump, looked askance at each other.

"What are melon holes?" But neither had the answer.

Hetherington directed his troopers to proceed to the Mounted Native Police Reserve, while he diverted his horse and the packhorse on his lead, along the track under the overhead telegraph line.

"I'll drop you three off at the Telegraph Office. They have a small general merchandise shop nearby, where you'll probably get fresh clothes, hats and boots." He pointed to a corrugated iron building nearby. "That's the butcher shop."

At their drop-off point near some cabbage tree palms, he shook Ed and Henry's hands before he threw a nod Smiley's way.

"Good luck with the rest of your journey home."

"Before you go, Constable, can you tell me what are the melon holes you talk of?" Curiosity had the better of Ed.

Hetherington smiled. "They're a right nuisance is what they are. They're wide round holes like a dish, about four feet deep, in which the horses often slip and break a fetlock. The limestone under the soil dissolves and the ground collapses." He waved and nudged his horse forward.

"He's in a hurry," Ed observed.

"I guess he wants to get his men sorted and prepare for a quick return to Coen before more of this rain settles in," Henry proposed.

Three bedraggled men, two white and one black, watched the constable make his way back to the police reserve leading two animals.

They walked over to the steps of the Mein Telegraph Office.

The door above opened.

"G'day, can I help 'ee?" The words fell out of a wide toothless grin broken only by two off-colour canine teeth on the top jaw. With chipped dirty fingernails the owner of the grin dragged at his unkempt grey locks.

Ed glanced at Henry one step below him. His eyes danced.

Henry furrowed his brow in a warning glare. He spoke to their host.

"Good evening, Sir. I'm Doctor Henry Baldwin and this …," his own chipped and dirty nails pointed to his friend, "… is Doctor Edward Benton. We were en route to Cooktown from London when we caught a lift with a pearling schooner in the Arafura Sea. The vessel sank during a storm, we were eventually tossed up on the west coast of Cape York. For about two weeks we travelled east until we met up with the troopers led by Constable Hetherington who has guided us here."

"Who's the native with 'ee?"

"His name is Smiley – he lives in Cooktown too – with my family."

"Well, I'm sorry, but no natives are allowed inside the telegraph station building – that's a Guvment law." The man's grin did not alter. "He can sleep over in the changing stables as long as he don't disturb the animals." The grimy hand and fingers raked the hair back from his face again before pointing to a corrugated iron shed near a set of horse yards about one hundred yards from where they all stood. "Me name's Irish and if 'ee wanting a lift to Cooktown, 'ee out of luck. The last wagon went through three days ago on its way south. It won't return till after the monsoons leave." As if on cue, the skies opened in a deluge of rain. "Come in, out of the wet." He invited Henry and Ed inside. "You can tell the native I'll send food over to him later."

Henry and Ed did as they were instructed. Ed unslung the two rolls of canvas from his shoulders and set them on the floor beside the front door. Henry wasted little time doing the same with the canvas satchel holding the water-bag.

PART THREE

LAVINIA DOWNS

LAVINIA DOWNS HOMESTEAD

Max Young	Co-owner with his brother David Young.
Lavinia Young	Dead wife of Max Young.
Gordon Young	Eldest son of Max and Lavinia Young.
Peter Young	Middle child of Max and Lavinia Young.
Victoria Young	Youngest child of Max and Lavinia Young.
David Young	Co-owner with his brother Max Young
Miriam Young	Dead wife of David Young
Summer	Native partner of David Young. Cook at Lavinia Downs' big house.
Velvet	Daughter of David Young and Summer. Helps her mother in the kitchen.
Stockmen	Hans and Bevan

Homestead consists of the following buildings.

The big house:	Two houses with a large dining room acting as a breezeway between.
Sheds:	Stable and Hay storage
	Workshop, Blacksmith forge and cow bails.
	Men's quarters

Twenty-five miles from the homestead is a hut situated above the bay where the current Flagman lives. Below on the water is a small jetty and a flagpole.

CHAPTER NINETEEN

The Telegraph Station

Before the Telegraph Station door shut behind Henry, Ed and Irish, the sound of galloping horses heralded the arrival of two riders on chestnut mounts. They were unrecognizable under the torrents of water running from their drooping hats and long coats. On the heels of the riders rumbled a large wagon pulled by four heavy Clydesdale horses. A dark tarpaulin covered the supplies loaded behind the driver. The man peered through the stream of water running over his sagging hat brim as his adept hands guided the team.

The larger of the two outriders veered over towards the Telegraph Station building.

"Hey, Irish, we'll be here the night – once we get the horses settled in your stable." The man's voice boomed across the flat.

Irish pushed past his new arrivals to call out through the open doorway.

"Awright, Mister Young, just come up when 'ee ready." The answer from Irish struggled to be heard above the drumming of rain on the corrugated iron roof. Irish turned, shut the door and ushered Henry and Ed along the hallway through to the back verandah, where he seated them at the rough-hewn table outside an open doorway leading into the kitchen. "Me wife'll be 'ere shortly. 'Er's just shutting up the merchandise store across the way. Now sit 'ee down and tell me more about 'ee selves."

Light footsteps clattered up the back stairs. A small woman with grey hair dripping water onto her faded black dress, struggled to hold the door against the rising wind as she entered. She hauled a length of canvas from around her body and tossed it on a nail inside the doorway.

"We've got people popping up from everywhere, I see, Irish. I do hope you've put the kettle on the heat and added another log to the stove, eh." With a grunt, she scraped off the muddy boots from her feet. Each landed with a thump on the hessian bag lying on the floor. The woman sighed as her arthritic feet slipped into the soft house shoes waiting by the mat. She bustled closer to her first visitors of the day. "G'day, my name's Doreen. How do you like your tea?"

Henry and Ed rose and touched their forelocks. "Good evening, Missus. I'm Henry and my friend's name is Ed."

The already numerous wrinkles in Doreen's face almost swallowed her eyes, when she concentrated on taking the tea order, before slipping into the kitchen to check all was as it should be. The volume of the voice from the scrawny body now inside the kitchen came as a surprise to Henry and Ed. The gaze of their sparkling wide eyes met. Henry's quick frown warned Ed not to smile. Doreen had no trouble being heard over the noise of the pelting rains crashing down upon the tin roof.

"Was that Max Young I saw arriving a minute ago? He'll be back with his daughter, Victoria, no doubt." Her head poked out through the open doorway to explain to the guests. "He's been to Cooktown to pick her up from the boarding school. He's hoping to make a lady of her in the image of her dead mother."

Irish butted in at this point. "Not much chance of that with 'er determined ways and those scallywag brothers to lead her astray." His raucous laughter echoed along the verandah.

Grey strands of hair still wet with rain clung to the side of her face as Doreen nodded and showed a rueful smile.

"What do you expect, she's her father's girl that one. He dotes on her and being brought up in this wild country, with only men and natives for company, hasn't helped. The nuns in Cooktown will have their work cut out trying to turn her into a lady, I should think."

A kerfuffle was heard at the front door as the next group of visitors entered, stamping their feet on the top step and shaking rain-sodden coats and hats outside, before coming in and closing the door.

"That'll be 'em now." Irish rose and moved through the house to welcome his guests.

He led them onto the back verandah and introduced them to Ed and Henry.

"This 'ere is Max Young," Irish pointed to the tallest of the three before turning to the second tallest of the arrivals. "This 'ere is his son Peter – it is 'ee, Peter, ain't it? 'Ow old 'ee be now, eh, Pete? Must be eighteen, if a day. 'Ees getting as big as 'ee older brother Gordon, I see, and we celebrated 'is twenty-first at the beginning of the year." Irish grinned as he looked up into the face of the father. "Now who is this other young fellow, Max? I didn't know you had a third son?" A wicked chuckle brought smiles to the members of the Young family.

"No, Irish, I've no third son, but sometimes I think I might have. This is my daughter Victoria." Max's piercing blue eyes danced.

A red flush rose in the cheeks of the young woman who stepped forward. Bedraggled blond curls haloed her face. Wet shirt and trousers, similar to those worn by her brother and father, clung to her promising fifteen-year-old body.

"With me around, Dad doesn't need another son. I can do everything my lazy pair of brothers can do." Her blue eyes flashed as she tossed a cheeky grin at Peter.

"Aw, Sis, come on now. That's a bit harsh." Peter Young rolled his laughing blue eyes.

Chairs scraped on the floor when Henry and Ed stood again, this time to greet the family. To his surprise and consternation, Henry's heart thumped erratically inside his chest, when the girl's striking blue gaze pierced into his own green eyes from across the room. In only a matter of seconds, her long-lashed eyelids dropped and Victoria bowed her head. A short-lived frown marred Henry's brows as he pondered this unusual sensation caused by the sight of the tomboy-styled girl on the opposite side of the table. Several women he met during his sojourn in London had set his heart into a wobble, but this young woman before him was hardly more than a child. Mentally he shook himself. *Must be my failing physical condition after all we've been through.* He struggled to return his attention to the conversation going on around him.

Irish turned to the earlier guests.

"This 'ee fellow with the fire-red head is Doctor Henry Baldwin, and 'is friend's Doctor Ed Benton. They've appeared out of nowhere, 'aving been shipwrecked in the Arafura Sea and walked across country to 'ere."

It was Max Young who stepped forward.

"Did you say, Doctor Henry Baldwin?"

"Yes, I'm Henry Baldwin. We were heading back to Cooktown."

Max's frown deepened. "You'd be Miss Abigail's son, would you?"

"Yes, that's correct."

"Have you telegrammed her, you're safe? When I left Cooktown a few days ago, she was checking out all the ships expecting you to arrive by sea. I have to admit she did sound very anxious, last time we spoke."

Henry looked over at Irish. "Will I be able to do that as soon as possible? And Ed will be wanting to let his people know he's safe too."

"No trouble, we'll do it first thing in the morning."

"Thank you, Sir. I have no money with me – everything we carried except our pearling knives was lost at sea." Henry patted the scabbard on the belt at his waist.

Max Young spoke up before Irish had a chance to answer. "You can put the telegrams and accommodation on my account, Irish." He turned towards Henry and Ed, "And anything you need from Doreen's merchandise store over the road." Max Young went on to explain. "Miss Abigail and Doctor George Goldfinch have done me and my family more good turns than I can count."

"Mr. Young, I appreciate your assistance, but of course, we will pay when we can make our way to Cooktown."

"You are more than welcome and may I suggest you and Ed travel with my family tomorrow to stay with us at Lavinia Downs until we can arrange transport back to Cooktown? And was that Doctor George's handyman, Smiley, I spoke to in the stables?"

"Yes, Smiley has had an adventure of his own."

"He is welcome at Lavinia Downs also."

Irish butted in. "Please, please, can 'ee all sit down, I'm feeling overshadowed by all 'ee tall fellows 'ere." Chairs scraped as everyone sat around the table.

Doreen moved over to Victoria and wound a skinny arm around her shoulder.

"Come, Victoria, come and stand in front of the stove. The heat will dry you out." She turned back to the men. "I'll bring you a fresh pot of tea, and the stew will be almost done."

Irish picked up the teapot to hand to his wife. "Doreen, can 'ee do a serving for a native friend of Henry's who's gone off to sleep in the stables."

Her eyebrows raised under her hairline. "Did he get shipwrecked too, Henry?"

"No, Doreen, he left Cooktown to come and get me."

Her eyebrows returned to their place but a deep cleft separated them.

"How did he know … no, no, it doesn't matter …; I've seen some strange things since being up here on the Cape. I'll get you to take him a feed in a minute."

After the sound of Henry's footsteps walking down the back stairs faded, Ed turned to Max Young.

"Max, it sounds like you know Henry's mother quite well. I've yet to meet her and his Uncle George. He often talks of them. I'm due to take up practice at the Cooktown hospital."

"Well, son, if you're half as good as Doctor George you'll be doing alright." Max placed his empty teacup on the table. "He and his sister, Abigail, came to Cooktown …," he paused to consider, "It was a few years before my wife and I with our first born arrived, along with my brother, to take up Lavinia Downs. They must have arrived just under twenty years ago – when the Palmer River goldrush was at its height. The town was desperate for medical care at the time. George set up his surgical practice under his house. There was no hospital in Cooktown then."

"And don't 'ee be forgetting his sister, Miss Abigail. She knows every bit as much about doctoring as her brother. Word has it she studied every book her brother did, but her father wouldn't allow her to go to the university. A crying shame it be – a crying shame. She a good caring woman that 'un."

"Irish is right there," Max took up his tale. "Abigail is a diamond, that's for sure. When my Lavinia became poorly after Victoria was born, Abigail travelled all the way up here on a coastal trader, *The Northern Orchid*. She cared for Lavinia as if she was her own sister. Sadly, when the fever catches you in this country, there's little chance of surviving. Abigail stayed until we buried my wife, and then, until she was satisfied the native woman, who served as our cook, was capable of suckling my daughter, beside her own babe at the time." Max gazed at his fingers as they stroked the china of his empty cup.

Over in the stables, Henry watched Smiley blowing onto each spoonful lifted from the meal on the plate. Saliva drizzled into his mouth as he watched his friend dunk the fresh slice of bread into the stew.

"Those lacerations on your wrist are healing nicely. Are they still painful?"

Even in the gloom of the evening, Henry saw Smiley's eyes gleam. "Them good."

"Thanks, Smiley, for coming to fetch me. Do you want to tell me how you learnt I was in trouble?"

"My father, he tells me." Smiley recognized the curiosity his statement raised in Henry's expression. Henry had always been full of questions about things when they were kids. "In a dream, he tells me to go fetch you."

"Again, I say thank you from me and from Ed too. Ed's the new doctor coming to Cooktown hospital."

"Doctor George, he tells me this."

Henry sat silent for a moment watching Smiley as he satisfied his hunger in the gloom of the evening.

"How is my Uncle George these days?"

"He still all the time busy. He looks after the big hospital much of the time now too. The lady matron there she a big help to Doctor George, but he say she bossy and he hides from her much of the time. He calls her, The Dragon. He show me a picture of a dragon and tell me this." Smiley paused in his chewing on the meat in the thick stew. "Doctor George, his eyes still sad all the time. He carries the spirit of his friend inside him long time now."

"Uncle George and Thomas had been together a long time in life. Thomas rescued Uncle George on more than one occasion, I understand."

Smiley snorted with laughter. "Like you and me, eh, Henry? How many times I save your miserable life." Smiley's smile lit up his face.

Henry laughed along with his childhood friend. "I hope you're counting the times I saved your life too?"

Lamplight reflected off the empty spoon as Smiley waved it back and forth between them both.

"Tell me again when that was, Henry?"

"Where's the gratitude?" Henry's brow furrowed for a moment as he struggled to think of one time at least when he rescued Smiley from life-threatening danger. His face cleared. "How about the day I helped you escape the wrath of your mother when she would have happily fed you to the dingoes after you tossed your sister into the river? Remember? You were teaching her how to swim?"

Both men laughed out loud. "My mother still in shock after hearing someone talk as fast and as long as you did that day. Anyway, my sister needed to learn to swim." Smiley struggled to breathe. "If I remember neither of us hung about the camp too long."

"Are your family still at the camp outside Cooktown, Smiley? Uncle George told me about your father."

"He resting with his ancestors, Henry."

"Sorry to hear that, Smiley." A silence fell as Henry recalled the tall dark man with the aristocratic air and abounding courage, and a smile as wide as his son's. A man he had seen only briefly, as a child. He asked with a wry grin, "Your mother still wielding her big waddy over everyone in the camp?"

The smile once more split Smiley's face in two. "She has competition now with her …," Smiley paused as he searched for the English words he wanted, "… daughters-in-law. I am married and my older brothers."

Henry jumped up and reached over to slap Smiley on the back. "Married? Congratulations. How come I did not hear?"

"You not old enough to understand, I guess." Smiley's face remained deadpan as he reiterated their often-used retort when young boys – Smiley being older than Henry by a few years.

Henry's hand slaps of congratulation turned to light punches of response. Once more the laughter rang out. Eventually, a hush descended on the pair in the shed and the spoon scraped at the near-empty plate, Henry asked the question he so desperately wanted to hear the answer to.

"Have you seen my mother lately – how's she been?"

"Miss Abigail, she work too hard every day beside Doctor George. She every day misses you much – she tell me this."

Henry's arm reached out to press Smiley's shoulder. "We'll go home together, my friend. Nothing will stop us now."

Smiley used his last piece of bread to clean the plate before handing it back to Henry. "You tell the nice lady she cooks good food."

"You sure you'll be okay sleeping here in the stable?"

"Better than out in the rain. Better than in handcuffs. Yes thanks, Henry, I will sleep good here."

"I'm off to the telegraph house. I'm starved. You're lucky I didn't eat half your meal before I got here." Henry touched Smiley's shoulder as he stood up.

"Sleep tight, Smiley. See you in the morning."

"Good night, Henry."

On his way back to the house, the strange design of the building claimed his attention. He had not noticed it on their arrival, with the rain catching them out. Now, with the moon struggling to shine through breaking clouds, he thought there were turrets built on each corner of the building. He looked forward to examining them in the light of the morning.

The rattle of the back door announced the return of Henry.

Doreen greeted him with a large plate of stew and fresh bread. Henry swapped it for the empty plate in his hand.

"Henry, sit down now and eat up. I've been hearing how you and Ed's diet over the past couple of weeks left much to be desired."

"Doreen, this looks better than anything we ate in the finest restaurants in London."

"I thought doctors were usually broke and struggling to survive." Max wiped at a drop of gravy on his bottom lip with the empty spoon.

"Believe me, it was always my uncles or aunts who were footing the bills, not me."

"What do they think of you returning to the antipodes and the land of convict settlements?" Max laughed.

"Not too happy, I have to admit. But they have lots of other children and now grandchildren to comfort them." Reluctantly he slowed his eating. "Does Australia have any convict settlements left?"

Convicts and convict settlements of Australia filled the conversation until Henry remembered the house design he'd noticed earlier.

"'Ee right, son, they be turrets 'ee seen – one on each corner. The guvment built all the telegraph stations the same – in case of marauding natives. Don't think there ever been an attack, mind 'ee. They sometimes steal the wires and the insulators from the poles and even the poles sometimes."

"Do they know how the telegraph works?" Ed's eyebrows rose. "What would they do with them otherwise."

"They make spear points with the flakes from the insulators and multi-pointed fishing spears with the wires by sharpening the ends."

Henry struggled to retain a yawn. "Sorry, sorry, if you can point me to where I can sleep, I'd be grateful."

Irish pushed back his chair. "Of course, what we be thinking." He lifted his voice to be heard above the clatter of dishes in the kitchen, where Doreen and Victoria were tidying up. "Doreen where 'ee be wanting Henry and Ed to camp tonight?"

She appeared in the doorway wiping her hands on a cloth.

"Well, young Victoria will use our spare bedroom as usual, and her father and Peter will sleep outside her door on the verandah where the staff sleep. Can you grab a couple of blankets and take Henry and Ed downstairs to camp on the stretchers between the tanks?"

Holding the hurricane lamp, Irish led Henry and Ed down a narrow winding staircase within the south turret corner. Henry's gaze caught sight of two rainwater tanks protected within the bottom section of the house.

"Why are the rainwater tanks inside here?"

"That be another guvment decision. The marauding natives can't shoot holes in the tanks nor can they shoot poisoned arrows into the water."

"Is that a likely scenario?"

"Never heard of it meself."

Henry accepted a blanket and threw himself onto the nearest stretcher. He shut his eyes, but after a few seconds, they sprang open. The stretcher creaked as he rolled onto his left side. It creaked louder when he rolled over onto his right side. A groan rose from Ed who also tossed and turned in the neighbouring stretcher.

"You alright there, Ed?" Henry mumbled.

A grunt came back in answer. The shuffle of Ed's bare feet whispered in the darkness as he threw himself upright, pushed the stretcher aside, folded the blanket double and lay upon the ant bed floor.

"Red, those stretchers must have been built for men with deformed spines."

Henry chuckled. "Maybe that's why they have deformed spines in the first place. We've got used to sleeping on bare earth. I think you have the right idea." He arose and prepared a bed on the floor himself.

In a short time, the snores of both men followed Irish's footsteps up the staircase. Neither man stirred during a second downpour of rain in the middle of the night.

The squawking of the guinea fowl roosting in the trees beside the butcher's shop brought the two men to their feet. They lifted the solid bar and opened the door leading to the outside of the building. The sun rose in a cloudless sky, but the heat and humidity promised rain later in the day.

Doreen's voice modified with respect for her guests called from the top of the staircase.

"If you men want some clothes you can come over to the store now – just up from the butcher shop. If you want, I'll trim a bit of that hair off while the porridge is cooking.'

"Thank you, Doreen, we will. Would you have a razor and strop over there? These whiskers are driving me mad," Ed called back.

"Everything and anything."

Within the hour, Henry and Ed joined the household at the breakfast table each dressed in a set of clean stockman's clothes with the skin of their faces red after a cold shave – their excess hair now trimmed somewhat, if not stylish. Both men wore brown neckerchiefs over their collars. Henry carried in his hand an old dark, wide-brimmed felt hat. The brim on one side appeared to have been chewed on, by a local dog.

Irish handed Henry a piece of paper and a pencil.

"'Ee be writing a message to 'ee mother on that and I'll get it sent right after we eat."

Another piece of paper and a pencil were issued to Ed with similar instructions.

Irish then rose and went off to discuss the day's duties with the telegraph linesmen living within the station also.

When Henry finished the task at hand, his eyes lifted to discover Victoria's unconcealed gaze boring into him. His red face became redder. Yesterday's heart wobble rolled in his chest. He shook himself – *This is ridiculous*. But he did dare another glance in her direction and felt satisfied to see her squirm. He rose and went to see if Smiley had been given breakfast.

Smiley's head and hands were absorbed in the sketchbook on his lap as he sat cross-legged in the morning shadows sketching the small township. Henry tossed a new set of stockman's clothes on the rail beside him.

"There's a set of new clothes for you. Can't have you with the arse out of your trousers and the ladies about. Did they give you a feed, Smiley?"

Smiley's grin shone as bright as ever. "Yes, the young lady, Miss Victoria and her brother Peter delivered a fine meal of porridge, steak and toast along with a pannikin of tea, thanks."

"Victoria?"

"Yes, Miss Victoria and I met in Cooktown. Her and Miss Abigail are good friends."

"Oh."

A voice bellowed across the yard.

"Come on, you lot. If we're hoping to get home before the floods set in, we'd better make tracks soon." Max Young called up his young and his additional three guests as he strode across the yard."

Victoria ducked her head as she and the chestnut horse exploded out through the opened double doors of the stables. She egged her brother on. Peter exited with the wagon and horses in a more sedate manner, before pulling up in front of Henry, Ed and Smiley.

"All aboard."

Henry and Ed stowed their canvas rolls and satchel which now carried a spare set of clothes each, with the razor and strop to be shared. They swung up onto the buckboard, one on each side of Peter. Smiley, in his new clothes and with shining eyes and white teeth glistening, found a niche within the load in the wagon for himself and his sketching satchel.

Irish and Doreen waved until the cavalcade disappeared over the horizon with Max Young and his daughter leading the way.

CHAPTER TWENTY

Cooktown

"Gina, I think we deserve a cup of tea and a piece of Mrs. Buetel's rainbow cake, don't you?" Abigail swapped the overflowing cane basket from her left arm to her right, rubbing the aching muscles of her forearm as she did so. "Who would have thought choosing materials for bandage-making could be so time-consuming?" She removed the lace-edged handkerchief from inside the sleeve at her wrist and patted her face where the perspiration glistened.

Gina Dougall, with a basket of her own overflowing with packages, looked up at her mentor and grinned.

"I don't think anyone within a hundred miles can talk as much as our haberdasherer."

Abigail chuckled. "It has been a while since I went to school, but I'm not too sure if haberdasherer is a word. I think it might be a haberdasher."

"You know who I mean, though."

"Oh, yes, my ears are bruised with the listening. I doubt she missed making a comment on anyone who lives or who has ever lived within our district. Nobody has escaped an airing."

The younger and older woman stepped under the lintel of the doorway into the tearoom and stood in the cool shade for a moment while adjusting their eyes to the light changes.

The pair seated themselves at an empty table and gave their order, when the local sergeant of police, Charles Beaumont, and a young police constable entered the shop. The tall, dark-haired Charles's eyes lit up at the sight of Abigail Baldwin. While enjoying the dip in the sergeant's admiration, Abigail did not fail to notice the shy, but admiring glances, which were thrown by the constable in Gina's direction.

"Charles, good morning, up and about early, I see."

"Miss Abigail, you are no laggard yourself, it seems." The sergeant's eyes opened wider and he smiled at the sight of the two overloaded baskets on the floor beside the ladies' feet. "I'm taking our new constable on a tour of the town." He turned to the equally tall uniformed man at his side. "Constable Nelson, I'd like you to meet Miss Abigail Baldwin, sister and right hand to her brother, our Doctor Goldfinch."

"Please to meet you, ma'am." The constable removed his cap revealing snowy blond hair. He bowed his head, but his eyes devoured young Gina at Abigail's side.

"Constable Nelson, lovely to meet you, welcome to Cooktown." Abigail thought she had best put the constable out of his agony. "Constable Nelson, may I introduce Miss Gina Dougall, our nurse at the practice." Her red hair, caught in a knot resting on the base of her neck, wobbled beneath the wide-brimmed soft straw hat as she turned to her companion.

The constable's bow was lower than that he had bent to Miss Abigail, but not low enough to drag his gaze from the blushing Gina whose trembling fingers lifted to tidy the errant dark curls from her face.

Sergeant Beaumont's eyebrows lifted, when he glanced at the exchange before he spoke again to Abigail. Their gaze met. Green eyes and dark eyes sparkled with knowing amusement.

"I was heading towards the surgery. I have news for you, but I think it will need more private surroundings than here. May we call on you at the surgery later – after we talk to the editor next door?" He moved aside as the shop girl, almost hidden by a large tray, began to unload two small teapots, milk, sugar bowls, cups, saucers, and spoons, along with two plates each holding a large serving of the legendry rainbow cake layered with thick cream.

"Yes, Charles, of course. We'll return home as soon as we have finished our morning tea."

Heat and humidity had lifted along with the sun by the time Charles arrived at the surgery to be greeted by Doctor George Goldfinch.

"Charles, come on through. Abigail has only this minute left to prepare cool drinks for us out the back, in the shade."

They found Abigail sitting in the protection of a large tree, behind a small table holding three bottles of cordial and three tumblers.

"Oh, Charles, I've been all a dither wondering what this news is that cannot be spoken of in public. Have you bad news about our family? Is Henry safe? Don't tell me something has happened to him. We're expecting Henry and his friend home any day now."

George leant across and patted his sister's hand. "Perhaps if you gave Charles a moment to sit down, we might learn what he has to say."

"You're right, George. I'm sorry, Charles. I don't normally get into a dither like this, but we had a strange incident with Henry's childhood friend, Smiley. Something happened, which we couldn't explain." Abigail drew in a deep breath. "No, of course, you don't want to hear all this, please tell us your news."

George nudged the third bottle of cordial across to Charles who emptied it into the tumbler and drank deeply.

"A report from the Native Mounted Police up Coen way came through late yesterday. They had been on a mission to take delivery of a prisoner from the Mein district for transfer to Coen en route to the Cooktown Police Station. They met two men at the Archer River who appeared out of the scrub. One had long wild red hair and the other's brown hair hung just as unruly. They claimed to have been on a pearling ship, *The Pink Pearl*, shipwrecked in the Arafura Sea. Having drifted on debris to the west coast of the Cape, they travelled east on foot, planning to eventually meet up with the telegraph line. These two claimed to be Henry Baldwin and Edward Benton ….."

Abigail's face paled. She gasped. George reached over the table and held her hand tightly. Her words felt wedged inside her throat.

"Yes, that sounds like Henry, his friend is named Edward Benton."

"Henry has certainly got ginger-red hair and if it hasn't been cut for a while he might very well look like a wild man." George nodded.

"The Inspector has sent messages off to Port Kennedy to seek confirmation of a ship going down in the area within the past few weeks."

Abigail sat quietly trying to digest this news. She refused to consider the horrors her son may have experienced – to know he was alive was the most important thing to focus on. An idle thought entered her mind. *What of Smiley? Did he know Henry was in trouble? Is that why he went off in the middle of the night last month? Where is Smiley now?*

It was George who recovered first.

"Charles, I have never met Edward Benton, but I understand his father has a fleet of pearling luggers up that way. He will need to be informed also."

"Yes, that is in hand at the moment. The Troopers left Henry and Edward at the Mein Telegraph Station along with a native fellow called Smiley. No doubt you can expect a wire through in the near future – that's if the lines aren't down again."

"Please, God," whispered Abigail.

"How long will it take for them to get back to Cooktown do you think?" George posed the question.

"That could be another problem for the men. The wet season is threatening at the moment, and the creeks and rivers are beginning to rise. You know what that country is like in the wet, nothing and no one moves anywhere until the dry season returns."

"At least they've reached civilization so they'll just have to sit and wait it out at Mein. Did the report say if the men were wounded or anything?" George turned to Abigail. "Max Young lives up that way, they might meet up with him."

Abigail's eyes brightened and then her face fell. "Max will be well home by now. He planned on making a rush trip back to beat the rising rivers they'd need to cross on their own property."

CHAPTER TWENTY-ONE

Overland Again

Before they had gone five miles, Henry and Ed's heads swayed with the wagon, as their bodies slumped with exhaustion.

The thudding of the hooves of Victoria's horse altered to a long slide in the mud, when she reined in beside the Clydesdales.

"Are those two alright, Pete?"

"Yeah, Sis, they're both out to it. I've been left to talk to myself."

Victoria grinned. "That'll make a change – you talking. It's like pulling teeth to get a word out of you."

Victoria tightened the rein a little more to let the wagon pass her by. She veered in near the back wheel and spoke to Smiley.

"Are you alright there, Smiley?"

Her consideration earned her a reward of white teeth in a wide smile.

"Yes, Missy, I'm good."

A flick of her wrist accompanied by a nudge in the flank of the chestnut horse with her boot, and Victoria galloped ahead to where her father encouraged his animal to keep up a smart walk.

"You getting bored already, Victoria?"

"No, Dad, just checking up on our passengers. I don't suppose there's any mustering left to be done on Lavinia Downs when I get home?"

"I should hope your brother has all the cattle up on the high ground by now."

"Do I have to go back to school next year? I can look after the house and help Summer and Velvet with the cooking, and maybe help you and the boys with the cattle."

A tolerant smile filled Max Young's face. Already his daughter was starting with the reasons why she should leave school and help on the property. The smile faded as memories of her mother's last days returned to haunt him. If he reached out his hand, he felt sure he would touch Lavinia's hand as he did on that last morning.

"Promise me, Max, you'll not let our baby girl run wild out here in the bush. You'll send her to a school where she'll learn to be a lady. Promise me that, Max."

Tears threatened to fall once again, as they had fifteen years ago. He recalled his last words to her. "Yes, my dearest, Lavinia. I promise to bring our Victoria up to be a lady. But you'll be better by tomorrow. You will choose a good school for her when the time comes."

Perspiration flew from his face as he shook his head. Lavinia had not been better the next day. She was buried the next day. With near forty-degree temperatures and extreme humidity, bodies were interred as soon as possible after death.

It had been Abigail Baldwin who kept the family going for weeks after that day. And now she has offered to board Victoria in Brisbane. Max's thoughts splintered at the call from his daughter.

"Dad, are you going deaf? I called you twice. Sounds like you're getting old. Perhaps I'll need to stay home from school and look after you and Uncle David."

Max struggled to smile. *Got to hand it to Victoria, she never gives in too easily.*

"We're almost at Ironwood Crossing. Do you think the water will be over?"

"I'd be surprised if it wasn't, but at this early stage in the wet season, I don't think it will pose too much of a threat."

"Do you want to stop on the other side to boil the billy and have a bite to eat?"

Max paused deep in thought before he answered. "Not this time, Victoria, we'll push on to the Homestead Crossing. I'll not be happy until we're over that river." He watched as Victoria and her horse pranced along in front of him. He smiled again as he observed the excitement of their reunion thrilling both horse and rider. "Do you know, where on the load the sandwiches Doreen made for us, have been packed?"

"Yes, of course."

"Well, dig them out and offer them around to eat as we go."

Clouds heralded an early evening when the riders and Clydesdales drew to a stop at the Homestead Crossing on the Batavia River headwaters. The Young family jumped to the ground and walked over to inspect the swirling brown flow.

"It's not too bad," Peter offered encouragement.

"Maybe, son, but it's almost dark and I don't fancy finding out, when we're halfway across, that we've unanticipated problems to deal with. At the moment, the water is at a level when one is never quite sure whether to haul the wagon across or strip it down and float it. I'm thinking it may be a mite too deep to take the wagon across, as it is."

"Do you want me to ride across and see just how deep it is, Dad?" Victoria's eyes glistened with anticipation.

"No, young lady, I don't. Any risk-taking will be done in daylight. We'll set up a bit of a camp here." His gaze ran across the sky. "With any luck, the rain will hold off and the waters may have receded by morning. We've got the spare tarps; we'll sleep under the wagon. I hope there are a few sandwiches left. I don't like our chances of boiling a billy though. Everything's pretty damp."

A light breeze overnight cleared the clouds of the previous evening. The cloak of darkness still hung over the camp, when Henry's eyelids sprang open as a piercing whistle filled the air. His eyes closed again just as quickly, but the sound of the whistle echoed within his skull for a long while. From the other end of the line of bodies, he heard Max clear his throat and mumble to his son lying next to him.

"Is that our little lady, Pete?"

After a soft laugh, his son answered, "I see the nuns haven't dampened her whistle then."

Henry felt a tired smile tweak his lips. Silence returned for a short moment before the tinkle of the horse bells in the distance lifted Henry's eyelids again. He realized someone other than Victoria was up, when scuffling noises at last night's fireplace, courtesy of Smiley, warded off further sleep. He rolled onto his back and glanced over to where Ed lay snoring softly on his right. He then turned to his left, to the sleeping site of the absent Smiley who now tended his fire. A faint aroma of cooking meat drifted over the campsite. Hunger put an end to any chance of further rest. He sat up and spoke softly.

"Smiley, it's the middle of the night. Don't you ever sleep?"

"Henry, it's soon morning. You lazy fella. Time to go to work."

"What's that I smell?"

"Chicken."

"How did you get a chicken out here?"

"An old tough turkey, then."

"Geez, I hope you gutted the thing. I hate it when you cook them with their guts still inside."

"Oh yes, Master, I take out the guts just for you." A deep chuckle came from near the fireplace.

Henry thought for a minute, anticipating the taste of roast turkey. He lifted his head.

"What did you use to remove the guts? I'm sure your pocket knife wouldn't do the job. You had nothing else with you. I'll know by the taste if you're trying to fool me."

Sparks flew into the air as Smiley lifted the bird by its legs and rolled it over in the coals.

"I borrow your knife."

Henry's hand snapped down to the vacant knife scabbard at his belt. The flap hung loose.

"How the hell did you do that without waking me?"

This time a prolonged chuckle drifted over from near the fire.

"Henry, how many times I tell you to sleep with one eye open? I could steal all the toes from your feet and you not wake up." Smiley reached down and clasped the handle of the knife almost buried to its hilt in the sandy loam. He lifted it and wiped the blade on the leg of his trousers before spinning the knife in his hand. With the blade now between his thumb and forefinger, he held it out towards Henry. "There you go, one knife returned. Turkey guts now feeding the ants."

"Thanks, Smiley." Henry dragged himself upright just as Victoria and the horses returned to camp.

"I could smell breakfast from a mile away. Who's the cook? Not you, I bet, Pete," she called as she slid down from the bare back of her horse.

A hint of morning lifted the gloom as Max sat cross-legged admiring the style of his daughter. Beautiful as her mother yet with the survival skills her mother never had.

A grunt rose from the last sleeping body. "I really must complain to the management. This establishment is not conducive to a peaceful night's rest."

Laughter rang out around the camp in time to accompany that of the kookaburras in the tall gum trees by the river.

They ate the dissected fowl from plates of bark and shared the three cups to drink their black tea, as they had done the night before.

While Smiley cleared away the detritus of their meal, Henry and Ed helped Peter harness the Clydesdale horses into the shafts of the wagon. After saddling their horses, Max rode off to assess the river crossing with Victoria, on her mount by his side, offering a dozen or more reasons why she should come with him to check the crossing.

When Max noticed the water level had fallen somewhat during the night, he agreed to her wishes. Sunrise glinted in the water as it splashed up from the legs of both horses. At the deepest point, the water did not touch the horses' bellies.

Wagon timbers groaned and the leathers creaked as the Clydesdales, under Pete's guidance, pulled the wagon to a stop on the west side of the river crossing.

Leading his horse, Max walked over to speak to his son.

"Right, Pete, I'll take the wagon across." Max passed his reins across to Victoria sitting waiting on her restless horse; a horse almost as impatient as herself. He turned back to Pete. "You keep close to the near-side wheels. Add your muscle if one or the other gets jammed up." Max looked over at Ed. "Do you mind helping at the off-side wheels, Ed?"

"No, Max not at all. What exactly do you want me to do?"

"If a wheel drops into a hole or baulks at a rock, grab the wheel rim and a wheel spoke as they come around and lever them up to help the wheel forward. Whatever you do, be careful the current doesn't suck you under the wagon."

Max focused his attention on Henry. "Can you and Smiley lend your shoulders to the rear of the wagon?"

"No trouble, Max."

"Right, I'll take it slow. If I feel the wagon slipping in the current, I'll give you a yell, Pete. You get the hell out of there, quick smart before it slides over you. The rest of you back off quick, too." Max took one last look at his preparations. Strong hands gathered the reins, which he danced lightly along the backs of the Clydesdale horses.

"Walk up, there." His voice echoed above the noise of the rushing waters. His glance shifted towards his daughter with her sparkling blue eyes and hair straggling out from under her battered felt hat – as steady as a rock on her prancing horse with the lead rein of his own horse in her hand. Admiration shone in his eyes. Max nodded his head. "Lead on, Victoria." Under his breath, he whispered to the ghost of his long-dead wife, "Lavinia, ride with our girl, will you? Keep her safe."

The offside, rear Clydesdale, a recent addition to the wagon team, threw up its head and pawed at the brown water. Max's long whip flicked lightly over the animal's ears.

"Lead on, Blaze," he yelled to the lead horse of the team. "Haul him up."

The wheels rumbled on the stony track as the wagon entered the water. Pete and Ed, on either side, assisted by grabbing the spokes of a wheel, putting their weight behind their pull and push to help roll it forward. At the rear, Smiley looked sideways at his friend and grinned.

"Let's see those muscles, Henry. Too much idling around London town, I think." He ducked his head and leant into the rear panel of the wagon also.

Henry lifted his head and returned the grin.

Water splashed up around the horses' legs. In minutes, everyone was drenched. When they reached the deeper water, Max felt a slight shudder through the seat of his pants as the current caught the wagon wheels. When they approached the halfway mark, he felt the jar when the off-side front wheel dropped into a hollow.

He heard Ed yell, "This wheel's stuck, Max."

Max turned his head to see the grimace on the reddened face of his helper at the off-side wheel. The young doctor's muscles bulged as he strived to help roll the wheel up and out of the hole.

Max cracked the whip above the heads of the four horses. He swung around to the rear.

"Henry, give Ed a hand?"

Henry felt the drag of the current at his legs, as it threatened to pull him down. Holding onto the edge of the wagon, he splashed around to add his muscle power to Ed's endeavours.

On the front seat, Max gritted his teeth, prayed and urged the horses onto greater efforts with the sting of his whip. The shudder in the timber of the front seat increased as the rushing river waters rose in a bow wave against the paused wagon. The crack of the whip echoed around the horses' ears. The lead horse lifted its head and snorted harshly. The muscles of the brown shoulders and thighs rippled as his powerful legs forged forward dragging the equine team and wagon along with him.

The wagon lifted up out of the hole in a rush. The shudders of the water pressure on the timbers stuttered. Max glanced back to check Ed was safe when his body froze. His gaze fell upon the sight of a floating debris island heading directly towards the wagon in an unrelenting current. A flash of memory filled his mind. A day of horror many years ago, which occasionally still filled his dreams. A day at this very same river, in a higher flood than now. A day when a large tree trunk rushed towards the wagon of the time. The broken tree roots had caught the back of the wagon behind the wheel. It spun the other end of the log around to smash into the backboard of the vehicle killing two good stockmen. The men disappeared into the water. One man was never seen again. The other decomposed body they discovered many months later, jammed in a crevice in the river bank many miles downstream, with evidence of feasting crocodiles and dingoes found in the rotting flesh. Only by the grace of God had he been able to grab his five-year-old son Gordon, and jump into the upstream waters hauling them both away from the splintered timbers of the broken wagon, the twisting traces, and the flailing feet of the four horses screaming out their fear as they drowned.

Max's shudder joined that of the timber seat. *Was the horror of that day about to repeat itself?* He screamed a warning to Pete, Ed, Henry and Smiley. His arm ached as the whip cracked like repeated gunfire.

CHAPTER TWENTY-TWO

Lavinia Downs

David Young dragged the soiled rag from beneath his pillow. He wiped the perspiration from his haggard face. The cloth gathered up the trickles of blood leaking from his nose. Blood stains, dried and darkened, marked the pillow. The mattress beneath him held no linen cover either. This did not bother him as much as the sharp ends of the fibre-stuffing inside the uncovered mattress ticking.

"Summer!" He attempted to call the cook, but even to his own ears, it came out little more than a squeak. *Where is that damn woman? Never here when I need her.* In fact, when he thought about it, he had not seen her all day. It may even have been longer.

His stomach churned inside him. The feeling, which had been with him since he awoke at dawn, resurfaced to kick and squabble inside his belly. He felt sure he and Summer had a blazing row in the night, or perhaps that might have been this morning. Screamed words echoed in his head even now.

"I know you've been poisoning me, you cow. Well, I won't die, and you'll go to prison and be hanged by the neck."

David found it hard to believe he raised the strength to get up and confront Summer, let alone scream abuse at her. But his throat felt red raw and his body felt as weak as a newborn lamb. His eyes closed, while the sun edged past the meridian.

When they opened again, he struggled to focus his mind on his earlier thoughts, but along with his failing body, his mind felt weak and useless. The thrum of a brief rain shower falling on the tin roof above his head tempted him back into sleep, but determination whipped the reluctant beast – his body.

A groan escaped his tightened lips as he rolled onto his side and edged his long legs over and onto the floor. Wearing only a dark singlet and his loose cotton pants, what had once been well-muscled arms and legs developed by hard gut-wrenching work, now sagged with empty pale wrinkled flesh wobbling with the movement of his limbs.

The effort shook remnants of memory to the surface of his brain – *the rat bait*. That's what he had been thinking about earlier. An article he had read in an old newspaper – was that last week, last month or the year past – it was all too hard to pinpoint – a report on an investigation by the Brisbane Police. Using the walking stick kept by the bed, he stirred the pile of papers askew on the chair. With a thud, papers splattered onto the floor. Even a curse posed too much effort. How much did he really want to look at the papers? What had seemed so urgent moments ago? Was that moments ago or hours?

Focus David, concentrate, this is important. He berated himself.

Pain ripped at his insides producing another deep groan. *Rat bait and the signs and symptoms. The court case of the wife poisoning her husband. It's here in one of these papers. Does it matter now?*

His head hung low from the prop of his arms and his upright shoulders. One inch at a time, he slithered over and onto the chair. Breathing slow deep breaths, he struggled to override the pain before he reached down to recover the first paper at hand. It sat on his lap while one arm searched under the pillow for his magnifying glass.

It seemed a monumental task to spread the paper out on the mattress. In bursts of concentration, he traced the articles in the old news between bouts of resting his head down on the printed word. Weakness tempted him to give it up, but the thought of Summer, his cook and concubine, poisoning him, drove him on. He may be past any chance of living, but he needed to know. He needed to leave a note for his brother Max, to ensure the woman would pay for doing this to him, and for thinking she was going to get away with her dastardly deed.

The gods were with him. The article was on the first page of the second paper. He knew there was little chance he might last the distance if it was to be found in the last paper lying on the floor.

The list of symptoms of arsenic poisoning was long. As he read, David realized he could tick nearly all of these symptoms, having experienced each at one time or another in the past months. He rested his head on the printed word, fighting off the desire to sleep. His next challenge awaited him. Trembling fingers searched through the report for the ways and means the accused had poisoned her man. According to the article, this tasteless white powder was easily disguised and presented no problem for anyone cooking food containing flour. *No wonder Summer made his favourite chilli bread every day.*

If he needed any reminder he was going to die, the hot knife of pain through his belly and the frequent blood-producing cough, convinced him. When the attack eased, his head fell onto the report on the bed. Blood dribbled onto the paper. A bony finger poked into the wet blood and after several attempts, he painted a circle in blood around the list of Signs and Symptoms.

David had no idea of the amount of time passed since reading the report, but he felt tears on his cheeks when he lifted his head. His body's weakness and his determination fought a valiant battle and the latter won – for the moment. David pushed himself upright taking up his walking cane at the same time. He shuffled over to his writing-table under the window. Shaking hands fumbled underneath the desktop to feel for the slot where the key to the top drawer lived. He flopped onto the chair in front of where he worked and tried again. He felt the slot, but it was empty. His gaze fell to the floor. *Had the key fallen out? It never had before.*

His body still retained some reserve of anger, as demonstrated, when he shook the drawer expecting it to be locked. The drawer slid open with ease. On top of some papers lay the drawer key. *Am I going mad? No, nothing, not even senility, would induce me to leave this drawer unlocked.* He slipped his fingers to the back of the drawer where the key to the poison cupboard usually lay in a flat tin. A strong whispered curse prompted a drawn-out whistle of air sucked back into his lungs. His hand scratched around the pencils, papers and a ruler which usually resided there. An instant flash of recognition registered. His fingers lifted out the key ring holding not only the poison cupboard key, but the silver charm his wife Miriam had always worn around her neck. He slumped against the backrest of the chair and rode the wave of torture tearing at his gut, but his hand held fast to the two keys now pressed against his chest.

While his trembling hand slipped the keys into the one pocket in his pants, his mind struggled with the calculation of the distance between his bedroom and the work shed where the poison cupboard hung, bolted to the wall. At least fifty yards here and back. To his mind, it may have been fifty miles the way he felt right now. But then, he believed he was as good as he was ever going to be with the poison eating at his insides. *Perhaps I should leave a note for Gordon and Max.* The thought had barely materialized before he knew he should see the evidence with his own eyes, first.

Leaning heavily on the walking stick, he stood. His feet scuffed across the floorboards. At the doorway, he slipped into the now-hardened leather boots, fur-lined with fungus. He reached up and took the battered felt hat from the nail on the wall and jammed it tight on his head.

At the top of the steps looking out over the backyard, David lifted his hand to ward off the glare of the sunshine. A wave of vertigo washed over him. He gripped the walking cane. With the fingers of his other hand wrapped around the slats supporting the steps' railing, he lowered his body to sit on the top step. Perspiration ran from his face and upper body. The tremble began deep inside his belly like the rumble of a train in the distance. His head rested against the timber slats until it passed. He breathed deep and slow. This had to be done and he was the only one to do it. With the few teeth left in his head gritted together, and using the stick and the slats, he lifted himself upright once more. One step at a time he descended. Blood trickled down his legs and into his boots, but David neither felt it nor cared.

The achievement of having reached the ground afforded him a small satisfaction. The shed appeared a long way away. He almost fell over the long washing stick used by Summer to stir the clothes when boiling them in the copper. Now he had a stick for each hand to lean on. Half a dozen trees along his route provided six places for him to pause and lean against for a few moments, but he dared not sit down knowing there was every chance he might not rise again. Despite intermittent dark clouds cruising the sky above, his sallow skin burnt cruelly in the fierce sun.

David Young stumbled through the partially opened doorway and into the shed. He paused. Some time elapsed while his eyes grew accustomed to the gloom. In front of him stood a long table littered with leatherworking tools, where during the slack season, the stockmen counter-lined their saddles, or repaired and created leatherwork including bridles, harnesses, hobbles, belts and other accessories. Three saddles hung over their individual racks waiting, like patients at a hospital emergency department, for attention from the doctor. He moved further into the shed and leant on the bench against the wall. His target, the poison cupboard, rested upon the same bench in the corner. With his goal in sight, he felt consciousness slipping away. His hands reached out seeking something to grip onto. A tin of bolts rolled over, the contents rattled across the bench and some fell to the ground raising miniature dust explosions in the dirt. Frail fingers wrapped around a wall post and held tight. His weight fell to his forearms and elbows across the bench. Stertorous breathing haloed a blood spray from his nose.

"No, I've got to do this." The message fired from his brain as a yell, but rated no more than a whisper from his mouth.

It was enough to drag him upright and shuffle his feet onwards to stand in front of the poison cupboard. Even in his depleted state of awareness, he noticed the absence of the large tin of hoof nails which he had always left in the same position; where the two doors of the cupboard met when closed. It always sat centred between the two middle letters in the name 'HOOF' in the sign on the tin of HOOF NAILS. The bench surface, usually thick with dust, now disturbed to such an extent by human intervention, to be almost clean. The lock had been relocked, but it hung upside down.

He felt his legs slipping from under him and leant his body weight against the shelves of the bench. Shaky fingers removed the key from his pocket. It clattered against the lock several times before he succeeded in slipping it into the slot and turning the mechanism. Once the door hung open, it only took one glance to see things were not as they should be. The bottle of arsenic powder used in making the rat baits stood at the front of the top shelf of the cupboard. He always kept it hidden behind the other tins and bottles.

Habit alone guided his hands to shut and lock the cupboard. He sank to the ground. Pain, misery and despondency pulled him down. It was true then. She had poisoned him. The cloak of darkness eased over David, but he refused to accept it just yet. Using his last remaining strength, he dragged his body through the dirt towards the door of the shed. His mind kept asking the question – *Why, what had he done to deserve this?*

He failed to understand what he had done to earn Summer's hatred to such a degree. *Had he not, with his own hands, helped to build her a room attached to the house for her daughter Velvet and herself?* A short-lived vision filled his mind of their roustabout Hans, an ex-sailor, who had danced across the roofing frame like a sprite without any fear of heights. A skill gained when hauling canvas sails, he had presumed. Previous cooks and the house staff on Lavinia Downs always lived down at the native camp near the river. *It was at her instigation they had ever begun co-habiting, after all.* A reluctant fleeting confession reminded him of how Summer relieved the loneliness after Miriam had died of fever out here in the wilderness.

And then like a flash in his head he recalled the look in Summer's eyes when she asked why he did not marry her. She wanted to wear a white dress and have a shiny ring just like Miriam had worn. His amusement echoed through the house at the time. The dark stare of steel had chilled his laughter. Now he felt the chill inside his body once again.

David's thoughts turned to his brother. He must leave him a note. His hand tried to smooth the dust to write two words, but his strength failed him. All he managed to write with one dirty finger was:

RS

POI

Thinking he had completed his task; he closed his eyes. He felt his wife Miriam wrap her familiar arms around his body and hold him tight. Death slipped in without further protest.

CHAPTER TWENTY-THREE

Bad Spirits at Lavinia Downs

Max felt as if his head, like his attention, was divided into two. The gaze of one eye focused on the horses and his effort to keep them moving. The gaze of the other eye followed the approaching island of floating debris. It seemed to barrel towards them. His son, Peter, and the other three men dragging themselves through the water on the upstream side to safety edged ahead of the wagon.

His brain clicked out the distances in his mind's eye: fifty feet away, forty feet away, thirty feet away, twenty feet away. It seemed inevitable the debris and the wagon were on a collision path. Then, at the ten-foot mark, where something underneath the water caused a swirl, the debris island shot off into the deeper current towards the middle of the river.

"Dad, it's gone. Holy cow that was a close call." Peter yelled back as he grabbed the stirrup leather on his sister's saddle. Victoria held the animal steady, while the men each followed Pete's example to pull themselves up the bank of the creek using the leathers for leverage.

Max heard the shout of his son's voice but took some moments to acknowledge and translate the sound. It released a rush of unspent adrenaline throughout his body. He winked and lifted his hat in salute before a burst of air whistled through his teeth.

A bow wave rode up against the four front legs of the team as they also pulled up the bank onto solid land.

"Whoa, whoa," Max called. "Easy now, easy."

He secured the reins and jumped down from the wagon. Trembling hands clasped the edge of the front board for a few seconds as the strength flowed back into his limbs and soothed the quiver in his legs. A soft whistle brought his own horse to his side.

Max called to his son, "There you are, Pete, it's all yours. Only another twenty-five miles to go. We should be home by mid-afternoon."

Victoria rushed into her father's arms.

"I thought you were done for, Dad."

"It'll take a bit more than a soaking to bump this old codger off, my girl."

Henry and Ed approached Max with hands outstretched.

"Mister Young, Max, you have a fine team there," Henry smiled as he pumped the hand of his host.

"You did a fine job, Sir, thank you." Ed shook hands also. "How often do you have to bring a load across swollen rivers?"

"I need to thank you blokes. By helping the wheels out of the hollow, you enabled the horses to get us all out of trouble." He stroked the mane of his mount and stared back into his memory. "I cannot count the times we've taken the wagon across deep water, but few have been as hairy as the trip over today."

The dogs on their chains raised a noisy welcome, as the cavalcade pulled up near the homestead verandah. Surprise and premonition stirred inside Max in equal measure, when they found nobody in sight. Why had neither Summer the cook, nor her daughter Velvet, been standing on the verandah shouting their delight as they usually did? At least David should be here to greet them.

Victoria did not wait for her horse to stop completely before she jumped to the ground as gently as a feather on a light breeze. She dropped the reins into the thick grass. The horse, trained not to move away when ground-tied, nibbled the green pickings. The girl's booted feet clattered up the five steps and onto the verandah.

"Velvet! Summer! We're home. Gordon! Where is everyone?" Her lithe body swung back to look askance at her father.

"I'll go see if your Uncle David's alright." He stood in the stirrups and swung his right leg over the horse's rump to land as lightly as his daughter despite his size and age. Leaving his mount ground-tied also, Max turned back to the lumbering wagon. "Pete, you start unloading the house things here and then take the wagon over to the shed. When you've finished the unloading, you can release the horses." Max ran up the steps across the verandah and into the house with Victoria hard at his heels.

Peter nodded to his father's disappearing back and secured the reins before joining Henry and Ed as they jumped to the ground.

The three men began to do as Max had instructed. On the back of the wagon, Smiley stood upright his head swivelling back and forth. Slowly he levered himself to the ground.

"Henry," the whites of Smiley's eyes flashed, "Bad spirits, Henry. I feel bad spirits."

Henry swung back to listen to what Smiley said. "What kind of bad spirits, Smiley?"

"Plenty big bad spirits, Henry. Here, at the house."

Peter and Ed paused in their chores listening to Smiley's words. The four men looked up at the sound of Max's approaching footsteps from inside the house. When he stepped out onto the verandah, his anxious eyes peered out from under a deep frown.

"David's not here." Max's hand reached down to rest on Victoria's shoulder. "Victoria, will you take a fresh horse and check the two top paddocks for any sign of Gordon or one of the other stockmen." Max's gaze looked up into the heavens, where the clouds thickened as they raced across the sky. "It looks like we'll be in for a drenching again tonight. We've just made it home in time, it seems."

"Yes, Dad." Before she'd finished speaking, Victoria lifted her horse's reins, threw herself up into the saddle and left to catch a fresh mount from the horse paddock near the barn.

With his daughter out of earshot, Max turned to the men now unloading the wagon.

"I fear David may have died while we were away. It can only have been in the last couple of days or we would have received a message at Mein. With this heat, they may even be burying him as we speak."

"Do you want me to have a look at the family burial ground to see if Gordon's there, Dad?"

Max paused to consider his options. "Yes, Pete, and if you don't find them you can help Victoria look for everyone while you're in the saddle. We'll manage this lot."

Henry could not help but notice, how Smiley stuck close by his side as they placed all the items destined for the house store room and the pantry, onto the verandah.

It took the four men to manhandle the large tarpaulin into a neat fold and throw it into the back of the wagon.

Max explained to the others. "We'll take the rest of this lot over to the shed and stack the grain bags. These horses will be wanting out of their harness." Max reached over and stroked the ears of the leading Clydesdale. The wagon rocked back and forth as the now restless horses made their feelings known.

After they unloaded the grain bags onto a large platform built five feet off the ground in the shed, Henry watched Max as he dug out four containers planted on the ledge of the wall. He checked their contents. Henry noticed the furrows deepen between Max's eyes.

"What's in those tins, Max"

"This is the rat bait we lay here in the grain store. We also keep two similar bait tins inside the pantry in the house." He scratched his head. "It seems the rats have been hungry; I'll need to fill these in the next day or two."

Henry helped Ed and Max release the Clydesdales from their harness. The men watched the horses kick and buck their way over to a water trough. Once the animals' thirsts were satisfied, they rolled their sweat-coated bodies on the grass.

The men made their way back to the house. The sound of galloping horses drew their attention to the three riders and a small dray approaching from the east. Henry admired the expertise with which the riders handled their horses. Victoria and Peter showed equal determination to outrun their older brother if the looks and style of the unknown third rider were anything to go by.

When they halted their mounts, it was obvious to Henry, that Gordon Young was a copy of his father – down to the slow smile and quiet voice.

"Sorry, Dad, we found Uncle David dead, when we arrived back from herding the cattle yesterday afternoon. I knew we had to bury him immediately with this heat as bad as it is."

"Thanks, Gordon. Did he say anything before he died? And where are Summer and Velvet, I thought they'd be with you at David's funeral?"

When the buckboard came to a halt beside them, a grey-haired man eased himself to the ground. A droopy felt hat protected a sun-hardened face, and his hands, seen below the long sleeves of his blue shirt, were rough with long years of manual labour. The younger man with him jumped to the ground on the opposite side. He lifted the wide-brimmed hat from his head as he joined the older man to walk over and shake Max's hand.

"My condolences, Max." The grey-haired man spoke first.

"Thanks, Hans." Max turned to shake the hand of the second man. "Thanks, Bevan." His gaze returned to Hans. "We'll have a drink later to see David on his way. Will you both join the family for dinner tonight?" Max drew the older man into a bear hug before he stepped back and introduced the newcomers to Henry and Ed. "Hans has been roustabout here at Lavinia Downs almost as long as I've been here. Bevan is one of our stockmen. He joined us last year – been working in the Cloncurry area for several years. Reckons he's going to show us up here, how it should be done." At this point, a grin lit up Max's face dissolving the lines of strain dragging at his flesh.

Hans shuffled from one foot to the other as if uncomfortable in the presence of so many strangers.

"This horse won't let itself out." He mumbled and nodded as he led the horse and buckboard over to the shed.

Max turned and sighed as he addressed his further chores.

"Everyone can carry something in," Max pointed to the heap of stores on the verandah before asking his daughter, "Victoria you'd best make a cup of tea and sandwiches for us all, seeing as Summer and Velvet seem to have disappeared." Max turned to Gordon. "Any idea where they've gone?"

"I presume they're in mourning. The whole native camp on the creek is quiet. I've never heard such a silence. It's a bit spooky actually. None of the stockmen from the camp turned up at the burial, but they don't normally do that anyway when I think about it."

Peter and Ed paused in their chores listening to Gordon's words.

Max grunted as he lifted a bag of flour. He turned back to his eldest son. "I presume you buried David near your Aunt Miriam. The poor woman lived less than two years after we arrived, you know. Your mother did not live much longer. It's a damn hard country out here – particularly on the women."

Henry felt Smiley's nudge on the back and his quiet whisper.

"Plenty bad spirits, Henry. Plenty bad. I go make smoke and sing."

Henry felt the shiver run down his spine from the top of his neck to the tip of his tailbone.

Henry was in the pantry when Max carried in a carton of dried fruit. He looked up at the sound of Max cursing.

"Bugger it, will you look at this tin of rat bait too. It's all but empty. I must ask Hans when he last filled them. And by the way, where is Summer? Has anyone seen the damn woman?"

Victoria, with the help of Hans, filled the wood box in the kitchen, lit the fire in the stove and filled the largest kettle, and placed it on the stove plate. Victoria prepared enough dough for two large dampers while the stove heated up.

"Dampers will do tonight. I'll make bread in the morning, Hans," she explained before he left the kitchen to go out to the hen house and select three or four volunteers for the evening meal.

The clatter of bottles filled the kitchen when Victoria went to the pantry to choose preserved vegetables to add to the main course.

Dusk fell softly around them as the members of the Young family, plus Hans, Bevan, Henry, and Ed, sat around the table on the verandah behind the kitchen. They each drank a glass of rum to salute the passing of David.

"Henry, where's your friend, Smiley?" Max asked.

"That will be him making all the smoke you can smell coming from every corner of your garden. I believe he is singing to his ancestors. I'm sorry, he is cleansing the house for you. He believes there are bad spirits in the house."

Everyone's eyes looked up from their dinner at Henry's words.

"What sort of bad spirits?" Max asked the question, but the expression on his face did not present any sign of surprise. He glanced across at Gordon. His son nodded as if he'd read every word in Max's mind.

Gordon leaned closer to his father and whispered. "We need to talk."

The old clock in the lounge room chimed nine o'clock. Everyone made their way to their sleeping quarters. A central living and kitchen area separated the large house into two. Max and his family plus the property's office occupied one side, while David's bedroom, a large sleepout, and a storeroom occupied the remainder. Henry and Ed slept in the sleepout.

"You sure you and Ed won't mind sleeping so near to where someone died, Henry?"

Henry placed a hand on Max's shoulder. "After seven years of taking catnaps on the nearest bed/trolley/horizontal surface and even on the morgue slab, on more than one occasion, sleeping on this verandah on a bed will be no obstacle."

The house settled for the night. Even the creaks of the iron roof and timber house frame quietened by the time Gordon slipped on silent feet into his father's room.

"You still awake, Dad?"

"Yeah, I thought you'd be in. You looked like you had something you wanted to tell me earlier." Max placed the paper he was reading on the bed beside him. He reached over and turned the lantern wick lower. He pushed himself higher against his pillows. "So, what has you so worried?"

"I did want to talk to you alone. It may be nothing, but I'm feeling a bit unsure about David's death."

"Oh, in what way, unsure?"

Gordon sat on the chair beside his father's bed. He stretched his legs out and leant back.

"Hans thought he heard an argument in the middle of the night – that was on the Sunday night. I hadn't heard it, but then from this side of the house, it's not surprising. Uncle David's room opens out towards the men's quarters. Hans assumed it was one of the nightmares Uncle David had been having in recent weeks. We left to herd the cattle across to the higher grounds on the Monday morning, first light. Hans came with us. We only expected to be away for the one day, but we ran into a few problems and ended up camped out overnight. We did not get back to the house until Tuesday afternoon. Before we left on Monday morning, Summer and Velvet were both at the house. They cooked the breakfast. Everything seemed normal. Uncle David looked tired, but that was not unusual. He never said anything was wrong. I just wished I had left Hans behind." Gordon sat up and raked his fingers through his hair.

"Son, none of us could have predicted the disappearance of the women."

"The thing is, Dad, I have a suspicion they disappeared shortly after we left. The stove was stone cold when we got back the next day and you know it takes a long time for that big old stove to cool down. Summer had it going when we had breakfast on Monday morning."

"What are you saying? Do you think Hans may have been right – there had been an argument on the Sunday night."

"Yes, and I think there is something suspicious about his death, but I'm not sure what exactly."

"David had been unwell for months, Gordon. I doubt if you can blame Summer for his death. She may have been careless and sometimes lazy when the mood took her, but a murderer …? Maybe she couldn't be bothered keeping the stove going."

Gordon sat in silence as he digested his father's words. He drew in a deep breath and went on.

"Dad, we found Uncle David dead on the ground near the shed door."

Max's eyes snapped up. "What was Uncle David doing out of the house?"

Gordon continued, "He had been to the poison cupboard. His keys were on the ground in front of the cupboard."

"How on earth did he walk so far? He could hardly make it to the commode chair in his room." Confusion filled Max's eyes.

Gordon lifted his head to gaze at his father's face which appeared pale in the dull lantern light and the feeble moonlight flickering through the open window.

"Reading the marks in the dirt, I believe he collapsed in front of the cupboard. The ground was scuffled up, where he had dragged himself from there to the shed door." Gordon's eyes burned with passion. "And, Dad, there's something else as well as the cold stove. Uncle David had been out there for many hours – certainly overnight – his body was covered with ants and …," Gordon paused unsure if to say more.

"Go on, Son."

"The crows had eaten his eyes out and torn a lot of the flesh on his face. That does not happen within a few hours."

"Holy cow. Poor sod."

Silence lay upon them as both men looked inwards at the scene within their heads. It was Max who moved first. He threw his legs over the edge of the bed and sat facing his son.

"Gordon, you cannot blame yourself. You weren't to know any of this was likely to happen."

"You don't blame me then, Dad?"

"Of course not, Gordon. I would probably have done things exactly as you did."

"But why do you think he took it into his head to go wandering out to the poison cupboard?"

"Maybe his mind was wandering. I've noticed in the past few months he seemed vague at times."

"Anyway, I've bolted and locked his room up as it was. It seemed a bit of a mess, I can tell you." Gordon stood up and dug into the top pocket of his shirt. "I've got Uncle David's keys and the room keys here." He removed the three sets of keys and placed them on the table beside his father's bed, one at a time. "The writing desk drawer key, the poison cupboard key and the room key."

Max reached out and held Gordon's wrist. "Thanks, mate, you have done me proud. I'll think about what you have said. Now you go to bed and sleep. Tomorrow's another day."

With one hand on the doorknob, Gordon swung back.

"Oh, I forgot. On the ground near his hand, it looked like he may have been trying to leave a message."

Gordon went on to tell his father of the letters seen in the dirt near his uncle's dead body.

CHAPTER TWENTY-FOUR

Cooktown

"Mrs. Baldwin, I've a telegram 'ere for you." The youth, with his sun-blond hair and grubby fingers, reached into the bag hung from a leather strap around his head and shoulders. String laces held the dusty boots upon his feet. "Mister Booth at the Post Office said I'm to deliver this to you and the other wire, which came through at the same time, to the hospital. Dad said that one's from the new doctor coming there soon."

Abigail clutched the small envelope in her hands. The lad's words were almost drowned out by the pounding of her heart in her chest. At the mention of the words, new doctor and hospital, her gaze lifted. She bit her bottom lip. This cannot be a coincidence. This will be news of Henry and his friend Ed. She slipped a threepenny bit from her skirt pocket to the delivery boy and returned to the surgery room.

Her brother lifted his gaze from the chart in which he had been writing when she flopped into the chair beside his desk.

"What have you got there, Abigail?"

Abigail did not answer. Her fingers tore open the envelope and stretched out the page within. Green eyes concentrated on the words. Tears leaked down her cheeks.

George replaced the pen in the inkwell on his desk and blotted the writing of his report. Anxiety furrowed his brow. His sister crying – that cannot be. Abigail never cried.

"Abby?"

Tears continued to fall, but they drifted past a wide smile as Abigail read.

Met Max Young at Mein – stop – joining him at Lavinia Downs – stop – hope to catch Mail Ship at Weymouth Bay to Cooktown – stop – Smiley with us – stop.

"It's from Henry. They met Max Young at the Mein Telegraph Station and they plan to stay at Lavinia Downs. Max will get them onto the Royal Mail ship, which delivers their mail to Weymouth Bay. It's about twenty or thirty miles from the homestead if I remember."

"Has he seen or heard from Smiley?"

"Yes, George, Smiley is with Henry and Edward."

"Well, that sounds all good news to me, so why the tears?"

A soft sob burst from her lips along with a quiet laugh. "Oh, George, you may be a wonderful doctor, but you have no idea what it is like to go through 'that time of life'."

"Great Scot, I never think of you being that old." He knew better than to show any more crinkles at the edges of his eyes.

"Don't you laugh, brother, remember no matter how old I get, you'll always be that half-hour older."

The small room filled with their laughter.

CHAPTER TWENTY-FIVE

Sleuths

Henry delivered his breakfast dishes to the kitchen, where Victoria stood at the large wash tub on the bench with her arms up to the elbows in soapsuds.

"Thank you, Henry." Victoria's blue eyes shone. Blond curls danced from the confines of a red ribbon at the back of her head.

"My pleasure, Victoria. Is there no sign of the return of the regular cook – did you say her name was Summer?"

"Dad's sending Gordon down to the camp this morning to ask for the whereabouts of Summer and her daughter, Velvet. Between them, they usually look after the cooking and the running of the house." Mischief lurked in Victoria's eyes as they lifted. "I'm sorry Uncle David has died, but maybe Dad will not send me back to school again. He'll need me to help him here."

"I thought you'd rather be out with your brothers than chained to the kitchen." Admiration and amusement glinted in his green eyes.

Victoria's forehead crinkled as she pondered her preferences.

"Anything is better than going back to school. Anyway, Dad said I'm to ride to the coast this morning with Pete and Doctor Benton." Her frown disappeared and laughter filled her eyes again.

Henry's eyebrows lifted. "Doctor Benton? My friend Ed, gets to be called Doctor, while I have to make do with just Henry?"

A pink flush infused Victoria's cheeks. Her eyes dropped.

"I'm truly sorry, Doctor Baldwin. Miss Abigail talks so much of you; I think of you as a close friend already even though we've only just met. I do apologize."

Henry laughed. "If I'm to tell the truth, I'm glad you think of me as a friend and not a stuffy old doctor. Please, keep calling me Henry."

A short time later, after sorting some papers in the station office, Max Young came out to wave goodbye to Peter, Ed and Victoria as they headed their horses towards the rising sun. The animals' hooves splashed water up from the puddles in the yard left by the overnight rain showers. The two black and white dogs ran in circles around Victoria and her mount. Max walked over to the stables where Gordon and Hans saddled their horses.

"What's Bevan doing this morning, Gordon?"

"He's out working those two young horses we brought in last week. If you get a moment, you should go and watch him. He has a fine hand on a rein."

"Maybe after I sort out David's room, I'll do that." Max reached into his pocket and slipped a lump of sugar between the willing lips of Gordon's horse. "Make sure you both take your guns with you. You shouldn't run into any trouble, but I feel a restlessness in the air since I've arrived back. Maybe Henry's friend, Smiley, has put the wind up me with all his talk of bad spirits and his smoke fires and singing during the night."

Gordon patted the leather gun scabbard on the offside of his black horse.

"Already thought of that, Dad. We'll take care. I can't understand why our stockmen aren't up here at the house this morning, though. Things seem very quiet over that way." Gordon's head nodded towards the direction of the native camp on the river two miles west of the house.

"There could be a simple explanation. With the cattle all sorted for the monsoon weather, maybe they think we won't need them here today. It's most strange how Summer and Velvet have disappeared, particularly with David having been so ill." Max walked beside the two men as they led their horses out into the open. He watched them swing up into the saddles. After a brief wave, the riders nudged their animals into a canter.

Henry sat on the back step watching Smiley working at his sketch pad. The homestead took shape upon the page.

"Smiley, are you satisfied all the bad spirits have left?"

Smiley's hand kept moving the pencil in light marks on the page for several moments before he paused and looked over at his friend.

"Bad spirits not all gone, Henry. Something bad happened here."

"What sort of something?"

"I don't know yet."

Max's voice disturbed the conversation.

"Well, Henry, now we have got the others out of the way, I need to go in and look through my brother's room. Would it be an imposition if I asked you to come with me?"

"Of course, Max, no trouble at all. I'm not sure if I'll be of any use, but always glad to help if I can."

Smiley looked up from his sketching. "You want me do something, Mister Young?"

"No, Smiley, not at the moment."

As they walked up the stairs, Henry asked Max where everyone had gone.

"Pete, Ed and Victoria have gone to leave a message for the next mail ship passing out in the channel. We have an old prospector,

Johnny Hayden, who lives in a hut near the beach. He controls our signal flag post. He flies a red flag when we have a message to be collected by a passing mail ship. When a seaman collects the message, he lowers the red flag. If the seaman leaves us mail, newspapers or a message, he flies the yellow flag. Johnny goes down to collect it from the mailbox under the flag pole. He rides up here to deliver the collection at least once a fortnight."

"Communication is not easily achieved this far north, I see." Henry pondered the situation of those on properties in the Cape. "Nothing happens in a hurry, then."

"Not a big hurry, I can tell you. Once the monsoons reach their peak, we have no chance of riding to Mein. The beach mail is the only communication we have at all then. Sometimes we still have to wait for flooded creeks to go down."

"Is that how you plan to get Ed, me and Smiley back to Cooktown – on a passing ship?"

"Yes, it's the only way you'll get home before next year, and I don't want to be on the receiving end of your mother's wrath if I don't get you home before Christmas." Max laughed.

"Maybe I should stay here and hide. I'm sure I'll cop some of her wrath for causing all this upset to her plans."

The laughter of both men came to a sharp end when Max unlocked his brother's room and they first laid their eyes on the filth and untidiness.

It was the stench of stale body excretions, which assaulted their senses first. Henry thought he had seen it all during his training in the hospital, but he struggled not to curl his lip in disgust at the state of the bed with its blood-stained bare mattress and pillow. Newspapers scattered across the bed, overflowed onto the floor. Fungus flourished in an old tin used as a sputum mug and wedged in beside the pillow. Three food trays with partially eaten contents wrapped in mould almost covered the writing table. Two dead rats lay nearby. Dust blanketed everything.

"Stone the crows, I've got to empty the commode first thing; that smell is life-threatening." Max went to lift the lid but drew back retching. "That bloody woman hasn't been in here for days." He moved to attend the commode again but was stalled by Henry who stood looking at the upper paper on the bed, where David had marked in a circle of dried blood, an article, which caused Henry to pause.

"Wait, Max, wait. Do you see what David has marked on the paper? Do you know what this article is about?"

"Eh, no. How can I read the paper when the stink in here is tearing the lining from the inside of my nostrils?"

Henry moved closer to the paper on the bed. With one finger he smoothed the page to make it easier to read.

"This is an article on Arsenic Poisoning. I remember reading it myself just before I left England, I think." Henry read the article again and pointed to the ticks made by a bloody finger beside each of the Signs and Symptoms listed. "Can you see that, Max?" But Max had moved to the open doorway to suck in the fresh air. "Come over here, Max, you need to see this."

Hesitant steps approached the bed. "What am I looking at?"

"Can you see the marks beside each of the Signs and Symptoms of the poisoning? I think David may have been trying to leave a message to say he has all of these symptoms."

Max looked more closely. "Strike me, they are most of the things he complained of at different times. Are you saying you think he has been poisoned?"

"That I don't know, but I think David thought he was."

Max slapped his forehead with the palm of his hand.

"I should have suspected this last night when Gordon told me what he had found in the shed near where David had died." Max retreated to lean on the doorframe and draw in more clean air as he went on to repeat Gordon's findings of evidence of David's visit to the poison cupboard, and his consequent collapse. "He left a mark in the dirt near his body – RS and POI. He could have been saying Arsenic Poisoning."

Henry moved towards the doorway and took Max by the elbow.

"Max, shut this room up again for a bit. You and I need to talk about what we've seen here. I think a cup of tea might be a good idea."

Just then the sound of a distant gunshot came from the direction of the native camp on the river. Max froze, his head cocked. Within a few moments, another shot echoed in the west.

"Hopefully they're only shooting a couple of wallabies to deliver to the camp folk for tucker." Max did not move for at least five minutes. When no further gunshots reached their ears, he moved again towards the kitchen. "Yes, that's what it'll be."

The aroma of cooking from the kitchen helped clear the unpleasant odours of the bedroom from their nostrils and palate. They found Smiley at the stove, cooking.

"Henry, Mister Young, I make Miss Abigail's favourite flat cakes and have boiled the billy." Smiley's grin broke some of the tension in the room.

"Thanks, Smiley, you'll take some too?" Max raised an eyebrow as he turned to Henry. "Smiley has many talents, I see."

"My mother and Uncle George ensured we both had a working knowledge of how to survive in a non-serviced kitchen, and in return, Smiley taught me many skills on how to survive in the bush – which contributed to Ed's and my recent survival." Henry turned to the dark-skinned man turning the flat cakes on the hot plate. "Thanks, Smiley, that looks good."

Henry and Max sat at the table on the kitchen verandah. In front of them lay a large plate of flat cakes beside two pannikins of tea from which steam drifted into the morning air.

"So, Henry, you pulled up inside that room like you were about to step on the head of a brown snake. What's on your mind?"

"Did you see the two dead rats on David's writing desk – near the leftovers on the trays?"

Max's jaw dropped. His eyes opened wide. "You're saying – you really are thinking David has been poisoned."

Henry dragged his hands across his face. "Max, I don't have any solid evidence, but things seem to be adding up." He used the forefinger of his right hand to touch the fingers on his left hand in turn, and he began to list what they knew. "One: The similarity of David's medical signs and symptoms and David's markings on the newspaper article related to these. Two: His unexpected and almost incredible trip – given his condition – to the shed just to check the poison cupboard. We have to ask what motivated him. Three: The enigmatic note written in the dirt as he was dying. Four: Dead rodents near left-over foods of which one can almost safely presume they ate." Henry drew a deep breath. He hesitated at this point, to remind Max the cook and her daughter had disappeared.

The muscles on Max's face writhed as his expressions travelled through a journey of horror, disbelief, guilt, and at last, acceptance of this possibility. He opened his mouth to speak, but could not formulate his words.

"Max, please remember, none of this is proof of anything, but I feel there is probably circumstantial evidence that we need to consider."

"B-b-but who would do such a thing? He may have been a prickly sort of cove at times, but there was never any reason to kill the man."

Henry watched Max's silent struggle with this new possibility in his life to contend with.

"Max, if my suspicion is correct, my guess would have to be the poison was delivered in the food and therefore the guilt will lie with the person who delivered his food each day."

"Summer!" A rush of air accompanied Max's one word.

A silence fell between the two men. The wind began to swirl the foliage in the trees outside. It blew grey clouds scurrying across the sky. A rooster crowed from the fowl house followed by the clucking of laying hens. Smiley appeared from the kitchen carrying a large empty bucket heading towards the water tank. A repeated clang of a loose sheet of iron on the shed roof lifted Max's head.

"I'll send Hans up there to fix that later." He spoke more to himself than Henry. Unseeing eyes followed the path of a sheet of newspaper dancing in the winds across the backyard. Gradually Max brought his attention back to Henry.

"What am I to do now? I cannot let my brother's death go unavenged." His fingers of one hand tapped one side of his pannikin. "Yet, I'll have to be careful not to set off a war with the natives. Summer was from the local tribe. She has worked for us for years."

"Max, we have no solid evidence, remember. I can take samples of things from David's room and have them sent off to Brisbane for analysis."

"Please don't say we have to exhume David's body. That is too terrible to contemplate."

Henry sipped at the tea and chewed on another flat cake while he considered his words.

"As far as I have read, the bodies of those having been poisoned with arsenic do not decompose in the normal way. Some have remained intact for years. Let me get the samples sent off to Brisbane and then, we'll look at what we have."

Max stared at a hen scratching in the dirt near the bottom of the steps. Henry was unsure whether he had heard everything he said or not.

"Max?"

"Hmmm, yes, Henry." Max looked up. "Sorry, did I miss something?"

"Max, without the proper preservative fluids for the specimens, any negative results cannot be guaranteed accurate. A positive result can be a more reliable indicator."

"Henry, I'm not sure if I really want to know." A sigh drifted off on the breeze.

"Max, I am obliged, as a doctor, to report a suspected murder, and that is what we are talking about here – a likely murder."

"Damnation, you're right, I know. Let's get these specimens collected and clean that bloody room."

Chairs scraped on the wooden floorboards as both men stood.

"I'll need some small tins, or bottles perhaps, to separate and keep the specimens in. Perhaps larger tins for the two rats' bodies. All these will need to be wrapped in separate paper bags or newspapers and identified. Everything will need to be sealed inside a solid box for me to take back to Cooktown before postage on to Brisbane."

Max scratched his head. His frown deepened.

"Victoria collected empty tobacco tins when she was younger. I'll get them and my wife's preserving bottles. There's an assortment of tins in the shed and no doubt a wooden box or two. You get on with your collecting and I'll find everything for you."

Henry removed the diving knife from the sheath on his belt. His thoughts were of the *Pink Pearl* and its skipper as he ran his thumb along the edge. The blade felt blunt. He doubted it would even cut butter. He detoured via the kitchen to collect a large fork and a sharp knife. Max handed him a handful of empty tobacco tins from inside the pantry before exploring further for the bottles. Henry retreated to open David's room with hesitation, and a large deep breath of air in his lungs. He placed his feet with care amongst the debris of months gathered since last being swept. He moved towards the window and turned the latch. Henry found it necessary to lean his weight against the frame to push the window open.

Samples from the contents of the commode bucket were the first specimens collected. Henry felt sure if he collected what he needed from here, and removed the container to soak in a bucket of water out in the backyard the room's odour might not be so offensive.

Disappointment rolled in upon him to find the dead rats' bodies reached highlights of their own on the scale of foul odour. Much to Henry's relief, it was then Max returned from the shed with the lidded tins. Henry grabbed two tins from Max's hands and tossed a dead rat into each one before tightening the lid with haste. He rushed through the doorway, stood near the verandah railing and sucked in the fresh air.

Samples of each food and drink container were allocated labelled storage containers and wrapped in newspaper, also labelled, using a pencil from David's desk. The newspaper, marked by David, also became a specimen for analysis. Henry thought to cut out bloodied pieces of the mattress and pillowcase and treated them likewise. He held the sputum tin upside down over a specimen container, but the thickened mucous clung determinedly to the sides of the tin. With a vision in his mind of sputum flying over his hands, he gave it a gentle shake, to no avail. A stronger shake and the pull of gravity moved the contents forward half an inch. The large congealed blob of sputum contents hung like an obscene alien body. Should he use the blunt knife to scrape it out? A grimace tightened his face at the thought of ever touching the knife again if he did. While he procrastinated, the dollop fell away with a slurp and a plop to land in the container awaiting underneath.

With the containers safely inside a wooden box now sitting on the verandah, Max and Henry stripped the rubbish from inside the room, including the mattress and pillow, assigning everything to the heap to be burnt out in the yard. Max felt his courage would not go so far as to address all of David's paperwork just now. The desk remained locked.

"At least the wind has settled. I'll get some kerosene from the shed and set this lot alight. Henry, once it's caught, you and Smiley can keep an eye on it, while I go and scrub that room and furniture from roof to floorboards."

On his way to the shed, Max descended the back stairs two at a time. When his feet hit the dirt, he spun back and grasped the rail of the steps for balance. He rested one foot on the second bottom step.

"Er … Henry, I'd appreciate it if you'd not mention our findings here today to Victoria – not until things become clearer."

Henry looked up from where he was tidying the contents of his sample box.

"Of course, Max, I'll not breathe a word."

CHAPTER TWENTY-SIX

Riders Return

It was Gordon and Hans who returned to the homestead first. Blood dripped from the body of the wallaby hanging over the horse's withers. Gordon slid to the ground and handed his reins to Hans who went to unsaddle the horses.

"Thanks, Hans."

Gordon's boots pounded up the back stairs as he called, "Dad! You there, Dad!"

The door slammed against the wall when Max rushed out to see what was wrong. Henry followed close on his heels.

"Everything alright, Gordon?"

With one step left to climb, Gordon stood leaning on the railing.

"The tribe's gone. Only about nine or ten old people and a couple of sick kids are left in the camp. Snowy seems to be looking after them."

"Good grief, Snowy is probably the oldest of them all. Who's looking after him?"

"They looked pretty hungry. We shot a wallaby for them. Snowy was throwing it on the fire when we left." Gordon took off his hat and rubbed his hair. "According to all of those still there, no one knows where Summer and Velvet are – or if they do, they're not saying."

"Did you ask them, when the rest of the tribe will be back?"

"'They back when bin finish bizness, Boss,' is all they'd answer to that question."

"I heard two shots."

"We brought a wallaby back for a stew tonight. Hans is going to fix tea shortly."

It was late afternoon before the other riders returned. The noise of the barking dogs pre-empted their arrival followed by the plod of the tired horses' feet. Gordon and Henry waited on the east verandah. When a halt was called, the horses stood with heads hung low. Pete approached his father, while Victoria and Ed Benton swung down to the ground and led their horses off towards the stable.

Max called to his daughter, "Victoria, Hans has fresh wallaby bones in the kitchen to give to those dogs, when you tie them up." He shifted his attention to the remaining man in the saddle. "Pete, you look all done in."

Peter smiled a rueful smile at his father. "What a day we had. We swam a few of the smaller creeks and had to detour quite a way upstream at Nugget's Gully." Peter reached down to the saddle bag near his thigh. "Here's some mail and papers Johnny had for us. He was planning to head up this way with them tomorrow." Gordon trotted down the stairs to collect the bag. "Before we left, Johnny saddled his horse to go down and leave your note at the beach for the next mail ship."

Max shuffled through the papers from the saddlebag.

"Thanks, son, now go unsaddle your horse and come on in. Hans has cooked us up a fresh wallaby stew."

"I'm starving."

Later, as the family and guests sat around the dining room table, the activities of the day were discussed. Max's comments on his occupation consisted of an edited version of how he and Henry had cleaned up most of his brother's room. Henry watched Max as he spoke, amazed at how the lines on the man's face had multiplied and deepened since early morning.

"Did I tell you that old scar on Snowy's thigh is swollen up to twice the size and it's dribbling blood-stained pus down his leg, Dad?"

"Gordon, that thing's never healed properly since he sliced it open with the axe."

Henry stirred a spoon of sugar into his pannikin of black tea. "Can Ed and I take a look at that for you, Max?"

"Would you mind, Henry? We don't carry much more than basic medical gear here, but your opinion will sure be welcome."

"No trouble at all." Henry turned to his fellow medical officer. "What do you think, Ed?"

"Something to keep us out of mischief, I guess. It'll be good to feel useful again."

"Thanks to both of you." Max nodded.

"What's on the jobs' list for tomorrow, Dad?" Gordon asked.

"Well, first of all, I'll get you to take Henry and Ed over to look at Snowy's leg. The rest of us can drag out all the saddles and leather gear to sort through. It's been a big season. I'm sure there'll be hours of repair work in that lot to keep us busy during the monsoon months ahead."

As the chores were discussed, Henry glanced across to where Victoria sat munching on a corner of damper dipped into her gravy. The drooping eyelids did not go unnoticed. When those eyelids lifted and her gaze fell along the same path as his own, Henry blushed and dropped his own eyes, but not before he saw the twinkle.

When he finished eating, Henry took his plate into the kitchen, where he found Smiley preparing to wash the dishes.

"Did you get a feed, Smiley?"

"Since when would I miss out on a wallaby stew."

The wide grin lifted Henry's heart. "Do you want a hand here?"

The grin widened even further to almost close Smiley's eyes. "Miss Abigail said you and I not work together in the kitchen. We make a bigger mess than we start with." Both men laughed at the memory.

Henry leant against the table, while Smiley began to soap up the plate in the wash tub.

"Smiley, do you think you can talk to the local tribe down at the river to ask where Summer and Velvet have gone? Can you speak their language?"

The grin disappeared – swallowed by a deep frown and collapsed corners of his mouth.

"Henry, I'm not of these people. Their language not too different, but there's every chance they throw a spear through my heart. That's usual punishment for a stranger arriving in another's territory without Welcome."

"Is that why you slept outside my door last night?"

"Yes, Henry, I don't think they'll touch me if I stay close to the house." Smiley dropped his concentration into the washtub along with the items to be washed. The splash of water and clatter of dishes broke the silence of the room for long moments. Eventually, Smiley's head lifted. His hands leant against the bench. "Maybe I sing my father to speak for me."

"Smiley, nothing is more important to me and my family than your safety. Don't do it, if it will put you at risk."

"We see. Now, why you stand about talking? Are there any more dishes outside there for this fella to wash?"

Shadows danced off the walls of the kitchen as Henry and Ed searched, with the assistance of the light of a flickering hurricane lantern, through the medical items stored in a worn Gladstone bag sitting open on the table.

Lined-up contents were examined closely. A pillowcase full of clean rags, a skein of wool, a bottle of disinfectant beside a bottle of cough medicine, and a bottle of tonic. Henry recognized the handwriting of his Uncle George on the labels. Also present lay a solid sharpened scalpel, metal forceps, several needles and reels of suture thread, scissors, and a small jar of iodine for wound care. A small container of Oil of Cloves for toothache and a bottle of eyedrops with several extra glass eye-droppers – two with the rubber bulbs showing signs of perishing. A small brown packet held new rubber bulbs packed inside two tin jugs, one large and one small, alongside two small containers, one of Sulphate of Copper and the other of Silver Nitrate.

A hard-covered notebook filled with reminders of treatments for different problems lay pressed up against the back wall of the Gladstone bag. Henry flicked through the contents of procedures on how to obtain the juice of onion for treatment of earache, different uses of the Sulphate of Copper present and Silver Nitrate, as well as how to care for the scalpel and how to use the needle and threads.

His finger traced the flourishing stroke of his mother's penmanship on many of the instructions.

Ed sat back in his chair. "There are enough supplies here to run St. Bart's waiting rooms."

Henry nodded with a grin as he began to replace the items. "I guess they need to have a bit of everything. A trip to the hospital is an impossible event more times than enough way up here."

"I have to admit, Henry, I'm looking forward to putting my skills back into practice."

"Hmmm – me too."

Several cows in the stable yard mooed impatience while waiting to be milked. The soothing voice of Hans called back to them. The morning sun crept over the horizon as the sound of departing hoof beats resonated across the flat. Gordon, Henry and Ed rode away from the homestead towards the native camp. Henry rode with the Gladstone bag balanced on the front of his saddle, held by one hand. He used his other hand on the reins to guide the horse.

"Are you alright carrying that, Henry?" Concern filled Gordon's query.

"Yes, Gordon. As a young fellow, there were many times I'd carry my uncle's bag like this when we were on our way to a call-out."

"At least this horse doesn't have one leg shorter than the rest, as that trooper's horse did." Ed laughed with the joy of the wind blowing over his face. His unruly hair streamed back against his head. "This is nearly as good as being on board a ship."

Ed's infectious laughter set Henry off. "Sailing on land you mean."

Neither Ed nor Henry had noticed Gordon lift his gun from the scabbard. The sound of the shot so close nearly sent both of them out of the saddle.

"Another wallaby for their fire," Gordon called as he rode over to collect his contribution to the tribe's sustenance.

The camp, set up on the bank of a wide stream, consisted of a disorderly assortment of shelters made from the bark of the nearby trees and rusty sheets of corrugated iron, no doubt discarded from the homestead. The squeals of several children swinging from a vine rope into the water ceased as the white men appeared in their midst.

The dozen or so members of the tribe present greeted the arrivals with enthusiasm. Two women fell upon the slaughtered game and began its preparation for cooking on the open fire set in the centre of a wide area cleared of shrubbery and thick with loose dirt from the traffic of many bare feet. The man they called Snowy walked over to thank Gordon.

Henry observed the large abscess on the tail end of an old scar on Snowy's left thigh. He turned to tell Ed, but he had already noted the wound. He raised his eyebrows at Henry. The two doctors remained in the saddle while Gordon, using broken English and scattered words of the local dialect, explained who the two new men were and how they were medicine men come to cure them. His spiel finished with, "Like Mrs. Young made medicine for the sick in the tribe long time gone."

Other than the two women busy at the fireplace, the remainder of the people hung back. Wariness and distrust filled their eyes as Henry and Ed dismounted. Gordon led the horses to the edge of the campsite, where they soon dropped their heads to nibble at the fresh young grasses.

Henry took the bag with the items of treatment over to where a large tree had fallen some time ago. He removed things one by one and spread them along the wide trunk. On skinny legs that appeared incapable of carrying even her frail weight, a short, wrinkled woman with thinning grey hair rushed with a squeal to where the items lay.

"Missy Vin, Missy Vin," she called and spoke in a gush of words incomprehensible to the ears of the white men. A calloused grubby finger brushed along the line of bottles until it stopped at the small glass bottle marked Oil of Cloves. Her harsh cackle filled the campsite. She opened her mouth and pointed to the gums vacant of all but one tooth. "Sore tooth, sore tooth."

Henry and Ed stood, surprised into silence. The old lady reached out and shook Ed's sleeve. She jabbed her finger into her mouth before pointing again with determination at the small bottle. "Sore tooth, sore tooth." She held her hand over her mouth and groaned.

"Well, Ed, lad, I'd suggest you paint some of that stuff on her one lighthouse before she tears you apart limb from limb." Henry struggled to keep a straight face.

Their gazes followed the little woman as she scrounged around the dirt to find a small twig. She held it up in the air and tried to say a word that sounded very much like an attempt at "Wool."

Henry's face cleared.

"Ed, may I suggest you tie a couple of knots of the wool onto her stick and dip it into the Oil of Cloves and dab it on her tooth before we are all speared to death and eaten for tea."

With the tooth painted, the lady held her head high and strutted around her family with her mouth wide open showing off her stained tooth. The group erupted into Ooohs, Ahaaas and laughter.

A small naked child of about three years of age sagged in the arms of a plump grandmother. The woman held the child's foot out to the strangers with Missy Vin's magic bottles. A seeping untreated burn scar ran along the external edge of the foot.

Henry looked around to find Gordon sitting on the far end of the log talking to the native they knew as Snowy.

"Gordon, will you ask Snowy how we get water to wash this wound?"

Before Gordon had time to put the request into the native words, the orders had been issued from Snowy's lips. The man obviously had some understanding of the white man's language.

One of the old men on the perimeter of the group carried a hollowed-out wooden container, filled with water from the river, over to the doctors. Ed tore off a square of clean cloth and dipped it into the water. He drizzled the cool water over the old burn. The child's eyes widened, the little mouth opened to its full extent, the child filled his lungs, but the expected yell did not eventuate. Relief from the cool water released a small sigh. The child's eyes and mouth relaxed.

Using the small jug from their supplies, Ed continued to drizzle water over the foot.

"Henry, can you slap a bit of the iodine onto a dressing and tear up some bandages to dress this wound?"

"Almost done, Doctor," Henry grinned.

With the child now contented in his grandmother's arms, Henry turned his attention to Snowy with the oozing abscess.

It took Gordon's soft voice speaking in his broken local dialect to convince Snowy he needed to have the wound looked at. By the time they had the man sitting up on the fallen tree trunk ready to receive treatment, his eyeballs wandered back and forth within the eye sockets.

Henry's voice, in barely a whisper, warned Ed. "I'm going to lance this in one swift jab." Henry turned his head to Gordon, still speaking softly. "Can you tell Snowy I'm going to clap my hands and chase the bad spirits from his leg? He will feel a short sharp pain as the spirits will not want to leave."

With the scalpel hidden in his one hand and the other hand held loosely over its mate, he approached the patient. Henry lifted the top hand and slapped the flesh on the thigh just above the leaking wound. At the same time, he swept down with the scalpel and opened the wound a good inch wide and nearly an inch deep. While Snowy froze with the shock of it all, Henry stuck his finger into the open wound and scooped out the gathered pus and blood – twice. The mess ran over Snowy's thigh. Henry pressed his fingers around the edges of the wound to encourage further bloody pus to rise like lava from a volcano and spew out over the top.

"I've never seen anyone do that as quickly as you do." Ed smiled his admiration as he drizzled water over the wound. "We'll need to leave it to drain for a bit."

"Yes, I'll cover it with a thick pad of cotton soaked in the iodine. We'll return tomorrow to see how things are going." He glanced up at Gordon who stood speechless watching the procedure. "Will it be alright if Ed and I come back tomorrow to re-dress this wound?"

Gordon nodded.

Between them, Henry and Ed wrapped several torn lengths of cotton as bandages to hold the dressing. By the time the doctors had washed their hands and re-packed their treatment supplies, Gordon's whistle for the horses echoed up and down the waterway. The members of the tribe present gathered to admire the white bandage on Snowy's leg. Pride replaced the shock and fear in Snowy's eyes as he instructed the others to beware, he had potent magic in his leg now.

Gordon delivered the doctors to the camp the following day and then every second day after, allowing them to treat minor ailments as they thought necessary.

It was nearly a week later and everyone had settled early for the night when Smiley received his visitor.

The soft rattle of the dog chain went unnoticed by the household. The black and white dog, tied up under the back stairs, rose to its feet. Teeth gleamed in the moonlight as the mouth opened, but the bark dissolved into a soft whine as the animal dropped to its belly and lay with its head and neck stretched along the extended front legs. The dog's counterpart, sleeping over at the shed door, let out a soft yelp before it also took up the subservient posture.

Dark eyes stared out into the yard. A humming noise spread gently across the backyard bathed in a soft moonlight glow. The sound resembled the noise made by a hornet building a nest but contained a wider variety of notes. It strengthened and burrowed through

Smiley's ear and into his brain, where he lay on the old couch on the verandah outside the kitchen.

His eyes opened, the eyeballs rolled and the whites glinted in the moonlight before the eyelids closed. A vision appeared within his head. Four cubes glowing with a luminous light stood in a row in front of him. An image appeared in the first cube. Two dark-skinned people ran across an open plain – women. One had the loose flesh of an aging body, while the other had a young nubile woman's outline. In the distance behind them rose a cloud of dust. The image faded.

The same women slowly appeared in the glow of the second cube. This time they ran on a narrow track, through large boulders, up an incline. Many black people watched from the base of the hill. This vision faded slowly.

The third cube filled with the sight of the two women at the top of a cliff face looking out towards a far horizon at dawn. The older woman took the younger woman's hand. They jumped. Smiley's body jerked before the image within the cube disappeared.

The fourth and final cube's vision appeared in increments, beginning at the edges and filling into the centre, where the two broken bodies lay on a wide flat rock within a perimeter of huge boulders, some smoothed and some jagged.

Smiley's body began to shake. His trembling increased until the couch beneath him vibrated. A sheen of perspiration covered his face and shoulders. His eyelids snapped open. The trembling ceased. He swung his legs around and stood up, stumbling to lean against the verandah post.

In a beam of moonlight unobstructed by any clouds, a man stood staring – a tall, dark-skinned man with snow-white hair. The humming noise Smiley heard drumming in his ears emanated from this figure. Smiley stood straight, he spoke using his own dialect – his voice quiet, but penetrating.

"I will tell them."

The head of white hair nodded before the figure turned. Leaning on his long stick, he shuffled off with his shoulders drooped – exhausted, following the physical and mental strength expended in the silent communication.

CHAPTER TWENTY-SEVEN

Cooktown

Abigail sat on a chair in front of the chest of drawers, the bottom one of which had been pulled out to sit on the floorboards. The contents lapped the top edge of the timber confines. Abigail's sigh filled the room. Her goal had been to go through all her belongings and discard unneeded items. This exercise was in preparation for their planned return to Brisbane in the next few months. *How did this drawer become so full?* Her first thoughts as she ventured into the drawer brought a smile to her face. *What else can I expect, it has been almost twenty years since we first came to Cooktown, for what was to have been a two years contribution to a humanitarian cause.*

A flat cardboard box sat on top of everything else in the drawer. She drew it out to place on her bed – the contents to be savoured later. These were her important documents. She knew it held papers precious to her such as her birth certificate, and documents relating to her son. Henry's father's birth and death certificate plus her marriage certificate had been preserved, all be it reluctantly. In all honesty, she did not classify them as precious – necessary, perhaps. Henry might need these at some time. The promise of perusing her prized photographs and sketches of her loved ones filled her heart with anticipation. In a brown envelope on top of the cardboard box, waiting for inclusion, was the copy of Henry's University Degree posted to his mother for safekeeping.

The drawer itself contained small treasured gifts from special people in her life. Abigail removed a cake tin patterned with red roses. The lid opposed her intrusion for a brief moment until her determination sent it spinning off and clattering across the floor. Inside the tin, a small blue velvet drawstring bag caught her attention. A moment later, the silver cherub given to Henry at his baptism lay in her hands. Tears lay soft on her cheeks. A vision of her friend Millie Carson, who had owned the Mariner's Rest Hotel in Brisbane, rose to the forefront of her mind. A no-nonsense woman who helped her during the birth of her only child, Millie had an infectious sense of humour and deep compassion. Abigail remembered her as a loyal friend and staunch supporter in those early years after they arrived in the colonies. Millie with the henna-coloured hair, ostentatious jewellery and flounced dresses, so alive, but now long dead – June 1873.

With the thought of Millie entered the vision of Millie's lover, Captain William Sloan. He stood tall and proud; the horrific scar on the left side of his face was the result of an accident on board his ship *The Northern Orchid*. William, who had helped Abigail understand not all men were self-opinionated, untrustworthy rogues out for their own satisfaction in life, as her husband had proved to be. Of course, she never thought that of her twin brother, George. The little carved replica of the captain's ship lived inside the blue velvet bag with the cherub.

From under the tin, she lifted the portrait of Henry as a youngster, sitting by a fire in the backyard with his friend Smiley – the frame now tarnished with age. Thomas, George's manservant, with his talented hands had been able to hold a sketching pencil or a hammer with equal ability. Thomas, a practical man had kept everything about the home and surgery in pristine working order. As Abigail held the replica of her son close to her heart, she remembered Thomas working on the painting of *The Northern Orchid*. Millie had commissioned it for her William, and it now hung in the foyer of the Mariner's Rest Hotel. Thomas, her unofficial brother and occasional confidant, now lay in the grounds of the Cooktown Cemetery, mourned these past four years.

Next out of the drawer, wrapped in wads of tissue paper wearing with age, she held the gold christening cup sent by her mother from London. Her father had remained uncommunicative until after his death in 1875 when a letter of reconciliation penned at a time unknown before his death, arrived – forwarded from the surgery in Brisbane to this address in Cooktown. Abigail leant back against the bed and analysed her feelings on the day of its arrival – how her heart had tossed around inside her chest like a ship on an unpredictable sea. Today she smiled. Her feelings now mellowed with age; not only on the issue of her father, but on many pig-headed opinions she held when a young woman.

A miniature replica of Brisbane's Victoria Bridge lay upon Henry's christening shawl. This gift was from her companion Jane, who, often reluctantly, accompanied Abigail on many of her escapades during their time together. Jane now lived with her husband, Mac, and their family in Brisbane. Ewan MacGregor, the previous Mate of *The Northern Orchid* in William Sloan's day, adored his wife.

For loving inspection upon Abigail's lap now lay the blue cap and booties gifted to the baby Henry and knitted by Eve, the young girl Abigail had rescued from the streets of London. Eve, now a mature woman married to Gus Dougall, the part-owner and current engineer on *The Northern Orchid*. Eve and her children lived only a stone's throw away and visited often. Gus always dropped in to say hello, when his ship anchored in the Cooktown harbour. Once more,

Abigail's gaze remained unfocused on the far wall as her mind journeyed along the hallways of time. A hint of a smile lifted her lips.

With her concentration back on her chore, Abigail took up a hand-painted card sent to baby Henry by Maureen Dougall. Maureen was the wife of Josh Dougall, the present captain and also part-owner of *The Northern Orchid*. Josh had followed Maureen to hell and back to rescue her from the evil Silas. Abigail shook the thoughts from her head – all that was years ago. Abigail admired Maureen for her indomitable strength. She picked the card up, smoothed it out with her long, now age-wrinkled fingers, and tossed it up onto the box on the bed.

Abigail held a cream-coloured baby rug made of the softest Australian wool against the skin of her face. The vision of Sarah Dougall, sister of Gus and Josh, and now married to Millie's adopted son, Jacko Benson, the current owner of The Mariner's Rest Hotel, filled her mind. Sarah had knitted this on those few occasions when her long days of work permitted any spare time.

Another misplaced item – a cutting from a Cooktown newspaper - she went to toss it up onto the box of papers on the bed. Abigail's eye caught the picture at the top of the article. Faint figures of herself and Henry standing on the deck of *The Northern Orchid* en route to Cairns where they were to catch the steamship taking them to London, ten years previously – 1882. She laughed outright at herself, who, sixteen years before then, had sworn long and loud never to return to London again. A soft gasp brought her hand to her lips at the rush of the excitement and pride she had felt when she stood with an arm on her tall son's shoulder. At fifteen years of age, he wanted to finish his schooling in London and go on to university to become a doctor like his uncle. A quiet sob of unknown origin caught her unawares. How close had she come recently to losing her son to the savage Arafura Sea? She gritted her teeth and gave thanks to God.

Henry was again safe in the care of a good friend, Max Young at Lavinia Downs. Impatience almost choked her. How long before Henry walked in through the doorway?

Nothing else of Henry's clothing remained in her possession. All had been given away over the years to either Eve and Gus's children or Jane and Mac's family.

A favourite ballgown, now a size too small for her, covered the bottom of the drawer. This should be given away, but somehow, she could not bring herself to do so. This was the gown she had worn at the church charity ball, when dancing with Max Young, two years following the death of his lovely wife, Lavinia. A sweet and bitter thrill scurried down her spine. The tears flowed as her hands busied themselves restoring order.

With the drawer closed and the box of papers on a chair beside her bed awaiting later perusal, Abigail stood and wiped her face with the bottom of her skirt. Her soft footsteps left the room. The door closed with a soft clunk of the latch.

A voice drifted up the back steps. It sounded like Gina, Eve's daughter.

"Are you upstairs, Miss Abigail?"

"I'm coming down now, Gina. Does George need an extra pair of hands?"

"No, I don't think so. Ma sent me over to tell you our dad is home for a couple of days. *The Northern Orchid* slipped into the harbour about an hour ago. Ma asked will you and the doctor join us for afternoon tea, later?"

"That will be lovely, Gina. I'm sure George will be there too unless called out to a patient."

Abigail watched Gina's lithe body spin around and run back to her own home.

Abigail's feet stopped. Like a bolt of lightning, a thought flashed inside her mind. *If 'The Northern Orchid' is in the area, Josh and Gus may have a freight delivery further north.*

CHAPTER TWENTY-EIGHT

Compromise

Henry felt at a loose end. Ed, Gordon and Max were in the office, with an early morning pot of tea, discussing the pros and cons of the pearling industry. Gordon had suggested to his father it may be a worthwhile investment. Max remained a loyal cattleman. Ed tried to remain unbiased and offered his experience both for and against the industry.

Henry hastened past the kitchen from where the crashing of pots and pans warned everyone within hearing; Victoria's day had not gotten off to a good start.

Clouds hung heavy in the sky as his feet carried him across the backyard to the stable, where Hans and Smiley were milking the house cows. As he opened the door, the mumble of their voices greeted him. The swish, swish, swish of the milk streams directed into the buckets and the munching of contented cows chewing on their token of hay, announced the start of another day.

Grateful though he may have been at being warm and safe – their recent experiences were still fresh in his memory – Henry's restless mind craved to continue his journey to Cooktown and home. He jumped when a sudden downpour of rain crashed upon the tin roof drowning out every other sound.

More damn rain. We'll never get home.

He knew inside himself; it was not only the delay due to the monsoon rains, which tormented him. Heavy upon his shoulders rested the responsibility of the knowledge David Young had almost certainly been poisoned by the long-term employee, whom Max had believed he could trust completely. Once the proof eventually arrived, after the samples he had packed securely in the box for travel reached the city, and were analysed, how was his friend Max and the family to cope with the outcome? What if the powers-that-be demanded the exhumation of the body? Henry's mind recalled the horror in Max's expression when faced with the possibility. But then, exhumations and autopsies were few and far between, although he knew the future promised a change if his London studies were anything to go by. Henry longed for a chance to talk all this over with his uncle, in Cooktown.

The sound of the milk being poured into the two shiny buckets for delivery to the kitchen interrupted his reverie.

Hans spoke, "I'll take these up to the house, Smiley. Let the calves out of the pen and with their mothers, will you? Then, can you push them all through to the day paddock?"

Henry looked up from his thoughts. He called good morning to Hans whose back disappeared towards the house.

"Want a hand with those calves?" Henry asked Smiley as his friend almost got stampeded by the three calves hungry for the left-over milk in the udders.

A companionable silence settled over the two friends as they ushered the animals into the paddock leading off from the stables. Henry placed the logs across the gateway to hang from the slots made in the large gateposts. Both Henry and Smiley leant against the top rail watching the calves butt their mothers in search of the promised milk.

"Henry, I had a dream the night before last. I wanted to tell you quietly between ourselves."

"What sort of dream, Smiley? Not another woman you've discovered?"

The grin flashed in the dawn light. "No, Henry, not another woman. I think you the one dreaming of women in the night." If it was possible, the grin expanded.

Henry gave Smiley a gentle punch on the upper arm. Both men laughed.

Henry's face lost its mirth. "So, Smiley, why do I need to know of your dreams?"

"It's a message to Mister Young and his family."

Henry's eyebrows lifted almost to his hairline. "How can you have a message for Max?"

"I asleep when these four pictures come into my head. In the first, two women, one old and one young, they dark skin like me, they run fast across the plains. A big dust cloud followed them. Then I see they climbing a steep hill on a narrow track between big rocks. At the bottom of the hill stand many dark faces of the tribe watching. Next picture they at the top of a cliff and look way out to the end of the earth. They hold hands and jump. Last, I see they lie broken on a flat rock way below."

Henry watched his friend closely. The dark skin glistened with perspiration. The whites of Smiley's eyes flashed. His friend retained the initial fear of his dream.

"Where did this message come from, Smiley?"

"A man visits me in the night. A tall dark-skinned man, like me, but he has only white in his hair like a cockatoo."

"That sounds like Snowy at the native camp near the river, but you've never been to the camp so how did you know of him? When did you meet him?"

"Never before I meet him, but I know he has the understandings, like my father, like my father teach me. He stays till I wake. I tell him, I will let the family know. Then he limps off, leaning on a long stick."

"Do you know what the dream means, Smiley?"

"The white-haired man wants the family to know these two women are gone forever. His people do not approve of what they did."

The sound of the meal gong shattered their quiet conversation.

"I will tell Max for you, Smiley. Now we'd best hurry, or Victoria may let us starve today. Those kitchen pots were given a fair thumping earlier this morning."

After breakfast, laughter and merriment rolled off the verandah, over the sheds and across the flats as Hans, with a comb and a pair of scissors in his hands, lined up the male population at the homestead from Max and his boys, to Bevan, the station-hand, and the two guests.

"I think you'll want something bigger than those scissors if you hope to trim the locks of Henry and Ed's scalps, Hans." The usually quiet Pete, now with only a half-inch of hair sprouting up over his head, laughed until the tears ran down his face.

"Hold up there, our locks aren't too bad. Doreen, at Mein, lopped off much of the overgrowth, when we were there." Ed pulled at the already shoulder-length brown hair. It must be all this rain you have up here it makes the hair grow fast."

Max moved over to sit in the chair Pete had vacated. He turned to the barber.

"Hans, you make sure you stop laughing before exercising those scissors near me."

This set everyone off laughing again. Victoria arrived with a large pot of hot tea. She watched the group at play, but her gaze slipped frequently to the one person with the unruly red hair who leant against the wall wearing a large smile under sparkling green eyes.

"Come on, Sis," Peter nudged her side. "I'll give you a hand to bring out the pannikins and the biscuits … or is it scones today."

Victoria smiled at her brother and turned with him towards the kitchen.

With his head feeling much lighter than it had for some time, despite Doreen's attempt at imposing order, Henry took an opportunity to corral Max, while on his own.

"You got a few minutes, Max?"

"Yes, of course, Henry. What is it?"

Henry led Max off on a walk around the house yard. He related the story of Smiley's dream.

Max never said a word for long moments. A frown burrowed into his forehead. He pulled off a stem of grass and chewed the soft end until it hung, demolished.

"You know, Henry, those magic men, and Snowy was a magic man in his earlier days, know things we can never guess."

"Yes, Max, I've seen enough between Smiley and his father, also a man of magic, to know they leave us miles behind in communication for all our pens, paper, postage systems, and telegraphs."

"What does Smiley say this message means?"

"Smiley said the young woman and the old woman have gone forever. He inferred the local tribe did not approve of the woman doing what they did to your brother. Apparently, they like living here near you and your family."

"Where will that leave us with your investigation and your samples for analysis, Henry?"

Without speaking, they walked out past the stables and watched the calves cavorting within the day paddock.

Eventually, Henry looked up at Max and spoke. "Max, to report this already-solved crime to the police will only be a time-waster for them. I think you and I should take the box of samples and bury them near your brother's grave. If you need to do anything more in the future, you'll be able to recover them at that time."

A long deep sigh whistled from Max's lips. "Thanks, Henry."

Max dragged his neckerchief over perspiration standing out across his forehead and dribbling down his stubbled cheeks.

"How the hell do I tell Victoria that the only mother she ever knew has killed her Uncle David?" Max drew in a long noisy breath before going on. He resettled the cloth around his neck. "Let alone tell her the woman has jumped off a cliff along with her daughter; the girl as close to Victoria as if she were her sister?"

Henry paused in the shade of the large mango tree on the north side of the house. He leant in against the rough bark of the trunk.

"Max, I'm not a father and never had a sister of my own. Smiley was my only real friend as a boy growing up. I cannot tell you what to do. I can only offer options." Henry scratched the back of his neck. "I'd suggest you reveal as little as possible of the facts – at this stage anyway. Keep it as brief as you can; perhaps, word has reached you of the death of Summer and Velvet due to an accident while on walkabout. Victoria is very sharp. She may guess at more than you might want."

The cicadas' drone outside almost drowned out the sound of the younger people saying their goodnights to each other as they packed up the playing cards.

Max threw himself into his office chair.

"Victoria, can you come into the office, please?" Max called to the form of his disappearing daughter on her way to her room. "There's something I'd like to talk over with you."

Victoria's eyes lit up. Immediately her mental processes began discarding all her school books to a place of no return.

"Victoria, my darling, I'm sorry to burden you with further sadness following the news of your Uncle David's passing." Max stood up and reached over to draw his daughter into his side. They both gazed unseeing through the open window. "I have received word from the native camp that our Summer and Velvet were killed accidentally while out on walkabout. It seems they slipped and fell from a cliff."

When she heard her father's words, the shock cleared everything but disbelief from Victoria's thoughts. Her mouth opened.

"That's impossible, Velvet was more sure-footed than a mountain goat." Her gaze lifted to stare at her father. "Besides, it's an odd time to be going on walkabout with the monsoon season upon us."

"Victoria, I cannot understand much of what the natives do or why. Perhaps the slippery terrain was the result of the rains and this caused them to fall."

Victoria's thoughts swirled inside her head like a torrent in a flooded creek. The two women, closest to her for her whole life, were dead. This could not be right. How can life be so cruel? Was it her own fault? Was God punishing her for trying to manipulate her father into allowing her to leave the convent? Tears trembled on her eyelashes but did not fall as another thought flashed within her mind.

What was Summer thinking about going on walkabout when she should have been home caring for Uncle David? Where exactly was God's hand in all of this?

Victoria felt the presence of her favourite nun at the convent, Sister Augustine. The vision of the nun's compassionate blue eyes and the sound of her voice as soft as talcum powder seeped into her head.

"God's reason is often hard to understand, my child. It is not our place to question his purpose. Keep your faith and pray to the Lord Almighty for strength and guidance."

The tears rolled down Victoria's tanned cheeks.

Henry had another week to curb his impatience. After morning sunshine, most days ended in heavy rain showers for short periods. Ed, Bevan and Henry ambled their horses on their way back from a session of treating the increased number of people now at the native camp. Bevan, the stockman, rode with the reins hooked over one foot slung across the saddle, while his hands manipulated the mouth organ between his lips.

Max greeted them at the back steps.

"I knew you were coming, I heard Bevan's music these past ten minutes." He turned to Bevan. "Did you talk to Snowy about sending Tilda and Sooky up to the house to learn how to cook and clean?"

"Yes, Boss. Snowy said he'll send them up first sun tomorrow."

"Thanks, mate. Victoria will really know she's alive. In my opinion, teaching someone to do a job is sometimes more trouble than doing the job yourself. We'll all have to tread lightly for a few days."

Max walked across to the stable where the men headed to unsaddle the horses, brush them down and release them. On the walk back to the house, the sound of galloping hoofbeats lifted all their heads. A rider approached. Water dripped from the horse's mane, from the rider and his wet trousers, and the saddle and the blanket roll. The grey horse's chest heaved.

Hans arrived from around the back of the kitchen with a digging fork in his muddy hands.

"It's Johnny with the mail, hopefully dry, wrapped in an oilskin in the bag on his back."

But Johnny had more than just the mail.

Smiley walked out from the verandah and relieved the man of the reins. He led the horse to the stable.

After Max had introduced everyone, he led them towards the house.

"Well, come on to the verandah and get a hot drink before you end up with the ague or something," Max then called to the kitchen. "Victoria, bring Johnny a hot cup of tea with a dash of rum in it, I think."

The kitchen window banged against the wall as Victoria opened it wide and poked her head through the gap.

"Coming right up, Dad. Hello, Johnny." Her head retreated inside.

While waiting for his drink, Johnny removed and opened the bag from his back. He unfolded the oilskin wrap around the bundle of mail before handing the lot over to Max.

Max skimmed through the mail passing two letters over to Bevan. He looked at Han's dirty hands and suggested he wash them first before he collected the one letter with his name on it. Most of the bundle contained newspapers – always a welcome arrival.

Max asked, "So, Johnny, where did you run into the rain?"

"It started before Deadman's Creek and continued right through to Rocky Crossing. I'll end up with webs between me toes if this continues much longer."

"You say that every summer, Johnny." Gordon grinned. "And if I remember, you're always threatening to go back to the desert."

Johnny attempted to look innocent but failed miserably. "A place'd be pretty boring if you had nothing to whinge about, I guess." Johnny sat on the step and withdrew a tobacco tin and his cigarette papers from his top pocket. With surprising delicacy, the thick work-hardened hands teased out a thin layer of tobacco and lay it along the length of the white paper before those same rough fingers rolled his smoke into a cigarette, thin at one end and thicker at the other. He looked left and right. "Geez, how's a man supposed to light a fag in this place? There's not a fire in sight."

Victoria's head reappeared at the kitchen window. "Here, Johnny – here's your tea and if you give me your cigarette, I'll light it from the fire in the stove." The cigarette and the pannikin of tea changed hands. Victoria disappeared again.

"Holy cow, Johnny, I've told you before, don't encourage Victoria to light your cigarettes. You'll have her smoking too," Max admonished.

More than a few moments passed after they heard the rattle of the firebox at the stove, and Victoria's appearance at the window. She passed the lit cigarette back outside.

"Here you are, Johnny, all fired up."

"What you done to me fag, girl, it's nearly all gone?"

"Rubbish, I only puffed it a bit to get it going."

Max rolled his eyes. "Now, Johnny, there must be more reason for you travelling up here through the miserable weather than to see us and get a drink of tea."

Johnny sucked on his cigarette and drizzled the smoke back out of his nostrils.

"There is, there is. The *Northern Orchid* dropped the last lot of mail off yesterdee. The captain, Josh Dougall, left you a note. He reckons you have two doctors stuck here who are needed in Cooktown. The *Northern Orchid* will pick them up on their return from Somerset, up north, in four days … so that will be three days now."

Johnny lifted his hat from his head and eased out a folded scrap of paper inserted within the leather band. The damp paper threatened to fall apart at each fold as he smoothed it out on the floorboards beside him. The words written in pencil presented a puzzle to read. He lifted the soggy paper over to Max.

"How am I to read this, Johnny?" Max lay the fragile note across his thigh with great care. "It's indecipherable. Why didn't you put it in the oilskin cloth with the other mail?"

Johnny scratched at his head. "Gus Dougall delivered it by hand and told me the message. When I realized it had been left out of the wrap, I just slipped it into me hat."

CHAPTER TWENTY-NINE

Transport

The smile on Henry's face was every bit as wide as the one dividing Smiley's face. Max Young led the group of riders from the homestead, east, towards the coast. Henry crammed the old felt hat discovered in the back room of the merchandise shop at Mein, down harder onto his head. Since having his red hair shorn recently, the sun had easy access to his naturally pale skin. Once more the sail cloth satchel hung around his neck and across his chest. It contained his and Ed's spare clothes now clean and mended by the hands of young Victoria.

The riders had eased into a single file due to much of the terrain of forest and narrow cuttings. Occasional glimpses of the coastline appeared as they approached their destination. The weather was in keeping with Henry's mood. Bright sunlight banished the clouds and dried up the land, even if only temporarily. It raised the heat and humidity, but the cessation of rain made travel more comfortable.

Max called a halt on the edge of another swollen creek. The large black and white dog which had been foraging along the side of the track raced back to flop on the ground nearby. Henry had lost count of the number of swollen creeks they crossed during the morning. The once pleasant sun of daybreak now beat down upon them with a vengeance. The suffocating heat engulfed everyone. Each creek crossing brought the relief of cool water splashing up around their bodies.

"Deadman's Creek," Max named the waterway as Peter and his sister Victoria, moved up to join him. The three of them spoke quietly together as Ed, Smiley and Henry watched the ominous flow of brown water rushing by. Henry untied the water-bag from his saddle and drank the clean water from the homestead tanks.

Max swung his horse about to speak to the group.

"Johnny reported a possible sighting of a crocodile near here last year. It's most likely the big lizard has long gone, but I'm not going to take any chances. I'll take the dog with me and cross first to stand watch on that high section of the bank on the other side with my rifle ready – just in case. Victoria will watch from this side until we're all across. You three will follow Pete." He nodded at Ed, Henry and Smiley. "Pete and I will then keep watch from over there until Victoria has crossed." Max watched the expressions on the three newcomer's faces and grinned. "Don't worry, she won't shoot you. She's the best shot of us all." All eyes turned to Victoria whose back was towards the group as she scrambled up the face of a huge boulder using the natural bumps and hollows as hand and foot holds. After taking up a position she turned to face the creek-crossing, where the men and horses were to pass. She settled herself and her gun steady against an outcrop of rock.

Max stretched out his right foot, still in the stirrup, and spoke to the dog. "Up, Caesar!" The animal ran towards the horse and leapt onto Max's foot, up his leg and across the saddle in a bound. Max caught the dog and settled it into position in front of him. "Crocs love dogmeat," he explained. He dragged his rifle out of its scabbard, lifted the reins and nudged his brown horse forward into the water.

In the middle of the stream, the water lapped the belly of the tall horse, but it was not too long before they reached the shallower area of the creek, where the sun sparkled like a waterfall of diamonds on the water running from the body and legs of the horse. Once across,

Max settled on a prime site from where he had a perfect view of the crossing. The dog and horse rested in the shade of the trees nearby.

Peter followed. His brown horse with the white slash across its forehead showed some reluctance to enter the water, but Pete insisted. He turned and threw a reassuring nod back to Ed riding another brown horse minus any blaze. Henry and Smiley's eyebrows lifted as they glanced at each other. Both smiles held some reservation, but Henry moved his chestnut horse along to follow Ed. Smiley came up behind him on his grey horse. Henry gave a last glance back to where Victoria remained steady on the rock with her weapon at the ready. Her concentration focused on the creek.

Meanwhile, twenty yards upstream in the shallows, where the foliage of the small bushes and long grasses danced with the current as they floated on the surface, the long thick body slithered along in water a little more than two-feet deep. The claws on the feet at the ends of its stubby legs toed the creek bed, while its amber-brown eyes glistened just below the surface as it moved smoothly along, visible to only the experienced. The reptile's snout with its uneven, but powerful teeth, moved towards the sound of voices and splash of water. It stopped only inches from the edge of the water-covered track. Muddy water and partially drowned foliage provided complete camouflage.

The swollen crossing was less than thirty yards wide, but Henry felt as if it may have been as many miles. His head swivelled from left to right hoping not to see any sign of a crocodile. Every second he expected to hear the sound of shots from the two riflemen – well, one man and a slip of a girl. The swirl of flood waters matched the swirl of anxiety in his stomach. A sharp sigh escaped his lips when he felt the horse's feet lifting higher to walk through the shallower water. His body relaxed.

Unblinking eyes watched the brown horse with the white blaze and its rider pass only feet away from its slack mouth. Water sprayed into the air as the hooves of another brown horse and its rider, Ed, splashed through the shallower water. The chestnut horse, now level with the crocodile, skittered and danced, warned by instinct alone. Henry tightened his grip on the reins and clenched his knees against the saddle. The crocodile lunged upwards.

Henry's head swung around. His shocked gaze struggled to make sense of the confusion inside his head. A brain in disbelief attempted to translate the danger rising towards him.

Behind Henry, adrenaline surged through Smiley's veins. He kicked up the grey horse and threw himself over the animal's head to place himself between the reptile and Henry. Both horses shied. Two shots rang out – close together. A curtain of blood sprayed up into the air. The bottom jaw of the crocodile hung loosely by a thread of skin – the skull shattered. The second bullet entered the opposite side before travelling through the heart. It disintegrated a front leg as it exited. The huge body slammed into Smiley. Sharp claws of the remaining front leg pierced Smiley's right shoulder and arm. The dark skin fell open as the weight of the dead animal dragged the claws downwards. The reptile's top jaw crashed down upon Smiley's skull and the stained, pointed teeth ploughed their way down his back as the dead crocodile began to sag.

Henry's horse threw its head up cracking Smiley's head near the temple bone. The full force of Smiley and the crocodile landed against Henry. He felt himself slipping from his terrified mount. He dug his heels into the stirrups and wrapped his arms around his friend as best he could, but the weight of the crocodile dragged both men down. At the last minute, Henry remembered to slip his feet out of the stirrups as the horse bolted out from underneath. Leather reins flew in the air around its head and stirrups thumped against its side, when Henry's horse bolted in a wall of water. The two men and the crocodile landed in the creek with Henry beneath the bodies of both Smiley and the reptile. To Henry, the attack seemed to have been in slow motion, but in fact, only seconds had passed.

Ed's head swivelled around at the first sound of the reptile's lunge and the gunshots. His glance took in the scene. Without another thought, he slithered from his saddle and jumped sideways to avoid Henry's horse as it raced off tossing its head in the air, while the whites of its eyes shone in the sunlight. The jangling of the hobble chains carried around each horse's neck did little to calm the animal's terror. Ed dragged his feet through the water to where Henry struggled to lift himself out from under the two bodies. Smiley's head remained under the water.

"Help me," Henry called as he strained to roll the corpse of the crocodile off his friend.

With strength only accessible in moments of intense fear and horror, the two men managed to roll the huge reptile over and off Smiley's body. Blood thickened the already opaque muddy waters. The two doctors each reached one of their arms under an armpit and the other under the torso of Smiley's unresponsive tattered body. With Smiley hanging between them, they lifted their feet high and rushed out of the water to the bank.

Peter jumped from his horse and ran back to help drag the inert Smiley higher up the bank where the grass provided a softer bedding.

CHAPTER THIRTY

Northern Orchid

"Whoa there," Gus Dougall's feet moved with the roll of the ship. His hands adjusted the angle of the two pannikins to prevent spillage. He stood at the open doorway to the captain's cupboard, the small room they now used as a chart room. "We'll be in for a bit of a blow before morning, I'll be betting, brother."

Josh looked up from the pages of his Log Book. "I guess we can expect no less – the monsoon season is fast approaching." He took up a pencil from the ledge and began to mark the large chart on the wall with notes copied from the book.

"I've brought you a hot toddy, Josh." Gus stepped inside and placed a tin cup in the circular rim of steel made for that very purpose and set in the corner of the room at waist height. He sipped his drink and watched as his brother entered the latest depth readings and other points of note onto the wall chart.

"Thanks, that will go down nicely. I've just about finished here," Josh stood back, as far as the narrow cabin allowed, to examine his entries. "We'll need to have these charts upgraded when we get back to Brisbane. This one looks like a drunken spider has been swimming in the ink well and then crawled all over it." He took up his drink and swallowed deeply. "The ship all settled for the night?"

"Yes, Josh. O'Brien's on the first watch, he's got things in hand."

Silence filled the room as both men analysed the map held firmly across the wall with light timber edging and small tacks. It was Josh who next spoke.

"Do you remember the first trip we made up this way with Captain Sloan?"

"How could I forget? The map he used was grey with age and indecipherable."

"To us maybe, but Captain Sloan seemed to read information in every crease."

Both men smiled at the memories of their mentor and friend. Gus held up his cup, "A toast to a good and brave man."

Josh lifted his pannikin from the holder and touched his brother's cup. "To Captain Sloan." He raised the pannikin again. "A toast to Jimmy Dougall whose spirit still walks these planks."

"To our dad." Gus followed suit.

Again, the comfortable silence fell within the timbered walls. Josh broke the silence again.

"I looked at those figures you left for me and your proposal."

Gus raised his eyebrows along with his gaze. He felt the excitement flow through his veins, but his face remained deadpan. It had been weeks since he first suggested they look to preparing for their future, but he knew from a lifetime of experience, how Josh loved life as it was and had little stomach for any change, particularly if it meant changing his sails for engines.

"Do you think we'll have enough money put aside to purchase a steel-hulled, motor-driven vessel within five years?"

"The bank manager seems to think so. He offered us a loan to purchase two if we wanted."

This time it was Josh's eyebrows that disappeared within his unruly hairline of dark hair splattered with grey streaks.

"You do understand you won't get me sailing in one of those noisy smelly machines, without the sails to break the monotony."

Gus's grin escaped. He knew better than to mention Josh was happy to have the auxiliary engine fired up when they passed through unfamiliar seas.

"Never thought for a moment you would, brother." He took a deep breath to contain his excitement. "The plan would be for both the second and/or third ship, which each require fewer crew members, to work the long journeys such as to the top-end. They'll have a quicker turn-around than the sailing ships. We can use the *Northern Orchid* on the shorter deliveries out of Brisbane – maybe as far as Rockhampton to the north and possibly Sydney to the south."

Josh stared into the dregs in his pannikin. "I take it this has all come about now your Eve and the kids are returning to Brisbane with Doctor George and Miss Abigail in the near future."

Gus's grin revealed itself in full. "I cannot deny that has crossed my mind."

Josh laughed. "You pair will be breeding like rats in the ship's bilge. Where are they going to live? Not in Jacko and Sarah's hotel, I hope. There'll be no room left for guests."

Gus shook his head and chuckled. "No, I wouldn't put that upon our sister. Sarah has enough to do. We bought the Turner's house over the back fence from Doctor George's Brisbane surgery."

"And when is this all going to happen?"

"What do you mean, the new house or the shipbuilding?"

"The house moving – give me a few more weeks to chew on the other."

"Once we pick up Henry and his doctor friend and Smiley from Pascoe River and deliver them to Cooktown, Doctor George will be about ready to make the move to his surgery in Brisbane. Eve and the kids will be travelling with them."

Josh threw the last of the tin mug's contents down his throat and handed the empty over to Gus.

"Will you clean these up for me? I'll just do this last entry and then I plan to get a sleep."

Gus took up the two mugs and turned to leave. "Night, Josh."

"Night, Brother."

CHAPTER THIRTY-ONE

Smiley

Henry, Ed and Pete stood. They took a moment to stretch their aching muscles before they knelt again in front of the wounded man.

"His back is shredded," Peter whispered in awe.

"I think most of the blood we saw was from the crocodile," Ed commented. "I can't feel any wounds on his front."

They rolled the body onto its back. Only minor lacerations were visible on the chest and abdomen.

"He received a nasty crack on the skull when he collided with the head of my horse," Henry explained. "That's what's knocked him out."

"Lucky whoever it was shot the lower jaw from the animal, or we'd have twice as much damage to his body."

Pete looked over to where his father and sister remained at their positions guarding against any further dangers.

"If you fellows are alright here, I'll go join Dad in watching Victoria come across."

"Yes, of course, Pete," Henry spoke without lifting his head as he examined the unmoving body. He turned towards Ed. "Help me roll him onto his side?"

Ed reached over and rested his hand on Henry's shoulder.

"He's still breathing, Henry. That's a good sign."

Both men gasped at the extent of the damaged tissue on Smiley's back, right shoulder and arm.

Henry bit his lip and drew in a long breath before he felt steady enough to speak.

"These lacerations will heal as long as he doesn't end up with an infection, which is possible considering the rotten flesh a croc eats. It's this coma that has me worried. There's not a flicker in him at all."

At that moment, Max and Pete joined them. Victoria remained in the background. Her watch on the dangerous waters of the creek never faltered.

"How's Smiley?" Max asked.

"Unconscious at the moment, Max." Henry slapped the side of Smiley's face in the hope of assisting the return of consciousness, but he received no response.

"How far are we from the coast, compared to the homestead, Max?"

"About ten miles to Johnny's hut and near twenty back to the house."

"I'm thinking we should move forward then. I know the *Northern Orchid* has a comprehensive medicine chest – or they used to. I'm sure Josh and Gus have followed Captain Sloan's practice in maintaining one." Henry dragged the satchel from his neck and pulled out his old shirt. He began to tear the cloth into strips.

"Henry, use my old shirt too. It'll take more than one shirt to cover this lot." Ed knelt to help Henry prepare pads and ties to cover Smiley's wounds.

"I guess with two doctors and a medical chest of note, Smiley will be in safe hands, Henry." Max stood up and turned to his son. "Pete, round up our horses, will you?" He turned back to Henry. "Do you want us to tie Smiley over a horse to transport him to Johnny's place, Henry?"

With his black felt hat long since disappeared downstream, Henry's red hair highlighted the pallor of his face, as the shock of his own whisper with death registered.

"It's the head injury I'm worried about, Max. If Smiley hangs with his head down, the rush of blood may cause more trouble. Do you agree, Ed?" Henry looked up at his fellow doctor who nodded in agreement. "If you all help to lift him onto the saddle in front of me, I'll hold him steady. Max, can you put the lead on my horse and let it follow you? I can then concentrate on supporting Smiley."

"No trouble, Henry. If you think that's best, that's what we'll do."

To Henry, holding the weight of the unconscious Smiley whose body tended to slip and slide with the movement of the horse beneath them, the last ten miles seemed a dozen times further than the earlier twenty had been. A tremble began in his thighs, which carried the weight of them both. The quiver spread up to his arms and dragged at his shoulders in a world of burning pain. Blood from Smiley's wounds mixed with his own sweat. He felt it trickle down his chest. Henry supported Smiley's skull, where it rested back tucked in between his head and shoulder. What felt like rivers of blood ran from the scalp wounds and down his back. The sensation sent accompanying shivers down his spine. It took all his concentration to focus on how best to deal with the situation instead of letting his imagination draw horror images in his mind.

Every one of his muscles screamed in agony. Relief flowed through his body at the sight of smoke drifting up from the rusty, crooked chimney of Johnny's slab hut. Max led them over to what appeared to be a stable, a short distance from the shack. Rust marks on a water tank close by matched those on the walls of the shed. Henry remained on his horse, while the others dismounted and tied their animals to the hitching rail in the shade of the trees. A whistle from Max called up the black and white dog which was sent into the shed with a single word of command.

"Snakes!"

With its head to the ground, the dog raced inside the three-walled stable. It sniffed into every corner and crack of the area where packed-down ant-bed made a hardened floor. It climbed over the six stretchers lined up against the back wall. The hessian bagging on each of these had been drawn taut over two poles supported by crossed timber, of different sizes and types, at each end. The far section of the shed had been separated from the human campsite for the use of animals by a few rough-hewn timber railings. The door of a dusty pot-belly stove in the centre of the area sagged open. In front of this, the dog growled. The busy nose became busier. Its tail threatened to wind itself from the canine body. The door of the pot-belly stove screeched when a long brown snake uncoiled itself and shot out of the gap. The black and white dog jumped – all four feet lifted off the ground. The snake slithered under the elevated body and off towards the animal section of the shed. The black and white dog followed in quick pursuit. The growls converted to noisy barking.

Max lifted his head at the chase but shrugged his shoulders before he returned to help with Smiley's transfer. The men supported Smiley's limp body as they lifted him with care to the ground. The horses under the trees shuffled restlessly when, nearby, the dog brought the pursuit to an end. The dog's jaw clamped around the reptile just a few inches behind its head. The weight of the snake almost proved to be too much for the dog, but the strong neck of the canine swung back and forth, belting the snake's head against, first the ground, and then a tree trunk. When satisfied with its endeavours, the dog dropped its prey and stepped back, daring the broken body to move. Even the arrival of Johnny Hayden did not break its concentration until Max walked over to inspect the snake's status.

Once released, the dog gave a half-hearted bark at the newcomer who was known to him, but he remained steadfast at Max's side.

"I see you made it here, then. What's happened to the young fellow?" Johnny dropped the box he held in one hand and the five-gallon tin he had been holding by its improvised handle to the ground beside him. "I saw you had someone wounded so I brung the medicine chest. I don't know all that's in it – me sister gave it to me, when I visited her in Brisbane ten year ago. I'm happy to use kerosene on any wounds meself. That always does the trick." He lifted a tattered straw hat and scratched his head. "Them's cooked crabs in that there tin, to have for your supper, and a damper I made this morning."

"Thanks, Johnny, that will be much appreciated. We ran into crocodile trouble at Deadman's Creek. Smiley saved Henry's life, but he's not in good shape himself."

Henry, Ed and Peter looked up briefly to greet Johnny but their attention fell right back on the patient. The doctors began to adjust those bandages disturbed by the journey.

"Oooh." Victoria's hand flew up over her mouth to cover the soft gasp at her first sight of Smiley's face where the claws of the crocodile had left one eyelid half torn off. Deep gouges to both cheeks and a split in the soft tissue of his nostrils also lay open exposing the underlying tissue. "Oh, his poor eye," she whispered. Max walked over and led his daughter away into the shed.

"Here, Victoria, can you sort out the bunks and set up these crabs and damper Johnny has cooked for us? Put Smiley's bunk close to the door so we don't have to carry him too far."

Max turned when Henry's voice called from outside. "Max, can you give us a hand here?"

With Henry supporting Smiley's head, Max and Ed took the weight on either side of the torso, while Peter and Johnny carried the lower limbs. The procession made slow progress to where Victoria had pulled the stretcher nearer to the open front of the shed.

With much shuffling and groans from them all, they lay the body down on the hessian stretcher.

"Was that a groan from Smiley I heard, Henry?" Max asked.

"It was, Max." A nod of his head accompanied the words forced out between Henry's clenched jaws.

"That's got to be a good sign, hasn't it?"

"It brings me hope, but experience has taught me not to build my hopes too early when dealing with a head injury." Henry realigned Smiley's body after he checked the heart rate and the bleeding from the wounds, while Ed walked over to inspect the contents of Johnny's medicine chest.

He held up items of interest one by one. "There are half a dozen pipettes – you may want to irrigate the eye using one of them. There are strips of clean linen and a pair of scissors. Ah, a needle holder, suture needles, catgut and also cotton thread." Ed held these up in the air. "We can stitch a few of those wounds together." Next, Ed held up a small jar with a rusted tin lid. "The writing is almost faded, but I think you'll find this is zinc oxide. Fancy finding that over here in Australia. It was hard enough to get in London." His fingers explored deeper within the contents of the box. Next to surface was a small tin about seven inches long with a lid; it rattled, when shaken. After a few grunts and growls, Ed released the lid to discover three solid scalpels with different sized blades. A small stone for sharpening the blades was included. Ed's hand pushed aside an enamelled kidney dish, a pair of forceps and more strips of clean cotton. Ed cut short an explosive laugh. "Will you look at this? I have in my hand a bottle of carbolic acid. A small bottle I grant you, but we can assume it is a concentrated solution. Diluted it will make an ideal wound wash." Ed turned the bottle around in his hand. "It will be better than nothing and hopefully better than Johnny's kerosene."

Henry sat back on his haunches. He looked behind him to where Victoria was lighting the stove with some twigs and sticks Peter had delivered.

"Victoria, when you boil the water for the tea will you pour some into a pannikin and put it aside to cool for me? I'll use it to irrigate Smiley's eyes and I'll want some to make up a weak carbolic solution."

"Yes, Henry, is there anything else I can do for you?"

"I think both Ed and I would kill for a drink of tea." Henry's gaze turned to Ed. "Once we have our disinfectant mixture, I'll try to patch up a few of these wounds, will you cut if I sew?"

The sun hung low in the western sky when Ed took up the scissors and knelt on the other side of the stretcher, while Henry picked up the needle holder and clasped a curved cutting-edged needle between the grip. Ed took up a roll of the catgut thread and measured out a length.

"Will you be sewing some internal stitches on the deeper wounds or leaving them all to drain?"

"Just a few in the worst of the wounds. I think a few mattress sutures will help hold the skin together, but I'll need to keep them slack for drainage, as you say. I'll use the cotton thread for the skin sutures."

Max, Johnny and Peter sat on a log outside talking softly. Victoria divided her time between keeping the fire going, checking the water in the billy on the stove and tiptoeing back and forth to watch the doctors at work.

It took a long time to make an improvement on most of the deeper wounds. When satisfied with his work so far, Henry sat back with his hands resting on his knees.

"Now we'll see if there's anything we can do with the eyelid." He stood and stretched his body and glanced over at Ed. "This will be like sewing a woman's lace collar with stitches of rope." He turned to ask Victoria if there was a hurricane light available, but she had already anticipated his request and was in the process of lighting a lantern using a burning stick from the stove. Henry selected the smallest needle and finest thread before again, taking up his position at the side of Smiley's still body. As he did so, the creak of his knee joints sounded loud in the quiet of the shed.

After Ed and Henry tied the last wound dressing over Smiley's right eye, both doctors stood up to look down upon their handiwork. Doubt at their success lurked in their eyes as they stretched their aching limbs. Victoria took it upon herself to collect and wash the instruments used in the surgical process. Peter was dispatched to refill her bucket with clean water from the rainwater tank outside.

Max led the two exhausted men outside to wash at the same water tank.

"You have done admirable work on Smiley. You have given him every chance of survival." Max reached over to shake the hands of both men. "Now, come and eat." He directed Henry and Ed to the log outside the hut to eat the cleaned crab and damper. A pannikin of tea for each of the doctors sat upon the stump nearby.

After a final check upon his friend and patient, Henry settled upon a stretcher placed beside the invalid. Despite his exhaustion following a day in the saddle, deep sleep eluded him as he relived the visions of the crocodile attack. By the time the moon rose over the horizon, only the creak of the stretcher under his restless body, the croak of the frogs in the many puddles, and the hoot of an owl in the trees outside broke the silence within the camp.

Several times during the night, Henry woke bleary-eyed to check on Smiley. He found some consolation in realizing the wounded man's condition did not seem to be deteriorating, but on the other hand, there was little sign of improvement. It was Ed who woke him with a drink of tea and a piece of damper in his hand as the sun broke through the gaps in the foliage of the trees outside.

"No change then, Henry, I see."

"No, Ed, I do hope the *Northern Orchid* arrives today as planned. I'll feel much better when we get Smiley back to Cooktown and into Uncle George's experienced hands."

Pounding hoofbeats broke the stillness of the morning. Johnny rode into the camp.

"The ship's here. I've been to the jetty to meet the mate. They're bringing a canvas stretcher to carry your friend. I told 'em I'd bring horses for 'em to ride back up here, without wasting too much time." A while later, they watched Johnny and a line of horses, heading back down the track.

Max walked over twice to speak to Henry but turned aside. On the third time, Max pulled a wrinkled grubby envelope from his top pocket.

"Henry … er … I'd appreciate it if you'd give this note to your mother. I hope you don't mind. It's just about the plans for Victoria next year."

With a nod, Henry pushed the letter down into his own stained shirt pocket, scrunching the epistle up even further.

"Of course, Max."

Later, when Gus Dougall, the mate and engineer of the *Northern Orchid,* approached their camp, Henry clenched his jaw and held tight to his emotions. The years fell away to when he was a young lad. Gus and his brother Josh, often visited his mother and Uncle George during the brothers' early days learning their trade on the sea.

The memories rushed into his mind like an ocean tide. He tried to smile.

"I see you've been working under those engines of yours too much Gus, you're rubbing off all the hair on your head."

It was nearly mid-day when Gus Dougall led the procession of Henry, Ed, Max, Peter, Victoria, Johnny, and four strong sailors, carrying Smiley on a litter of sail canvas stretched between two oars. They made their way on foot down the narrow two-mile track to where a small jetty reached out into the rising tide. Secured in position by two leather girth straps, the wounded man rocked with the motion of his frail means of transport. At regular intervals, the two teams carrying the man on the litter alternated.

"I figured the jolly-boat might have been too small to carry everyone along with the wounded man, so we brought the long boat instead," Gus explained the rationale for his choice made between the two rowing boats kept on the *Northern Orchid*.

Transferring the patient onto the long boat proved to be rather tricky with the tide running and the wind rising, but the years of experience between the seamen ensured no one took a dunking. Henry and Ed took up positions near the bow of the boat on either side of Smiley's head. As the oarsmen pulled away from the wooden jetty, Henry looked up, to be captured again by the piercing blue gaze of Victoria Young. Before his brain had time to remind him that she was only a young girl, his smile shone back. He lifted a hand and acknowledged everyone waving to them in farewell. The calls of best wishes for the recovery of Henry's friend rang out across the waters above the sound of the rising wind.

The ache in Victoria's legs, as she climbed back up to Johnny's hut from the beach, was nothing compared to the ache in her heart as she caught glimpses through the trees, of the *Northern Orchid* in full sail.

Henry filled her thoughts. How must he be feeling carrying his wounded friend home? From what she had seen of the two together, Smiley was more than a friend – he was a brother to Henry when they were children. This idea triggered her mind to uncover the memories buried inside her head for the past few days. The vision of her childhood friend, Velvet, and the only mother she ever knew, Summer, and how their laughter echoed around the house every day. Another pain, like the sharp stab of a knife into her heart drew forth a deep sigh. How can life be so cruel? How is it things can change so quickly? She appreciated her father's attempt to hide from her the fact that Summer had killed their Uncle David, but Victoria missed little of the goings-on in the house. As far as she knew, her best friend Velvet had nothing to do with Uncle David dying, but now she and her mother were gone forever.

Victoria looked up through a gap in the trees to see the *Northern Orchid* disappear behind the coastal headland. Her heart and thoughts rolled back to her initial contemplations.

How long was it going to be until she saw Henry again? She almost choked on a strangled sob as a more heart-breaking question posed itself. Images bounced around inside her head of numerous beautiful sophisticated women throwing themselves like petals along his pathway when he returned to Brisbane with his mother and Uncle George. He was ten years older than her. What chance did she have; an uncouth country girl with no social graces whatsoever?

Victoria gasped at the touch of her brother Peter's hand on her shoulder.

"Don't feel too bad. It's only a few months before you'll see Henry every day, Sis. I overheard Dad and Henry talking. Miss Abigail suggested you stay with them, while you go to school in Brisbane."

Victoria did not look up at her brother's words. She held her head down blinking furiously at the tears which refused to cease.

"I don't know what you're talking about," she mumbled.

Henry boarded the *Northern Orchid* using the rope ladder. The degree of difficulty of this task was compounded by the buffeting of his body by the rising wind. Several times, when his feet slipped off the rope rungs, he felt his weight dangling in mid-air, held only by the stranglehold grip of his hands on the ladder. With his arms and legs trembling, Henry felt like an awkward spider as he lifted himself over the bulwarks and onto the ship's deck where he landed in a heap at Gus Dougall's feet. A bell clanged twice, nearby. Henry's head turned towards the sound. He looked up to the sky.

"Am I correct in saying the bells are telling us it's about 1 pm?" Henry asked as he stood up.

Gus smiled. "Yes, each ring for the half-hour of a watch. Two bells mean one hour past the start of the afternoon watch, which began at midday. In your terms, it's 1 pm. I'll let the men settle you all into the cabins on deck. We have no passengers in there until Cooktown. Josh will be impatient to catch the wind, so I'll leave you to it. The boilers have not been fired up today, so the men will have to do it the hard way, without steam."

From their position on the deck of the *Northern Orchid,* Henry supervised three sailors as they hauled the stretcher carrying Smiley from the long boat. From down below, Ed and two sailors guided the stretcher as best they could.

No sooner had the sailors settled Smiley onto the bunk in one of the four cabins towards the stern of the ship, than they disappeared at the sound of Josh's voice roaring across the decks. Within a few minutes, the sailors hauled the long boat onto the deck for storage in its davit. Sunlight glistened in the water as it poured off the vessel and over the timber decking. The pad of the men's feet and the grind of the capstan they pushed around in circles to haul up the anchor, fell on Henry and Ed's ears as they rolled the patient into a more comfortable position. The rumble of the anchor chain running through the hawse access hole sent a vibration through the whole ship. By the time the doctors had checked all Smiley's wounds, the thundering noise of the unfurling sails caught on the wind echoed out over the sea.

"Did you notice, the swelling on his temple has doubled in size in the last twenty-four hours, Henry?"

"Yes, Ed, I'm in no doubt it's the head injury we have most to worry about, despite the horrendous skin lacerations."

"I'm surprised the journey down to the ship on the litter did not stir him to consciousness." Ed sat on the floor with his back against the wall of the cabin. A long yawn filled the air. He rubbed his bloodshot eyes. "Henry, have you thought about the risk of tetanus?"

"Ed, I'm trying not to think about that. There'll be no chance to access the new serum over here in the antipodes. Even in London it was classified as experimental use only, despite the successful testings performed."

"No, I suppose you're right." Ed stood up and leant against the frame of the open doorway, breathing in the sea air. "Nothing smells as good as the ocean." He turned back to watch the rise and fall of Smiley's chest. "Look at his tongue. He'll die of dehydration if we don't try to get some fluid into him. I'll go find a bucket of water. We can try to drip it in through a pipette if there is one on this ship." Ed turned to exit the cabin as the ship caught a large wave, which sprayed up and over the deck in a liquid wall. Ed crashed heavily against the doorframe.

Henry looked up and chuckled. "Oh dear, you've been away from the sea far too long. It looks like you're becoming a landlubber."

Ed rubbed his arm. "I'll give you another hour and I bet you're spewing up your guts, boyo."

"I didn't when we were on …," Henry paused. He did not want to think about the sinking of the *Pink Pearl*. He felt sure Ed would prefer not to be reminded of the loss of his pearling friends.

With Ed departed on his search for clean water and sitting all alone beside Smiley's unresponsive form, Henry listened to the crack of the sails in the wind. He felt the emotion rush up and down his body like the waves rolling in and out along the sand of a beach.

"Oh, Smiley, my friend, my brother. You saved my life. Are you now to lose yours?" The whisper fell, along with the tears that would not be denied. He dropped his head onto the mattress beside Smiley's shoulder.

It was the sound of voices outside which stirred Henry. He sat up rubbing his aching neck as he did so. Ed arrived with a lidded can of water in one hand and a large box in the other.

"Sorry I was so long. I took a wrong turn and ended up in the engine room. Gus was tearing a strip off his offsider who had dropped off to sleep during his absence this morning and allowed the fire to go out under the boiler. The steam pressure had dissipated and Josh was hopping mad in the wheelhouse calling for the engine. Apparently, he likes to have the engine at the ready, when he travels along these northern channels, even though he uses the sails. He believes there are still more reefs to be discovered and he'd prefer to have the engine available to get him out of trouble if need be." Ed sat the water can on the floor with the box beside it. He lifted the lid of the box and delved through the contents. "Josh sent down his medicine kit. There seems to be all of those things that were in Johnny Hayden's kit with a few extras. I'm not sure if we can use them. Dover's Powder for typhus, Sulphate of Copper for canker for example, but they do have some analgesics and a lot more bandages."

Ed grasped a small bottle in his hand and lifted it in the air. "Will you look at this, more Iodine? We can certainly use that on Smiley's wounds."

"Have they got a pipette?'

"Yes, here it is – several actually." Ed passed the small glass pipe with the bulb at one end over to Henry and pushed the water can across the floor before removing the tin lid.

Henry took the pipette and drew up a tube of water. Gentle hands placed the tip between the swollen cracked lips. He squeezed the bulb lightly to let the fluid drip into Smiley's mouth. Only ten drops fell, when Smiley's chest heaved, as he struggled to cough. Without any words passed between them, the two doctors rushed to roll him onto his side.

"At least he has a gag reflex. There is hope for him yet, Henry."

After several minutes they tried offering another few drops of water with a similar result.

"Henry, you look beat, why don't you go into the cabin next door and catch some sleep – there's no one in any of these cabins. I'll stay here with Smiley until you wake up. You can do the night shift later, while I sleep."

There was no argument in Henry, only gratitude. He made his way to the cabin next door. It seemed as if he was asleep before his head even hit the pillow.

Confusion filled his mind when Henry awoke to the sound of dishes rattling nearby. The movement of the ship puzzled him for a moment. Everything was in darkness. He jumped up and opened the cabin door to find dusk settled and lantern light pouring out from the cabin next door.

"You're awake then, Henry. You're just in time for something to eat. A lad named Sam has delivered our meals to the cabin behind this one. He said it's a sitting room for the first-class passengers when they have them."

Henry nodded. "Any change in Smiley?"

"No, Henry, I'm sorry. Now you go and eat first before you take over here. I'll grab a bite after you, and then I'll be off to catch a bit of shut-eye."

In the sitting room, Henry found three comfortable lounge chairs and a small table holding a large tray with two plates of food. It looked like a fish stew. Steam rose from two pannikins of tea. He shovelled the food into his mouth without tasting a morsel. The heat of the tea governed his thirst and the rate of each swallow.

At the door to Smiley's cabin, Henry watched the unmoving body of his boyhood friend, with his skin even darker in the poor lighting. A tremor shook his body at the memory of the saltwater crocodile rising from the muddy water less than thirty-six hours before. The fear and shock again rocked him. Henry marvelled at the courage required for Smiley to throw himself forward like he did – right into the crocodile's mouth. Smiley must have known the risk he was taking. Gratitude for his own life almost undid his composure.

He watched Ed struggle to his feet groaning all the way.

"Alright, Henry, I'm off to eat and sleep. Nothing here has changed. I did manage to get a few more drops of water into his mouth with very little coughing this time. I'm not too sure if that's good or bad, but he did seem to swallow it down."

Henry took up his position on the floor beside Smiley's head. He checked the heartbeat and the wounds as best he could in the light of the lantern hanging on the wall at the head of the bunk. He started at the sound of a voice in the open doorway.

"G'day, Henry, it's good to see you, even in these poor circumstances." Josh Dougall's tall frame moved inside to shake

Henry's hand as he rose to his feet. "I'm sorry to see Smiley in such a bad way."

"It's good to see you too, Josh. It's been a while – ten years about." Henry stared for a moment at the reflection of the lantern light in the greying hairs on Josh's head. He briefly wondered when that happened.

"Gus was telling me Smiley saved your life in a croc attack."

"He did." Henry drew in a tattered breath. "He is an amazing fellow."

"He always was, if I remember him when the two of you kids ran wild in the bush around Cooktown."

Henry chuckled. "We did, didn't we."

"Your poor mother – she spent half her life wondering where you were; although I don't think she really worried about you when you were with Smiley." Josh took in the strained face before him and had an inkling of the emotions Henry must be feeling for the state of his friend now. "Your Mother was telling me, when I caught up with her recently in Cooktown, you've been swimming the waters of the Gulf of Carpentaria and tramping across Cape York since I last saw you."

This time Henry's chuckle broke through. "Not by choice, Josh, I can tell you that."

"Well, one day, at a better time, I want to hear your tale." Josh turned to leave. "You know if you want anything, just give a hoy. The crew all know to get you whatever you need."

"Whereabouts are we now?"

"We'll spend the night here just south of Cape Sidmouth. Tomorrow night we should make Cape Melville and then the next at Cape Flattery before we reach Cooktown the following day."

"Thanks, Josh, goodnight."

" 'Night, Henry."

The night dragged on slowly. As the *Northern Orchid* rocked on a gentle sea, Henry struggled to keep his eyelids from drooping. Several times he tried to offer water from the pipette but was doubtful of his success. He rinsed the wounded eye with some of the water. The larger wounds had continued to leak a little serous ooze into the dressings. He made a mental note to change the dressings in the morning when he had Ed to help with the lifting. Subconsciously, he listened to the sound of the time passing as recorded in the half-hour bell code. The shuffle of the feet across the deck at shift change did not go unnoticed.

An hour pre-dawn, Henry's head rested on the bed. The green eyes closed. Dreams filled his mind. Dreams of Smiley and himself as children, sitting by a bundle of grass and twigs. Again, he heard Smiley laughing at his weak attempts at spinning the firestick to set up a spark. He felt the smile crack his lips as they raided an old log for its witchety grubs. He shook his head at how the taste of dirt in his mouth made him spit. He remembered the times when Smiley stood on the river bank, still and silent, for ever so long and when asked, explained how he was listening for the crocodile singing nearby. Once satisfied there was no crocodile in residence, he had no qualms about jumping into the water for a swim. If only we had taken the time to stand and listen to the crocodile's music at Deadman's Creek.

Henry woke with a start. The ship had become alive with footsteps, the grind of the capstan and the rumble of the anchor chain. Muted calls from the captain as piccaninny dawn threatened, but lanterns remained alight on the deck. He rubbed the sleep from his eyes and stroked Smiley's head.

"You awake there, Smiley? It's about time you stopped malingering about there and woke up." He choked at the last words when not even a flicker of an eyelid indicated his words were heard.

When relieved by Ed at breakfast time, he could only shake his head and remark, "No change."

Standing at the stern bulwark watching the mesmerizing roll of the waves beneath the ship, he heard the chug-choota-chug of the engine. Gus must be at work in the engine room. The sun lifted above the horizon. Henry turned back to the spare cabin to seek sleep.

The soft tap at his door brought Henry up from a light sleep.

"Doctor, the dinners are in the sitting room." The midday sun burned down upon the scraps of blond fuzz on the young lad's cheeks as he offered up this information.

Henry grunted a thank you and threw his legs over the side of the bunk to make his way out to clean up and eat. On his arrival at Smiley's room, he found Ed standing with his back against the bulkhead at the top of the bed. His eyes drooped.

"Ed, go and eat. We can change those bandages when you get back."

The removal of bandages, without causing further damage to the wounds, and the reapplying of clean bandages soaked in disinfectant took some time.

"Go and catch another forty-winks, Ed." Henry gathered the cotton cloth bandages up into a heap. "I'll ask Gus if someone can wash these for us."

The bells noting two o'clock in the afternoon – halfway mark through the afternoon watch – rang out.

Henry paced the room three steps one way and three steps back again with a regular rhythm in the hope of staying awake. At first, he thought it was another dream again when he heard his name called.

"Henry." The sound was barely above a whisper.

In one stride, he reached Smiley's side, only to find his friend lying still and unmoving with his eyes closed, as they had been for two days. He took up an unresponsive hand, his own pale in comparison.

"Smiley, are you awake?"

His heart fell when no response was forthcoming. He checked his friend's heart rate and lifted his one uncovered eyelid to check the pupil. He must have imagined it. Disappointment dragged his head down to rest on the bed.

"Henry." There it was again – very faint.

Henry's head lifted in a rush to find Smiley's eyes and mouth closed as before. His gaze never wavered from Smiley's face, when again he heard the words inside his head.

"Henry, goodbye my friend."

The white hand reached over and lifted the artist's long dark fingers.

"Smiley don't you dare go now. I won't let you. We will run through the forests again. You will teach me to make a fire after the drenching rains. I have yet to meet your woman and your son. Please don't go now."

Henry sat unmoving, as still as the body in front of him. He did not want to check the heart rate. He already knew. The ship's bells rang out the two bells of 5 pm, one hour after the start of the dog watch. The three bells of 5.30 pm chimed and the four bells of 6 pm and Henry had still not moved. And that is where Gus and Josh found him at the seven bells of 7.30 pm. Ed arrived in the doorway at the same time.

They did not ask. The answer was written in the colour and lines of Henry's face.

As the weak sun's rays spread a golden haze across the morning sky, Smiley, wrapped in a sail of the *Northern Orchid* and weighted with cannon balls, was buried at sea off Cape Melville on the east coast of Cape York Peninsula.

Henry forced a few words past the lump in his throat as he told of a wonderful friendship, a great artist and a brave companion. There was not a dry eye amongst those who had known Smiley during his life.

As the sea below opened up to receive the body, the skies above split apart to release the heavens' own tears. Rain barrelled down and along the deck filling the scuppers within minutes. Only Henry remained. Within seconds, water poured over his bare head to wash away his tears. It drained down his body as he leant against the bulwark of the *Northern Orchid* staring out across the restless waters.

"Goodbye, my brave and loyal friend."

CHAPTER THIRTY-TWO

Cooktown

Abigail lifted her eyes from the partly rolled bandage resting on her lap. She looked out from her rocking chair and through the back doorway of the verandah, now free of all but one patient, towards the roadway passing to the north of the house. She watched a group of native women walk past. They were dressed in the tunics worn when working as cleaners in the town area. They had barely disappeared from her limited vision, when two native men wearing trousers, as demanded by the law when in the town, travelled the same route. Other than the white ochre stripes painted on their skin, their chests were bare.

That's odd, the thought ran across Abigail's mind. She became conscious of murmuring voices accompanied by a repeated soft slapping sound. A smell of smoke from an open fire with something added, a sweet aroma, teased her nostrils. It was difficult to tell exactly what the unfamiliar odour was.

As her thoughts meandered, another small group of women and children walked by with heads bowed. The curious thing was the children were silent. This in itself was unusual. The native children were not often seen without laughter and squeals bursting from grubby faces with shiny eyes full of mischief. Two women and a man returned from the opposite direction. They nodded quietly to a family group of seven coming up from the direction of the river.

Curiosity drew her up. Abigail's feet, covered with her brown leather low-heeled shoes, led her down the two stairs and into her backyard towards the roadway. As she came out from behind the kitchen building, her breath caught in her throat. In her own backyard, in front of what they now called Smiley's shed, a group of about fifteen natives, male and female, sat around a small fire. She drew back amidst the banana trees and watched. In what appeared to be an inner circle of about six people, she recognized Smiley's sister and his mother. It was then she heard the faint melody of soft voices – a slow tuneless melody, almost the sound of a dirge.

Abigail froze as the thought registered. A dirge – it was a dirge they sang. There could be only one reason for them to come into the town and risk the wrath of the law to sing a dirge in front of Smiley's hut. He was dead. *Is this the tribal way of mourning their loved ones?* Her thoughts travelled on with reluctance. *If Smiley is dead, where is Henry? The pair are together, they met up at Archer River.* The telegram had reassured her of that fact. Henry would never let anything happen to Smiley unless he was unable to save him. *Is Henry dead too?* She groaned at the thought. *But how did they know Smiley is, or might be dead?* The *Northern Orchid* had not returned yet, although she did expect the ship's arrival any day now. Terror filled her heart at the thought Henry may not be on the ship as anticipated. Tears filled her eyes. Tendrils of auburn hair hanging down the side of her face flew up as she shook her head. *Stop this at once, Abigail. There is no sense worrying until you know what the facts are.* On the roadway, several more silent natives passed in either direction. Abigail stepped out from behind the thick leaves. She hesitated only a moment before she moved over towards where, what she believed was a mourning party, sat around the fireplace.

A grey-haired woman, Smiley's mother, sat cross-legged between two younger women – one with a baby on her lap. Abigail recognized the one on the left as Smiley's sister, having met her on several occasions when visiting Smiley. The other woman she assumed to be Smiley's wife of two years. Pain swam in their eyes. Smiley's mother's hands slapped at her cheeks and her arms as the grief washed over her.

As she approached Smiley's mother, Abigail paused. She gasped. Like a smack across the face, she realized, this was most probably the mourning party for the death of Smiley, a boy she had loved as a son also. Once more the tears threatened. Abigail drew a deep breath. She walked across to sit on the ground facing Smiley's mother. Abigail's understanding of the native language was very much inferior to Henry's, but she did her best to offer her condolences.

The bony, dark-skinned hand of Smiley's mother reached out and rested on the white fingers. Tears ran down the dark velvet skin of the woman's face. Her gentle words came fast and furious. Abigail may not have comprehended the words, but the meaning of gratitude and sorrow echoed crystal clear. As best she could, Abigail reassured Smiley's mother to feel free to mourn at Smiley's hut. Abigail would organize food for the visitors. She found rising to her feet not as easy as it had been only a few years ago.

In the kitchen, she informed the cook of her requirements before slipping through the gap in the fence and knocking on Eve's back door. With a baby on her hip and another tiny tot hanging onto her skirt, Eve appeared in the open doorway.

"Eve, I'm sorry to bother you, dear, and I do know it's Gina's morning off, but I really could do with a little help for an hour or so." Eve ushered her visitor into the kitchen, where Abigail went on to explain the odd situation occurring in the backyard next door.

"Oh dear, Miss Abigail, what do you think has happened? The *Northern Orchid* should be back at Cooktown within a few days. Gus did say they were collecting Henry, Smiley and Henry's friend at the mouth of the Pascoe River on their return from the north."

"I dare not think what may have happened. I will wait for the *Northern Orchid's* return to find out before I give up." Abigail removed a lace handkerchief from inside her long sleeve and wiped her eyes. "Would you send young Jack to the butcher's shop to deliver a note for me? Cook and I will fry up slices of meat for the mourners. What do you think; should I ask for half a goat?"

"Oh, Miss Abigail, that might be too much."

"Possibly, but any food not eaten can go home with them. Smiley was like a son to me and I want to contribute something."

"Well, you keep Gina all day if you wish. We didn't have anything special planned here today."

Within the hour, banana leaves covered two wooden tables placed near the fireplace. Slices of damper with jam and a pitcher of cool water with several pannikins held the leaves down in the light breeze coming in off the Endeavour River. Enticing aromas of frying meats drifted out to the family and friends of Smiley. The soft dirge did not alter, only the singers changed as some came, sang for a period of time, spoke with Smiley's mother, and moved off.

Abigail and Gina placed the cooked meats on two large metal platters on the table for the mourners. She watched as the guests tore off some banana leaves and picked up the hot meats. Another two dampers were added to the feast, this time without any jam. Just as the last additions were added to the collection, Abigail noticed Gina's rising blush and nervous fingers. She looked up to find the cause. Abigail smiled her first smile of the morning. Striding across the road came the handsome dark-haired policeman, Sergeant Charles Beaumont, and his offsider, the equally good-looking blond-haired Constable Nelson.

"Are you alright here, Miss Abigail? Are these people bothering you at all?"

"No Sergeant … Charles, not at all. They are joining me in mourning young Smiley." As she spoke the words out loud it really struck her. If she has interpreted this gathering correctly, her beautiful boy with the wide grin and shining white teeth was dead. A sharp breath almost choked her. Long eyelashes blinked away the threatening tears. She swallowed the wail rising from deep inside her belly. Speech felt impossible.

"We've had no word on his death. I thought you said he and your son were on Lavinia Downs. What happened?"

Abigail reached out her arm and ushered the two policemen towards the kitchen verandah. She turned to Gina, "Please ask Cook if we could have a pot of tea and any cake she may have over, dear? Ask Doctor George to join us, if he is back from the hospital. You will join us for tea, won't you, Gina?"

The deepening blush did nothing to detract from the girl's beautiful features. "Thank you, Miss Abigail."

While the teapot was drained and even the crumbs disappeared from the plate, Abigail explained to the men how she trusted the communication systems of the native people to know Smiley was dead. Her own fear for Henry's safety she kept locked inside her heart.

"Miss Abigail, that all seems a likely tale they've told you to get a free meal." It was Charles who presented the cynic's offering.

Abigail sucked in the air and bit her tongue. She swallowed her first response. Her glance at Constable Nelson and Gina told Abigail neither was listening to a word spoken on the other side of the table. Restraint tightened her throat around her words.

"Charles, we have seen many strange things since first coming to Cooktown and getting to know young Smiley. I don't know why I keep calling him young Smiley. He's older than our Henry and Henry is a fully-fledged doctor, and a man in his own right, now." Abigail shook her head and tried to recapture the essence of her conversation. Her breath caught – snagged on the deep worry inside her chest. "Smiley received messages from his people at times when the messages could only have arrived out of thin air. It was uncanny and often set the hairs on the back of my neck lifting."

The patronizing way Charles gazed at her almost caused Abigail to snap.

"Anyway, whatever is really going on here, tell the natives they must be out of town by dark. That is the rule."

She dropped her eyes to the clenched hands on her lap. "Yes, Charles, of course."

But Abigail did not have to tell anyone to leave. When the sun rested on the western horizon, Smiley's people rose and left in silence. Smoke dribbled up from the coals in the fireplace. The plates and pannikins were stacked in a tidy heap on the bare tables. The water container stood empty.

CHAPTER THIRTY-THREE

Heavy Hearts

Clouds hung heavy from the sky and the smoke from burning coal lay like a shroud over the *Northern Orchid* as it eased into the Endeavour River with its sails furled. The rolling thunder of the anchor, released into the dark waters in the middle of the river, echoed within the dome of shadows. At the sound of the captain's voice, bare feet sprinted along the deck on their way to release the stern anchor. The rattle of the chains almost covered the two chimes of the bells marking one hour into the afternoon watch. The rumble of the engine below ceased.

"So, this is Cooktown, Henry. Do you think it's changed much in the last ten years?" Both Henry and Ed were lined up at the portside bulwark.

Henry smiled. "If I could see it through this miserable drizzling rain, I might be able to say. The harbour jetty may have been extended since then though." The sound of cargo being loaded or unloaded onto the two ships at the jetty sounded loud in their ears. "Still as noisy." Henry leaned out to look upstream, but his vision was limited. "It's a wonder your father hasn't been to Cooktown with his pearling industry."

"Occasionally he ended up here for one reason or another, but I was only a young fellow then – maybe seven or eight. I can't say I remember it much."

"Well, this is your new home and your hospital. I can guarantee you'll find it slightly smaller than St. Bartholomew's in London."

"That in itself will be a blessing, I should think." Ed glanced at Henry's face. He empathized with the well of sorrow resting within the green eyes. "Will you be able to find Smiley's people to tell them what happened?"

"Yes, that will be the first thing I want to do, after I say hello to my mother and Uncle George."

Abigail looked up at the soft knock on the verandah post. She stood up straight from where she had been giving a patient his medicine.

"Can I help you, dear?" Her gaze took in the young native girl wearing a tunic made for someone twice her size. "Aren't you the young girl who works in the hotel laundry just down the road … Bubbles, isn't it?"

"Yes, Miss. I bin told to tell you the ship coming in."

Abigail's face lit up for a brief moment before the shadow of doubt stalked across her features. *What if Henry is not on the Northern Orchid?* Her feet refused to move.

"You right, Missus?"

"Er ... yes thanks, Bubbles. I'll be right along."

The girl turned and ran towards the harbour, while Abigail forced herself to move her feet. A dull voice inside her head warned her; *What if Henry is not on the ship?* She entered the office where George sat writing up some notes. He lifted his head at her voice.

"The *Northern Orchid* is here, George. Will you come down to the river with me?"

"Of course, Sis."

At the back steps, he picked up two of the large black brollies leaning against the railing and passed one to his sister. Together they ran down the steps and out onto the road making their way to the jetty through the light shower of rain.

"It looks like Smiley's family have come to greet the ship too," he pointed to a gathering of about twenty natives on the bank of the river.

"His poor mother, how must she be feeling?" At that moment, Abigail noticed the determined stride of Sergeant Beaumont heading towards the gathering of natives. She lifted her pace.

"What are you doing, Abigail?" George called as he sped to catch up.

Abigail whispered loud enough for him to hear. "It's Charles, he's hellbent on chasing the natives out of the town."

Both George and Abigail stood on either side of Smiley's mother as Charles arrived wearing a not-too-happy frown.

"Why, Charles, how nice to see you. It's not the best weather to stroll along the waterfront today. Do you think this weather will ever lift?" Abigail's smile sparkled in her eyes if not in her heart.

"Miss Abigail … Doctor George …," Charles nodded at each. "I really must ask you to move on. These people should not be gathered here like this."

"Oh, Charles, don't you know who these people are? They mourn for a son who should have been on the *Northern Orchid*." Abigail turned to encompass the group in the sweep of her hand. Like a kick to her chest, the thought that maybe neither Smiley nor Henry might be on board the ship cut off her breath as quickly as a butcher's knife slices through a side of beef. She gasped.

Smiley's mother reached out and touched Abigail's hand.

George walked over to stand at Charles's side. Their quiet conversation was not heard by anyone else, but when the sergeant of police spun on his heel, everyone noted his instruction.

"I'll trust your judgment on this then, Doctor George, but please ensure they are all gone before four o'clock."

"Of course, Charles."

"Step carefully there, Henry," Josh called as Henry, Ed and Gus climbed down the Jacob's ladder to board the jolly-boat where a seaman sat with an end of each of the two opposing oars resting in each of his large hands. A second seaman assisted the passengers into the small boat before he took his place at one of the oars.

As they neared the river bank, Henry caught sight of the group of people upstream about one hundred yards. He felt sure the two white people within the group were his mother and his Uncle George.

"Look, Gus," he pointed. "Can the men drop us upstream there?" The boat rocked perilously as he jumped up and waved.

"Geez, Henry, you'll have us all in the drink. Sit down." Ed laughed.

Henry's burst of spirits evaporated. He recognized Smiley's mother standing on the left of his mother. These were Smiley's people. *What will they say, when they discover I have not brought Smiley home?*

There was no stopping Abigail as she rushed down to almost haul her son out of the boat. The seamen barely had the oars on board, when she clasped Henry in a hug that threatened to choke him. Tears flowed as they stood back to look at each other.

"What is that stain on your shirt? It looks like … oh, it is. Is that blood?"

Doctor George broke the awkward moment when he drew Henry into an embrace.

"Look at you, boy, you've grown a foot, at least."

Henry smiled – a subdued smile. "Not quite, Uncle George."

Ed stepped forward and introduced himself to Abigail and then to Doctor George.

"Oh, I'm sorry, where are my manners?" Henry flushed.

It was Abigail who broached the subject heavy on her mind. "And where is … er … your boyhood friend?" Abigail had been in the area long enough caring for many sick natives to know the aboriginal people did not say the name of a dead one for a long time after their death.

"He saved my life, Mum." Was all Henry could say. He walked over to where Smiley's mother stood with tears rolling down her cheeks. Henry realized; she knew Smiley was dead. Somehow this did not surprise him. It seemed fitting. He struggled to dredge up the words from a sluggish memory of Smiley's native tongue as he held her hands and explained.

"The boy with the happy face lost his life when he saved my life in a crocodile attack. Thick scars may have weakened his legs, but his heart was as strong as a bullock's – as strong as the midday summer sun."

"His voice speak to me," she whispered through her tears.

Abigail leant in towards Henry. She pointed to the young woman with the infant in her arms by the side of Smiley's mother.

"Your friend's wife and son." She spoke the words quietly.

Again, in the language of Smiley's people, he pointed to the baby and addressed the young woman. "Your baby's father was a brave man."

At that moment the youngster's mouth widened in a smile of empty gums which covered its lower face.

Henry felt the smile tug at his own lips. "The son of my friend has kept his father's smile."

Tears glistened on the eyelids of the baby's mother. The dark curls surrounding her face bounced as she nodded her head.

Smiley's people began to disperse, moving further upstream, where they retrieved their bark canoes. The flotilla paddled across the water to the other side of the river.

Drawn into the reunion with his mother and Uncle George did not prevent Henry from watching Smiley's family withdraw into the riverbank trees.

Was it a trick of the muted light, the sprinkling of rain, and the black and grey clouds, which left an image of Smiley's smile and dark eyes in the sky above? Sadness at his loss, at the family's loss, crashed in upon Henry. He owed Smiley's people a debt for life.

George and Abigail led Henry and Ed to their home for refreshments. George pointed in the direction of the town hospital. He explained how he had been serving as a locum at the Cooktown hospital awaiting Ed's arrival. He promised to take Ed and Henry over and introduce them to the matron and staff after tea.

Abigail talked mostly of their plans to return to the surgery in Brisbane in the next few months.

"Henry, there'll be more than enough work there to keep you and George busy, if our cousin's word is anything to go by. He'll return to England next year. First, we'll have a Christmas celebration here in a few weeks." She watched Ed who turned his head left and right taking in everything around them. "You are to join us here to celebrate also, Ed. I know the matron has plans for your Christmas dinner at the hospital after church, but you must join us for a part of the day, at least."

"Thank you, Miss Abigail." He turned to where Henry sat quietly in the corner. "So, this is where you grew up, Henry. You know, you're like a two-sided coin. The city boy and the country boy all in one body."

Henry smiled and sat up straighter in his chair. His hand slapped at his shirt pocket. "Oh, Mum, I almost forgot. Max Young handed me this letter for you as we were leaving Pascoe River." He dragged out the scrunched-up paper and smoothed it with his hands. "Sorry, it's a bit wrinkled and stained. He said it's something to do with his plans for his daughter next year."

"Oh, Victoria, yes, a lovely girl. When I last talked to him, he was planning to buy a place in Brisbane and let the sons run Lavinia Downs, while Victoria went to a boarding school down south."

Henry and Ed laughed together. Henry spoke, "Somehow I think Victoria might be a challenge to any boarding school."

"Don't you be too hasty with your judgements there, my boy. Victoria was always the perfect lady, when she visited us at the weekends, while at the convent here."

Both Ed and Henry rolled their eyes as similar visions ran through their minds of a young slip of a girl, who rode horses as well as any man, who handled a rifle better than her brothers, smoked half of Johnny Hayden's cigarette, and threw the pots and pans around the kitchen.

At that moment, a woman with her grey hair drawn tightly back against her head strode across the road, towards where they sat on the kitchen verandah. A black parasol danced above her head on its rigid umbilical cord. The woman's navy uniform swished around her ankles and the fashionable bulge of the sleeves above the elbows flattened against her arm with her forward thrust.

George nodded to Ed. "Look out, here comes trouble. This is our nursing matron arriving at full charge. Looks like you are going to be thrown into the deep end with some drama or other." He laughed at the wide-eyed surprise on Ed's face. "Never fear, Ed, I'll protect you from her devil's tongue."

His face remained bland when Henry chuckled softly, "Well, Ed, my lad, sounds like you may have another Matron Ferguson on your hands here." Henry turned his head and spoke aside to his uncle, "Our Fergie was forever giving all the young doctors a hard time at St. Barts."

"Don't judge too hastily, boys. The matron here has been forged by time, heat and pressure into a true diamond. Scratch the surface and you'll discover a tough gem as is required in this tough country."

The men rose from their chairs to meet the new arrival.

THE END

Elizabeth Rimmington

Previous Books by Elizabeth Rimmington:

Shadow of the Northern Orchid – 2019

Shadows on the Goldfield Track – 2020

And now to make a trilogy

Shadows Across Cape York – 2022

Other novels by Elizabeth Rimmington

Burdekin Heartbeats – 2020

Rhylla's Secret - 2021

Elizabeth Rimmington

Elizabeth is an Australian author living in a rural area of South-East Queensland. Born in North Queensland, Elizabeth retains a deep love for Queensland and the north. During a career in nursing followed by several years driving a taxi cab, Elizabeth has met many and varied people from all walks of life. A storehouse of memories from which to plunder and develop story characters able to infiltrate the reader's heart by osmosis. Their laughter, their heartbreak and their pain will fill the book lover's soul with happiness, tears, fear and empathy.

Visit the website www.elizabethrimmington.com.au

Take advantage of her FREE monthly newsletter including a new short story every time.

Find her on Facebook – elizabethrimmington.author